SPINDLE

SPINDLE

A NOVEL

SHONNA SLAYTON

Entangled Publishing, LLC
2614 South Timberline Road
Suite 109
Fort Collins, CO 80525

Entangled Teen is an imprint of Entangled Publishing, LLC.

Visit our website at www.entangledpublishing.com.

Edited by Stacy Abrams and Lydia Sharp
Cover design by Louisa Maggio
Interior design by Toni Kerr

ISBN: 9781633754935
Ebook ISBN: 9781633754928

Manufactured in the United States of America

First Edition October 2016

10 9 8 7 6 5 4 3 2 1

For Mike,
who will always be my prince.

PROLOGUE

Two servants filled the largest fireplace in the castle with wood while a small gathering anxiously watched on. Small bits of kindling and cotton on the bottom and larger pieces of dry hickory on top. It would be a fire that lit fast and burned hot. One of the servants bent down, striking the flint and setting the kindling aflame.

Aurora's face immediately warmed with the heat, and she allowed herself to hope. Her nightmare would soon be over.

"Thank you. Leave us, please," she said.

The servants exited, closing the solid wooden door behind them with an ominous *thud*.

Aurora reached for her fiancé's hand and gave it a squeeze. He kissed her forehead in response. *Such a courageous, patient man.* She turned to the fairies gathered in the shadows. They nodded encouragingly. They, too, had been waiting for this to end.

Careful not to prick her finger, Aurora took one last look at the item that had cursed her. Such an ordinary object, aside from the pretty scrollwork carved in the wood. No one would suspect the power it wielded—and that was the danger.

One of the fairies coughed, reminding her to continue.

"The end," Aurora said with finality, and tossed the spindle into the fire. No one else would ever go through the horrors she had. Still, she held her breath, fearful of what might happen. Were they standing too close? Would there be an explosion of magic? They waited.

Nothing.

Not a crackle, a sizzle, or a hiss.

Aurora bent down and peered into the flames. What she saw made her heart pound with fear. She'd thought her ordeal was over. Her hundred years of turmoil had ended, and she had found love with a prince who was eager to show her what she had missed while she was sleeping.

"Why doesn't it burn?" she demanded.

The good fairies gathered around. "I was afeared of this," said one. "The curse still lives. You will not be able to destroy it until it fulfills its intended purpose."

"Isodora will be furious," said another. "Her powers are wrapped up in this unfulfilled curse. We must hide it in a place where no young girl can ever find it again. For if a girl before her seventeenth birthday pricks her finger..."

"We cannot help her," said the third fairy. "She will die."

CHAPTER ONE

Briar walked the length of her spinning frames, keeping a close eye on the whirling threads. She'd been shut down more often than not today and tried to keep her mind off of her lost wages. It was Saturday, so they'd be ending early, giving her time to go home to the country and spend the night with her young siblings and their nanny.

All she did at the cotton mill, she did for those children.

Out of the corner of her eye, she saw several threads break on frame number four. Her heart sank. "Drat."

Quickly, she pulled the shipper handle on four and waited for the spinning to stop. With her other frames, she could easily fix a few threads that had turned thin while the machine was running, but not this frame. It had a mind of its own and would likely pinch her fingers if she tried.

She looked around for Henry. He worked in the machine shop and had a knack for fixing this persnickety frame. His boss allowed him to come up to the spinning room and doff for her, tweaking the frame each time to keep it running. Most doffers were children, their small hands the right size for slipping through the frames and removing the full bobbins and putting on new ones. Henry, despite being seventeen, didn't seem to mind helping her even though the other boys his age gave him a ribbing. He had been her first friend when she moved to town with her family, and a loyal one at that, so she was thankful for his help.

Briar set to work tying threads and straightening out bobbins.

"Can't leave you alone for a minute," called a voice close to her ear.

Henry. He had to yell above the roaring noise of a roomful of spinning frames. He reached out and pulled off a bobbin, then pointed. "This here is your problem. Something's wrong with this spindle and it sets the others off." He took out his tools and straightened the metal spindle.

Briar finished tying the last broken thread. "Can't you replace it?" she yelled back.

Henry shook his head. "Already have. Every one I put in here goes crooked." He grinned. "Besides, if I fix it for good, I won't get to see you every day."

Briar rolled her eyes, which only seemed to encourage him further.

With a wink, he pushed the bobbin cart ahead and began swapping out the full bobbins for empties. While he did that, Briar started up number four again, staying long enough to make sure all the threads caught and were spinning evenly before moving on to check her neglected frames.

When Henry finished doffing, he waved to catch her attention, signaling he was done. She lifted her chin and smiled her thanks. Then he tapped the edge of number four—the same spot every time—and was off.

The only person completely dependable in my life is Henry Prince.

Sure, Nanny was always available for the children, but that was only temporary. Stiff and unyielding as the spinning frames, Nanny had only agreed to help out for a year, ending at Briar's seventeenth birthday. After that, if Briar hadn't come up with a more permanent solution for the children, they'd be turned over to the orphan asylum in town that would put them on the orphan train sure as anything. No one would take three children all at once. They'd be split up and would never see one another again.

Until last week, Briar thought she'd found a permanent solution. But now, instead of planning for a summer wedding, she was scrambling for ways to earn more money to bring the children back into town with her and was finding it nigh impossible. No matter how hard she worked at the mill or how much extra piecework she took on, it would never be enough on her own. Wheeler—her former sweetheart—had spoiled everything when he changed his mind.

Finally, the overseer shut off the power to the frames and the day was over.

Briar raced out the door and down the outside stairs to the mill courtyard, getting jostled by the constant stream of operatives leaving the buildings.

There was her room-mate Mim coming down from the weaving room. Briar waved.

"Let's go, then," said Mim, straightening her new Sunday bonnet that she had saved up several weeks for.

Mim was a few years older than Briar, the fashion expert of their boardinghouse and the only blonde in the mix. She was a gem with a needle and had been teaching Briar how to smock little girls' dresses, adding pleats with colorful patterns to the bodice and sleeves.

Briar had also worn her best hat to work. Not a new hat. It belonged to her mam, so it was dated but decent. She'd also risked wearing her best cotton dress, worried all day the hem would come away soaked in the grease that was liberally applied to the machines and often dripped onto the floors. They didn't have time to go back to the boardinghouse and change, if Briar were to make it home to the children before dark.

It was important she look presentable for where Mim was taking her: across town to where the wives of the mill executives lived and had their babies.

"You sure you want to do this?" Mim asked.

"Do what?" said Henry. He sidled up between them, his hands in his pockets.

"I'm looking for piecework," Briar said quietly.

He raised his eyebrows in surprise. "Don't you think you work hard enough at the mill?"

"You know why I have to take on more." It had been a long week and Briar was tired, more weary of soul than of body. She could push herself to work a little harder and, if nothing else, try to mask the hurt left in her heart.

"Let me—"

"No." Briar stopped him. Henry was the kind of guy who would give you the shirt off his back. "I can't. You can't. Your family needs what you bring in."

"Then let me walk with you."

Mim stopped. "You'll do no such thing." She looked him up and down as if to emphasize her point. He was covered in grease, wearing an old, torn pair of work trousers, and his shirt opened one button too many, on account of a button falling off and not being replaced.

Mim did have a point. It would be hard enough to impress these ladies that she could do the job neatly and cleanly without Henry hanging around in the background.

"Then I'll wait for you by the road to see you home. You *are* still going to the cottage tonight?" His forehead wrinkled in concern.

Briar nodded. She couldn't stay in town without telling the children first. They looked forward to her weekend visits. "Thanks, but you don't have to. Your mam will be worried."

"No, she won't. She'll know I'm with you." He turned and sauntered back toward the mill.

Mim snorted. "He doesn't know his mother, does he?"

Briar frowned, thinking of what she'd shared with her room-mates.

Henry had invited her to his house one day, not long after the children had moved in with Nanny. He was showing off, having never brought her there before. Their entire property was fenced off with ominous KEEP OUT signs posted everywhere, making Briar nervous from the start, even though she had already met his parents.

They had fed the chickens, petted the goats, and he was about to invite her into the house when his mother stood arms akimbo in the doorway. Her usual smile was gone, replaced by stern, set lips.

"Henry, may I speak with you inside, please?" she'd asked in a way that let Briar know she wasn't to follow. Trouble was, the window was open and Briar could hear everything.

"How could you bring her out here? What were you thinking?"

The white lace curtain in the window fluttered in the

breeze. Briar stared at it, straining to hear more. As if of their own accord, her legs started forward, taking her closer.

"I'm sorry, Mama." His voice came out whisper-quiet.

"We don't know what causes a girl to be drawn to the spindle. You need to be careful who you bring here. The farm is not a place for a girl, especially a girl like Briar. Take her home now."

Henry had come out with a basket, the first of many that he would bring to the cottage filled with food from Mrs. Prince's garden. His grin faltered when he saw her so close to the house, but then he smiled wide and led her out of the yard. He never explained anything.

Nor did he ever invite her back.

From then on, Briar not only avoided the farm, she avoided Mrs. Prince, who seemed to have something against girls "like her." She couldn't figure out if Mrs. Prince was against spinner girls in general or *Irish* spinner girls in particular.

Briar wanted to tell Mrs. Prince it wasn't that she was drawn to the spindle, it was simply the only job she could get. Options were limited, which was why, with Mim's help, she was hoping these housewives would take the time to judge her by her work.

Mim rang the doorbell of the first house, a new, two-story brick structure surrounded by a manicured lawn and a dozen purplish-pink azalea bushes. Mrs. Chapman opened the front door. Dressed in a pretty green dress with a lace collar and puffed sleeves, she beamed at Mim.

"Have you finished already?"

Mim handed Mrs. Chapman the wrapped package. "Yes, ma'am. And please meet my room-mate, Briar Jenny. I've been teaching her, and she is ready to start taking on her own clients. Do you have another dress that needs smocking, or do you know of another mother wanting fancywork done?" Mim pulled out a sampler showcasing Briar's stitches.

Meanwhile, Briar stood silently under Mrs. Chapman's penetrating gaze. She stiffened as the woman's eyes roamed over Briar's auburn hair, her freckles.

Making judgments.

This wasn't going to work. Briar sensed it before Mim could.

There was no physical sign posted in the window, but Briar felt it in her being. She wasn't welcome here. NINA. *No Irish Need Apply.*

CHAPTER TWO

Oblivious to Mrs. Chapman's reaction, Mim continued to sell Briar's work. "Look at how beautifully Briar makes the baby-wave stitch," she said. "Perfectly even: you'd think she was using a tape measure."

Finally, the woman shook her head. "I'm full-up on clothes right present. Thank you, Mim." With a final glance saying she should have known better, Mrs. Chapman snapped the door closed.

Briar shut her eyes, feeling the reverberations through her thin soles. And to think she dressed up for this.

Mim put her hands on her hips. "That's a surprise. She's always got work for me." Mim led Briar down the steps. "Let's try Mrs. Oxford."

Turning back to their side of town, Briar said, "I should be getting on the road." She had known none of these ladies would hire her. Too many immigrants had descended into Vermont too fast and some people didn't like it.

"Just one more?"

Briar pointed to her hair. Though Mim had done it up

for her in a Newport knot, the style didn't hide the color. "They can spot me a mile away."

"Oh, pooh. They're not all like that." Mim frowned, and then looped her arm through Briar's as they walked back to their side of town. "How about I take in the jobs and you can help me with the work? What they don't know won't kill 'em."

Briar gave a half smile. "Thanks."

They were passing a group of town girls, one of whom was wearing the exact same hat as Mim. One of the girls pointed and said in a loud whisper, "That mill girl's got your hat, Felicity." The rest began to giggle behind upheld hands.

The girl, Felicity, said, "I never did like this hat much. Too cheap-looking. I've been thinking about putting it in the charity box."

Briar felt Mim stiffen, but the two of them raised their chins and walked on like they hadn't heard.

"They're only jealous," Briar said, "because you can buy your own hats but they have to wait for their fathers to buy theirs for them."

"You're darn right," said Mim. "Spoiled lot. Wouldn't last a day on the looms."

They parted near the mill. "Give these to the children for me." Mim handed Briar a small paper bag with three lemon drops inside. "See you tomorrow."

"You need to stop sending me home with treats or they'll expect them every time."

Briar waved and started down the road out of town, wondering if Henry had waited or not. She quickened her pace, eager to be with her kin.

"Hey, wait up!" called Henry from a gathering of boys down the lane. He ran toward her.

Briar smiled, surprisingly glad for the company after the coldness of the ladies in town. "Thanks for waiting."

He grinned back. "I thought you'd be longer, but I saw Mim headed for Miss Olive's."

"Doesn't take people long to make a decision. Besides, it was time we got on home before the sun sets." She didn't want to tell him the reason she was walking empty-handed, no piecework for her. They walked in silence for a while until she felt his gaze.

"What?"

He shook his head. "Nothing. I just wish I could help."

"Something will turn up. That's what my da always said." Briar stopped. "Oh, no."

They'd caught up to a young couple walking ahead of them. The boy, handsome, tall, and lanky, leaned in close to say something to the curly-haired brunette he walked with. Neither of them lived out this way, so the only place they could be going was the pond. *Our pond.*

The brunette tilted her head to listen, laughed, and then touched the boy's arm. Wheeler and Sadie. Sadie was new at the mill and worked in the carding room, one of the worst jobs. Briar couldn't imagine how Wheeler had spotted her so quickly. He never went near the carding room since he'd moved into the machine shop. Unless they'd met during break on the fire escape when he was waiting for Briar to come out. She didn't want to imagine that; it was too painful to think how his heart was changing while she was unaware.

Last winter, Wheeler had spent hours with Briar, laying out their plans while they sat in the parlor at the boardinghouse. As soon as he was able, he was going to transfer to the new shirtwaist factory to work as a steamer, keeping an eye out for a cutter job—cutting out thick layers of material for the ladies to sew into the shirtwaists. Aside from being a boss or a dyer, it was the highest-paying job at the factory. And when he saved up enough, he'd leave rural Vermont to go back to the Old Country. He and Briar and the children.

Both their families hailed from County Wicklow in Ireland. Wheeler's mam liked to tell the story of how Briar's great-grandmother almost married Wheeler's great-grandfather, except he proposed to someone in the dark, thinking it was his girl when it wasn't. The proposed-to girl was so happy, he hadn't the heart to break it off. Everyone said it was inevitable for Briar and Wheeler to meet in the new land and get it right this time.

His new sweetheart didn't have a connection with him like that.

Everything had been settled. They'd had everyone's blessing. And then Wheeler changed his mind for no real reason other than he needed time to think things over. Briar didn't know how to stop him from getting lost in the dark like his great-grandfather did. Or if she should even try.

"If we walk any slower we'll start going backward," Henry said, pulling Briar back to the present. He stepped into the woods and came back with a tall walking stick. "Not that I mind this extra time with you, but I do have chores at home."

Briar set her lips and didn't answer. She never asked Henry to walk her to the cottage. But that was *the way with a Prince*, as everyone said. They acted out of habit, and once a habit was established, it stayed that way. His new habit appeared to be trying to keep her mind off of Wheeler.

"They're ridiculous," he said scornfully as the couple

in front of them touched hands for a few moments before separating again.

Briar's heart cracked a little more. She remained silent, but fingered the fancy comb holding up her hair. The comb that Wheeler had given her for Christmas. *And now they're going to our pond. Is there no other place he can take her?*

"You can hold my hand if it would make you feel better," Henry said. He held out his calloused, grease-laden fingers for her to grab. His hand had grown since the last time he'd offered it to her.

She sighed. *Henry*. He was there when her family moved into the valley and would likely still be there when they moved out. She was told there'd never been a time when Sunrise Valley didn't have a Henry Prince in it. From son back to father to grandfather and beyond, and none of them had ever gone anywhere. They were known as a reclusive family, hardly leaving their farm. Except for Henry. He was different.

Briar's family had only been in the valley since Pansy was born. They were supposed to be traveling through, but then Da got a job at the new factory and they stayed. Mam worked, too, but developed the coughing sickness from all the cotton in her lungs. She died when the twin boys were born, and then when Da died of consumption, the Jenny children were stuck there, like weeds that nobody wanted.

Briar didn't intend for them to stay any longer in Sunrise Valley than they had to. She would find a way out for her sister and brothers. Back to the Old Country like Mam wanted for them. Back to where they would fit in. And Henry Prince was not that way.

He wiggled his eyebrows at her.

Unguarded, she laughed. This particular Henry Prince was also known for being an audacious flirt.

"That's better. You're irresistible when you laugh."

But when Briar looked ahead and saw the couple again, she immediately stopped smiling. The pace they had set was torturously slow. If only she hadn't gone into town, she would have been far ahead of them now and she wouldn't have had to witness this budding romance. It was worse that Henry had waited to walk home with her. She didn't need an audience for her pain.

"I can't wait to leave Sunrise," she said.

Henry spun around and walked backward, facing her and blocking her view of the couple. "The way you say *Sunrise* makes it sound like you don't like the place. This valley has a lot to offer. Our town is booming, if you like that sort of thing. Thanks to the mills, we're getting electric lights installed, so we're as industrialized as anywhere you'd want to go." He cocked his head, holding up a hand to his ear. "Don't you hear the powerful roar of Otter Creek? Smell the fresh mountain air? And look: Solomon's Seal is already blooming in the forest. I can see the white bells from here. What's not to like?"

Briar refused to look. "All I hear is the echo of the spinning machines. All I smell is the cotton dust that's stuck in my nose. And all I see is a place filled with, with... nothing for me."

Henry didn't answer; he simply gazed at the scenery as if it were paradise and no other place on earth could be more lovely.

Despite herself, she followed Henry's gaze to the forest where she couldn't see anything at all blooming. The creek roared beyond the trees as usual, but there was no breeze coming down from the mountaintop.

As if to prove her wrong, the leaves on the nearest tree rustled like a gust of wind had blown through, twirling the leaves so they flashed silver and green on one branch only. The other trees and their leaves remained still. Briar stopped. A memory stirred.

"What is it?" Henry asked.

"Did you see that?"

"See what?"

"A cavalcade of fairies," Briar mused, remembering what her mother had taught her. "Whenever a wind seems to come from nowhere and affects only one tree or a strip of prairie grass, Mam would tell me it was fairies passing by, and she would pause to give them a moment to all get through."

"I didn't see a fairy go by. Is that an Irish thing?" he asked.

Go home came a whisper drawn out on the wind. *Go home.*

Briar cocked her head. "Hear that?" She brushed a hair back that had fallen out of her Newport knot.

"Is hearing voices an Irish thing, too?" he teased.

With determination, Briar returned her attention to the road. "Not everything I say is an Irish thing. Besides, what do you know, Henry? You've never left the valley. You don't know what's out there."

He laughed like she'd told the funniest joke. "Sure, I know what's out there. Another place, just like this one. And another. And another. If you can't be satisfied here, you won't be satisfied anywhere else, sweet Briarly Rose Jenny."

"Don't call me that," said Briar. "I wish I'd never told you my proper name."

"I like to say it," replied Henry. "You should go by Rose, a pretty name for a pretty girl."

Briar snorted. "Don't feel pretty today," she muttered,

watching Wheeler and his girl stand at the top of the lane and search for the forest path that Briar could find in her sleep. She definitely felt more briarly today.

For once, Henry was silent. Briar looked at him. He tilted his head as he examined her, his mop of sandy hair falling over his hazel eyes, but he didn't blink those long lashes of his. She put her hands on her hips. "Stop that right now, Henry Prince. I don't need your pity."

"Not pity. Curiosity. I was wondering what it would take to make you see what's right in front of you."

Briar rolled her eyes before she huffed and stalked away, almost colliding with Wheeler, who by this time had turned the girl around, apparently having given up on finding the hidden trail. Briar's face burned as she mumbled, "Excuse me," and brushed past them.

A heartache was what was in front of her, that's what. She may as well rip out her bleeding heart and hand it to Wheeler to toss in the river, all the good it would do her now.

"Hi, Briar," said the girl brightly. "Is this where you go on the weekends? I didn't know your family's cottage was out this way. It's quite a walk. No wonder you stay in town during the week."

Briar nodded and tried to get away, but the girl kept talking.

"Wheeler was telling me about a hidden pond in the forest. You must know where it is."

Briar looked up at the sky, slowly drawing in a breath. No way on earth was she telling them where her pond was. She was claiming it back. "Sorry, Sadie, I'm late. My sister and brothers will be worried."

Briar waved to Henry before she turned off the main road and strutted all the way down a long dirt path until she reached her home, not once looking back, despite the temptation to learn what the couple had decided to do.

The pot of geraniums near the door was always a welcoming splash of red against the brownness of everything. Brown dirt. Brown wooden shack. Brown smocks. Everything in her life was the color of dirt.

"Nanny?" she called out. "I'm home."

Like clockwork, Nanny would welcome Briar into the cottage and allow her a few minutes to rest her feet. Together they would drink hot tea and discuss the children before starting on the evening chores. Usually the discussion was about what naughty thing the boys had done that week while Briar was in town, working during the day and spending the nights at the boardinghouse.

"Nanny?"

But instead of Nanny's old wizened face, a new, peculiar one peered out the door, making Briar stop short with the shock of it.

A stranger was in her house with the little ones.

"Welcome home, dearie."

CHAPTER THREE

Briar stared at the strange sight welcoming her into her own home. The diminutive woman had bright eyes, pink cheeks, and gave off an underlying current of energy like she was a tornado about to tear across the earth.

"Hello?" A knot began to form in Briar's stomach. This was too soon. It was only May. Nanny said she had until her seventeenth birthday in July to find a new caretaker for the children. "Are you from the asylum? Where's Nanny?"

"Oh, is that what you call her?" said the peculiar woman. "Will wonders ever cease? I never expected her to get sentimental. Miss Prudence had something to do an' asked me to look in on the littles, since she might be gone a spell."

"You're not here to take the children?" Briar squeezed her fingertips nervously, waiting for the answer.

"Take the children? Goodness, no. They don't trust me to bring up children." The woman's expression altered. "Oh, my. That came out wrong. The children are perfectly fine with me while Miss Prudence is gone. Never fear." She held out her hands as if to stop Briar right then.

"How long is Nanny—Miss Prudence—going to be gone? A few hours?"

The woman's face took on a look like the kind the boys gave when they were caught in mischief. "Perhaps. Maybe longer." She cleared her throat. "A few days."

"Will she be home when I come back again next Saturday?" Briar suddenly realized it was time to have a serious talk with Nanny about the children. There was no use pretending everything was fine when it wasn't.

"Could be…but not likely. It might take her some time." She gave an awkward chuckle. "Not more than a few weeks, though."

The knot inside Briar's stomach tightened. A few weeks would bring Nanny's return close to Briar's birthday. Since Nanny was deliberate about everything she did, it was quite possible she was away making arrangements for the children without her. Briar chided herself for not speaking up earlier. She had avoided talking about their predicament for too long, and Nanny's patience must have run out.

"What is she—?"

"I can't tell you, so don't ask," the woman said, interrupting. "Biscuit?" She pulled a cookie from her pocket. "The children seem to love these."

Briar relaxed, relieved the woman was kind and not there to take the children away from her. "No. Thank you. And you are?"

"Fanny!" she said with enthusiasm. "Come in, come in."

Briar followed the lively woman into her house. "When I asked 'who are you?' I also meant how do you know Nanny—I mean, Miss Prudence?"

"Questions, questions." Fanny waggled her finger at Briar. "You won't be caught unawares if you remember to ask the questions." She stood close to Briar and sized her up.

They met eye to eye, Briar being on the petite side herself. Fanny didn't make much of an imposing figure. "Did Miss Prudence warn you the boys can be a handful?"

"Tut, tut. The children and I are going to have a grand time of it. Surely there is no place else I'd rather be than Sunset Valley."

"Sun*rise* Valley," Briar corrected, taking in the look of her one-room cottage. The curtain separating the sleeping area from the main living quarters was drawn back, and the two beds haphazardly made as if Nanny hadn't supervised the chore. The table was set with earthenware plates, a pot of something—stew, by the delicious smell—bubbled on the stove, and…and complete silence. Briar's heart skipped a beat.

"Where are the children?" she asked.

"Oh, I set them loose to catch supper."

"Excuse me?" Briar stopped her search of the bedroom. After working all week, it took a while to get the sound of spinners and looms out of her ears. "Did you say 'catch supper'?"

"Oh sure," said Fanny. "Those little boys thought it'd be great fun. The girl, on the other hand, looked at me like I'd suddenly sprouted wings. She was so earnest I had to feel my back to check." She patted her shoulders in emphasis, and chuckled awkwardly.

Briar raised her eyebrows. "Right."

She forced her tired self outside to see what trouble the twins and their older sister had gotten into. She also needed a minute to process the strange disappearance of

Nanny, not to mention the arrival of this…Fanny.

The twins were difficult to handle, playing tricks all week long. Their antics would tire any adult, especially one as old and cantankerous as Nanny. Briar frowned. Despite Nanny's crusty nature, she loved them, or so Briar thought. It struck her now, that she'd hoped Nanny would grow to love the wee ones so much she'd agree to keep them past her deadline. Especially now that any hope Briar had to marry Wheeler this summer was gone.

Given that Nanny could be out right now finding homes for the children, Briar realized her backup plan had been no true plan at all. She'd have to do more than find piecework if she were to keep the children with her in Sunrise. There was no way she could earn enough at the mill to support them all. Not with her persnickety frame holding back her production, nor the company continuing to cut wages. People were calling the 1890s the Gilded Age, but for the operatives working in the factories, there wasn't a glint of prosperity in sight.

She found nine-year-old Pansy at the edge of Nanny's rented land, arms straight at her sides, tears running clean streaks down her cheeks, and staring into the patch of forest that climbed up and out of Sunrise Valley. When she saw Briar, her lips began to tremble and she toyed with one of her long braids.

"They don't mind me, Bri. I tell them to mind me and they don't. I tried to tell 'em that new lady didn't really want them catching supper; she was just shooing them out of doors. But they told me they was going hunting. What can four-year-old boys hunt? They're going to get theirselves killed." She crossed her arms over her chest. "At first, I won't care. I'll feel bad about it later, but it'll be their own faults."

Poor Pansy. She took everything to heart. Those boys knew just how to get to her, too. "I'll go find them. Do you want to come with me or go back in the house?"

Pansy looked warily at the house. "I don't know. What happened to Nanny?"

"Did you ask Fanny?"

"Is that her name?" Pansy lowered her voice, even though they were far enough away from the cottage not to be overheard. "She didn't tell us nothing, just started giving us food. Nanny walked out this afternoon to use the privy and then Fanny walked back in. Did you know she doesn't make us wash up before eating? And she doesn't make us wait for dinner, neither; we can eat something small if we're hungry. But I made the boys wash up anyway 'cause I know Nanny would want us to even if she's not here. That other lady's not like our Nanny at all." A tentative smile spread across her face, revealing she was cautiously optimistic.

Like Briar, she'd had too many changes in her young life and wasn't too trusting. Their Nanny didn't have a gentle touch or an imagination. She'd been hard on Pansy, who was a daydreamer, while letting the boys run free. Fanny might be a welcome change if first impressions proved correct.

"Nanny didn't even tell you she was leaving?" Briar asked.

"That lady said Miss Prudence—that's what she calls Nanny—was in an awful hurry and didn't have time to take a breath. That lady said we were going to have some fun while Nanny was gone and the boys started jumping up and down on the beds, and that's when she kicked them outside to catch our supper."

"That lady's name is Miss Fanny. And until Nanny

comes back, we'll have to do our best to make our new guardian feel at home."

Pansy sighed. "You mean watch the twins."

"Yes, watch the twins."

A *whoop* to the right of the hedgerow sounded, and Briar set out into the forest to wrangle the boys. She found them kneeling on the ground, ten feet from the path that led to the backside of the Prince property, their strawberry blond heads together over a little bunny caught in a trap. *How in the world?*

"Benny! Jack! What are you doing to that innocent critter?"

They beamed up at her, cute little cherub faces that got them out of more scrapes than Briar cared to admit. Their matching grins and freckled noses were proud. All the Jennys had freckled faces, but the boys had them from top to bottom.

"Supper, Briar. We was hopin' for a spring turkey," Jack said, "but we caught him instead. He'll do, won't he?"

"One day that bunny might be supper, but it's too little right now. You've got to let it grow up. Now, let it go."

"Aw, can't we keep it, Bri?" Jack gave her his best pleading face. He was covered in dirt up to his elbows and had a fresh bruise on his right knee. Nanny would have had a fit if he came into her house so dirty.

"We'll take care of it," Benny piped in. "We'll give it food and water and Nanny'll never even know we got us a cottontail."

"'Specially since she ain't here."

"Isn't here," Briar corrected. She thought for a moment. Caring for a contraband pet might be the right kind of distraction to stop the boys from causing more trouble. "If you can find a way to keep it from escaping back into the forest, and keep it hidden from Fanny, then yes."

"Who's Fanny?" Jack asked.

Good question. "Let's go find out."

The walk back to the cottage took a considerable amount of time because the boys kept taking turns holding the bunny. They chose the back of the overgrown garden as the ideal location to hide it. Nanny did have a hard time growing things. The patch of dried and bent cornstalks was tall enough to hide a makeshift pen. The boys raided the junk heap for boards and chicken wire, then rigged up a temporary pen for the night.

When Briar and the children finally came around the house, Fanny was outside, sprinkling flower petals in front of the door and on the windowsills.

With a tiny squeal of joy, Pansy skipped over. "May I help?" she asked in her most polite voice.

"Of course, dearie. Here, you do that window. Make sure you get the corners." Pansy took a handful of petals from Fanny's little pouch while the boys ran inside, not interested at all in the strange decorating.

"What are you doing?" Briar asked.

Fanny looked up, surprise on her face. "Primroses. I looked for them in your garden, but I shouldn't be shocked not to find any. Prudence never was a gardener. Your family is Irish, yes? Didn't your mammy teach you about primroses in spring?"

"No," said Pansy, wide-eyed. She drank in any information that might relate to Mam. "What about primroses in spring?"

Fanny checked with Briar.

Briar shook her head. Mam had never spoken of such things.

"Primroses on the thresholds keep the bad fairies away."

CHAPTER FOUR

Pansy's face paled. Briar put her hands on her hips. "Please don't go putting thoughts into the wee one's head. She comes up with enough on her own. You'll have her up all night scared to fall asleep."

"Oh, she'll sleep fine, won't you, lass? Now that we've spread our primroses."

Briar stepped over the petals, into the cottage, and found the boys about to dip their fingers into the stew.

"Stop! Go wash your hands."

They grinned at each other before scampering out to the water pump while Briar set the table.

Fanny came in and ladled the stew into bowls. Then she placed thick pieces of bread smothered in butter at each spot. The twins raced back through the door, and their eyes grew wide. They'd never eaten this well under Nanny's watch. Nanny wasn't motherly or domestic, simply practical. She burned everything she tried to cook and left the majority of chores to Pansy, then Briar on weekends, so they would be "well-trained" for managing a future household.

Of all the potential mother figures in her life, Nanny was too much of a distant and stoic caretaker to be considered motherly. Miss Olive, keeper at the boardinghouse, was more like an aunt. But there was something friendly and warm about Miss Fanny. Briar could understand why the children had taken to her so quickly.

She caught Fanny's eye as the boys dipped their bread. "Thank you," Briar said, and she hoped Fanny felt the depth beneath her thanks.

"Where did all this good food come from?" asked Pansy, diving into a second bowl.

"Manners, Pansy."

"She just wants to know if it came from the magic cupboard," Jack said.

"Children, don't be rude," Briar scolded. *What would Fanny think of them making fun?*

"But I'm not," Pansy said. "She goes into the sideboard and brings out whatever we want."

"Pansy—"

"The children are so easily pleased," Fanny interrupted. She laughed, sounding like tinkling bells. "And I love to cook," she said, winking at Pansy. "It's the one thing I can do well. I hope you love to eat."

All the children nodded. Feed a stray dog and he'll be your best friend for life. Well, Fanny had certainly walked into a pack of stray dogs who hadn't received much food or affection. At the rate she was going, they'd never let her leave.

"When is Nanny coming back?" Pansy asked. "Soon?"

Fanny shrugged. "Soon, late, it's all the same. She'll be back when she's done her business."

"She's never had business before," Briar said.

"Yes she has," Jack said. "Lots of business when you're gone and she thinks we're not looking."

Fanny's eyes grew wide at Jack's confession, but then she masked her expression and turned back to Briar. "There you have it. Lots of business." She quickly plunked more food onto Jack's plate. "Fill your mouth."

"How do you know Nanny?" Briar again asked the question that had been ignored earlier. She took another bite. Fanny was indeed the better cook. The children would be well fed if not well supervised.

"We go way back," Fanny answered flippantly.

"To the Old Country?" Pansy asked.

Whenever someone in the countryside spoke of going back, it was when they were reminiscing about the Old Country. Briar had heard it often enough from Mam and her friends who used to gossip over tea on Sundays. They'd talk about the things they missed: sea air, the old folks talking about the free days, and the things they didn't miss: the hardship, the lack of food. The more they talked, the thicker their brogue, even from those who emigrated when they were wee things.

"I suppose you could say so," Fanny answered thoughtfully. "I hardly remember a time when I didn't know her."

"How come we've never met you before?" Benny asked. His spoon paused its rapid ascent to his mouth.

"You are young and there are a lot of people you've never met before. You might meet someone new tomorrow."

Benny and Jack looked at each other with wide eyes. Briar could see their brains whirling, wondering who would be sitting to tea in their cottage tomorrow. They were still so literal in their understanding.

"Did Nanny leave a note or a message for me?" Briar asked.

"She was in a bit of a hurry," Fanny said. "There wasn't much time for her to do anything but leave."

"Didn't she pass you on the road?" Pansy asked. "I thought she might have gone to tell you."

"No, she didn't," Briar said. "I wish she would have."

"Did Miss Mim send me anything?" Benny asked eagerly.

Briar smiled and pulled out a lemon drop for each of the children. She held them in her palm. "For dessert. Make sure you fill up first."

As Fanny buttered more bread for the boys, there was a knock at the door. Briar answered it to find Henry standing there with his straw basket.

"We had extra eggs today," he said. "Ma thought you might take them off our hands." He pushed his way into the room and set the basket on the table. When he saw Fanny, he gaped in surprise. "What are you—"

Fanny jumped up to shake his hand. "The name's Fanny," she said, pumping his arm up and down. "Nice to meet you."

"And you," Henry said slowly. "I brought eggs?"

Briar stepped toward the two. *Why did he say that like a question?*

Henry darted a glance to Briar and then back to Fanny. "Should I have brought anything else?"

"Oh, no," said Fanny. "We're fine. Nanny has only gone off to take care of a little something, and I'm here for the children while she's gone. Would you like to eat with us?" She stood and indicated he could take her seat.

"No, no, thank you." He jerked his thumb. "I should be getting back to my family?"

Briar cocked her head. Surefooted Henry Prince suddenly seemed so very unsure of himself. She narrowed her eyes. *What is he up to?*

"And how is your family?" asked Fanny.

"Fine. They're fine. As far as I know. I would know if they weren't…wouldn't I?"

Fanny nodded encouragingly.

Briar scrunched up her forehead, trying to figure out this odd exchange.

Henry nodded in time with Fanny as he backed his way to the door. He waved to the children. "See you, Briar." With that he was out the door, not even trying to find an excuse to spend more time with them.

"Anyone for dessert?" asked Fanny.

"Dessert!" yelled the boys.

Briar quickly transferred the eggs into a bowl on the counter. "I'll be right back." She flew out the door with the basket tucked into the crook of her arm. She looked up and down the lane, but Henry had disappeared with the sunset. She hurried to the corner and spotted him. Running.

"Henry!" she yelled. He heard and stopped, allowing her to catch up to him.

"What's the rush?" she said.

"Nothing." He slowly grinned. "Did you want me to stay?"

"No," she said, irritated. "It's just that you usually do. To play with the twins. They'll be disappointed you didn't stay longer." She pushed the basket at him. "And you left this."

"Thanks."

Briar stood awkwardly, waiting for him to say something else. He didn't. He was silent but fidgety, and kept wiggling his legs like he wanted to go. "Do you know Fanny?" she finally asked. "It seems like maybe you two have met before."

"There's something I need to tell you." He wiped his hand over his face. "I've been thinking on what you said. How we Princes never go anywhere."

"Oh?"

"I think it's time one of us does leave. Me. There's something I have to do."

Why does everyone have something to do all of a sudden?

"What is it?" She eyed his frayed pants and bare feet. How was Henry going to go anywhere? Didn't his family need him working at the mill, same as the rest of the young people in the valley?

He looked over Briar's shoulder. "Prove myself, I guess."

"To whom? Me?" She felt her face going hot and was glad for the twilight. "I was angry about Wheeler is all. I shouldn't have said what I did. You love it here. Don't leave because of me."

His gaze returned to hers. "Beautiful Briar."

He'd said it without a hint of flirting, and Briar caught her breath.

"It's something I have to do for my family. If we all continue the same thing that's gone on before, nothing changes, right? I've watched you, Briar. I see how hard you work so those children won't have to enter the mill too early, if at all. You're making a difference for your family. It makes me think I can be the one who makes a difference for my family." He took in a deep breath and gazed up into the hills. "Just because you love a place doesn't mean you don't ever feel stuck there."

Briar shook her head. "Where will you go? Next town over? The next one? You already told me they're all the same." Henry wasn't the type to feel stuck. Was he?

He laughed. "I did say that, didn't I? Well, that means I'll have to go farther then, maybe over the ocean to the Old Country where the Princes started out. Our old forest is now part of Germany. I'll find my roots. Settle some old family debts."

First Wheeler, then Nanny, and now Henry. Henry the dependable one. She had to convince him to stay. She couldn't imagine what the valley would be like without him. "How are your parents to survive without your mill wages?"

Henry avoided her eyes. "They'll be fine."

"Who's going to be my doffer if you go?"

He gave her a crooked smile. "I shouldn't be doffing for you anyway, Bri." He splayed his hands out. "In case you haven't noticed, I'm way too big to be climbing all over the frame, swapping out the bobbins. I have been for years, and it's only slowing you down. You'll see when you get a little one to help you."

"But—"

"And I can tell another machinist how to fix your frame when it breaks. I don't do anything special to keep it going. I just tweak it every time I doff."

As twilight turned to dusk, he was left in shadow, a silhouette. He *was* taller, and his shoulders broader, more like a man's than a boy's. When did this happen? While she was watching Wheeler? All the other boys Henry's age had moved on to other tasks at the factory long ago. It hadn't occurred to Briar that being held back to help her would bother Henry.

"Besides, you have more options than you think, Bri. I know about that book you keep in your apron pocket. I know you have dreams. Why don't you join the other girls in one of their Improvement Societies?"

Surprised, Briar absently touched her pocket and traced the edges of the book. So much had occurred since she got home, she'd forgotten to take off her apron. The slim book was a novel given to her by her teacher the day

Briar left school to start work at the mill as a doffer with Henry and the others. Years later, she still hadn't finished it. *How does he know me so well?*

"Not much time for learning when I get paid for doing." Annoyed he'd found her sore spot, she changed the subject. "Nanny left without saying good-bye. Is this *your* good-bye?"

He shook his head. "I'll need to make arrangements, so I can still walk you back into town after church tomorrow and then catch the train."

Why did everyone keep leaving her? She tried hardening her heart to protect it.

"Don't delay on my account. Good-bye, Henry Prince." Briar spun around and marched down the lane. When she got to the corner, her still-tender heart battled her pride to look back. She turned but couldn't see if he was still there. The way was too dark.

CHAPTER FIVE

Sunday morning, the boys woke Briar up early as they tried sneaking out of the house on their own. For all their effort, they were about as loud as the mail train pulling into town.

"Hurry," Jack whispered loudly. "'Fore she wakes up."

Briar opened one eye, but her back was to the boys. The other half of the bed she was in was empty and rumpled. Had Nanny been home, the sheets would have been made neat as a pin already. Judging by the amount of light, no one should be up and moving yet. Briar rolled over to see Pansy still asleep on the floor mat where she slept Saturday nights.

Carefully, she pushed herself off the bed and padded after the boys to the door.

"Where are you boys off to this early? We've got church today," Briar whispered, stopping them by grabbing the necks of their shirts.

"The bunny, Briar," Jack said, twisting loose.

"We've got to make sure he's still in his pen," Benny

added. "He might'a got out last night. Besides, we told you we'd take care of him an' he needs his breakfast."

Jack held up a squished slice of bread he must have put in his pocket during suppertime and then slept on.

Nodding, Briar followed the boys outside. "Did you see when Fanny got up?" she asked.

"Nope," Benny said.

"She was awake even earlier than Nanny," Jack said. "Didn't think anyone waked up as early as she did. Where did Nanny go, Briar? Is she coming back or is she gone forever like Mam and Da?" Questions asked, Jack ran ahead, not waiting for the answers.

Briar sighed. She didn't know what to tell him.

Benny took off running after his brother. By the time she'd caught up with the boys, they'd both climbed into the secret pen. Intuitively, Jack had cradled the bunny on its back, making it calm enough to endure the petting Benny was giving it. The food they'd left for it last night was gone, but it didn't seem interested in the bread.

"I'll get you some plants from the forest today, boys, but you'll be on your own tomorrow."

Briar left them making cute faces at the bunny and wandered onto the path, glad for the quiet and the slowly warming light. She peered through the trees to the forest floor trying to find some Solomon's Seal, not for the bunny but because Henry said they'd started blooming and she wanted to see.

Voices coming down the path made her pause. She didn't want to get pulled into neighborly chitchat when she needed more time at the cottage getting to know Fanny. Quickly, she gathered some clover, dandelions, and tall grasses, enough for two days in case the boys had trouble on their own. But then she distinctly heard Henry's voice.

He was just the person she needed to see. She'd stayed up late after the children had gone to bed to write a letter to someone she had never met and didn't know if she was even still alive. Mam had a sister who'd stayed behind in Ireland, and they'd lost touch. It was a long shot, but Henry was the first person she knew who planned to go overseas. He might be able to do what the general post had not.

But what was he doing back here so soon, and who was he talking to? It could be his mother if he told her his plans to leave the valley. She might be trying to talk him out of it. After all, no Prince ever left the valley. Under pretense of gathering more food, Briar inched closer to the voices. She peered through the leaf cover until she saw Henry. However, she couldn't see the person he was talking to unless she stepped out from behind her hiding spot.

"There is no need," said a distant female voice. "She's a good tracker. She'll take care of it."

"Aren't you tired of this?" Henry asked. His voice came out loud and filled with frustration. "Can't we end it once and for all and then we can move on with our lives?"

Briar strained her ears to make out what a second female voice was saying.

"You know your family has tried. What makes you think you can make a difference? We contain it. That's what we do. That's what you will do." Then the voice got whisper-quiet and Briar couldn't hear anything else. Whatever was said, Henry didn't like it because he threw his hands in the air and stalked off. In Briar's direction.

Briar spun around and trotted back to the boys, hoping Henry was so wrapped up in his own troubles that he didn't notice her.

The voices had been so quiet it was difficult to know who was speaking. One might have been Mrs. Prince, but what were they talking about? And what exactly went on at the Prince family farm? Before he could catch up to her, she darted around the back of the cottage and scooted into the enclosed space where the boys were hiding the bunny.

The boys lit up when they saw the food Briar had with her.

"I know how to pick those," Jack said.

"We both do. You don't need to help us anymore, Bri. We can do it ourselves."

Briar reached over to ruffle the hair on both their heads. "I know you can. You two are smart boys. But you best let the bunny alone for now. We've got to get breakfast and be off to church."

They climbed out of the pen and followed Briar back to the house.

"What do you think his name should be?" Benny asked. "Jack picked a stupid name, but I think it should be Hoppers because he hops."

Jack punched Benny. "Whitey is not stupid."

Briar was about to reprimand the boys when they turned the corner and saw Henry leaning up against the fence. His arms and legs were both crossed casually, his arms bare from his rolled shirt-sleeves, and he was biting on the end of a long piece of grass like he hadn't a care in the world. Like she hadn't been short with him last night. Like he wasn't about to up and leave them.

The boys tore away from Briar and rushed to Henry.

"We've got a secret!" Jack shouted.

"Hush, boys," Briar said before Benny could chime in to explain. "A secret isn't a secret if everyone knows it."

Henry bent down to the boys' level. "Briar's right. If you do have a good secret, you should keep it quiet until you have permission to tell it."

"What do you mean a good secret?"

"Well, the opposite of a bad secret. If someone asks you to keep a bad secret, you should tell."

Jack's eyes grew wide and Benny asked the question for him. "What's a bad secret?"

"One that you know in your heart isn't right, and you should tell Briar."

"'Cause she's responsible for us?" Benny asked, repeating what she told them whenever they asked about having a mam and a da.

"And loves us," added Jack.

"That's right. There isn't anything she wouldn't do for you if you were ever in trouble."

"And we'd help her, too," said Benny.

"I'm counting on it. You boys are sharp. You can help Briar by keeping watch at the cottage. Tell her anything unusual that happens. Like if the birds stop singing. Or the wind blows extra hard. Or the leaves on the trees curl and turn black."

Henry's tone had suddenly gotten serious. This change was so unlike him that the hairs on Briar's neck prickled and she gave a shiver. "Don't scare the boys," she chided him, forcing her tone to stay light.

"We've got a guard bunny," Jack whispered.

Benny nodded. "He'll let us know if someone bad comes along."

"Is that your secret?" Henry looked up and grinned at Briar. The old Henry was back. The dependable Henry. The Henry who didn't put scary thoughts into little boys' heads.

"We don't want Fanny to know in case she doesn't like bunnies. We have to watch her first before we decide," Benny said. He then took off, starting a race with Jack to the cottage.

"Why did you scare the boys like that?" Briar asked.

"They weren't scared. Boys like that kind of thing," Henry said, opening the door to the cottage and standing back to let Briar go in first. "Besides, if they're going to wander in the woods alone, they need to pay better attention to their surroundings."

Fanny was back inside and had breakfast on the table. Pansy sat at her seat with her hair already neatly braided and a scowl on her face. Likely upset she didn't wake up early enough to sneak off with the boys to see the bunny.

Fanny nodded at Henry and waved the boys over to their full bowls of porridge. Briar was trying to think up a way to explain their absence, but Fanny never even asked. She added a bowl for Henry and, as soon as everyone was done, had them all shuffled out the door and on to church.

"You've never walked with us to church before," Briar said. She slowed her step, hoping to be able to speak to Henry without the boys monopolizing his attention, but they had each taken hold of one hand as if they knew he was fixing to leave them.

"Let's talk on the way back to town tonight," Henry said, holding up the boys' hands.

Briar nodded. She let them bound ahead, leaving her with Pansy and Fanny.

"Briar is an unusual name," Fanny said.

"It's actually Briarly Rose. The girls in my family are named after flowers. Variations of the name Briar Rose go back generations. My mother was also called Briarly."

"And I'm Pansy Poppy," Pansy said. She looked torn between racing up with the boys or staying behind and listening to Briar and Miss Fanny.

"A perfect name for you, Pansy Poppy. Did you know that fairies like to use flower names to nickname children?

Since you already have a flower name, maybe the fairies will leave you alone."

Pansy smiled but then looked uncertain, as if she didn't know if she wanted a fairy to notice her or not.

"Briar Rose, just like Sleeping Beauty," Fanny said. "Pansy tells me you work in a room full of spindles. Best keep your fingers to yourself. That other Briar Rose was too curious for her own good."

"Good thing the other Briar Rose was a fairy tale, then," Briar said. Her workplace *was* rather dangerous. The operatives had to keep their hair up and watch that their clothing and fingers stayed a safe distance away from the machines. The doffers, usually small children like Pansy, got hurt when they weren't paying attention and accidentally wedged their fingers into the machinery. Briar set her jaw. She would do anything to keep her little sister from having to work there, too.

CHAPTER SIX

When Briar started work, she'd signed a contract, like all the other girls, that included a moral clause requiring her to attend church. Didn't matter if their denomination was available or not, a Catholic had to attend a Protestant church until a Catholic church could be built.

Briar didn't mind. She would have gone to services in the little country church no matter what, but some girls bristled at the idea of being forced to go, even if they wanted to. Now that Mam and Da were gone, her church family helped fill the void like aunts and uncles would. They took an interest in Briar and the children, and helped Nanny with repairs around the cottage. It was a small, poor community, fewer than ten families, mostly older folks, who lived even farther out from town. They met in a converted barn, one of the farmers doubling as the preacher. They shared what little they had, but no one had either the room or the energy for the Jenny children full-time, or Nanny would have already moved them on.

Today Briar struggled to concentrate on the sermon.

She found herself constantly glancing over at Henry's family to get any hints if they knew what he was planning and if they approved.

The Princes sat in her line of sight. Mr. Prince was a lumberjack of a man, with a graying beard and mustache and incredible concentration on the sermon, only belied by the occasional twitch of a facial muscle as he clenched his jaw. Mrs. Prince was his opposite: a lace parasol, elegant and frilly, hovering over Henry. She kept glancing at her son like she wanted to whisper something in his ear, but kept changing her mind and glanced at her husband instead.

They didn't approve. Or at least, they had reservations.

The service was ending and Briar lost what little focus she had after the preacher told everyone to make sure they said good-bye to Henry. The congregation stood to sing "It is Well with My Soul." They'd sung it so often she could say the words and be thinking about Henry leaving at the same time. But despite what she sang today, her soul was not well; it was troubled.

The children scattered as soon as the preacher said "Amen," and the rest of the congregation swarmed around Henry with questions and well-wishes: Where was he going? Why was he leaving? It was about time a Prince went on an adventure.

They kept him so busy with their questions he didn't have time to look her way as she hovered at the edge of the crowd. *Pesky Henry Prince.* As much as he could exasperate her, she didn't want him to leave. She'd never admit it to him because it would only swell his head, but she had come to rely on him for so many things. Not only for fixing her spinning frame, but for keeping her level-headed about Wheeler, and the business with the children.

Sometimes he was a better chum than her room-mates.

Meanwhile, several ladies busied themselves setting up the tables and laying out the food for potluck. The news must have gone out last night for all the church ladies to be prepared with food to share. The children were shuffled through first, and by the time the last adult had filled a plate, the kids were off playing again.

"So glad you're leaving, Henry," Benny said as he ran by with cake crumbs on his lips.

Henry caught Briar's eye and she shrugged. They knew what Benny meant. He was excited about a party. But as soon as the memory of a rare dessert left, he'd be missing Henry something fierce. They all would. Henry shared with the boys a love of the forest, spending much of his free time home exploring with them. And Pansy, she liked everything about Henry. Especially how he included her in their forest explorations. Since the twins were so close to one another, Pansy often felt left out.

Pansy shyly held out her hand to him now. "You'll never plough a field by turning it over in your mind," she said in her sweet voice, quoting Da and sounding very grown-up. "Good-bye, and Godspeed."

Henry solemnly shook hands. "Words of wisdom, Pansy. And I aim to act on them."

Unexpectedly, Pansy burst into tears. "Y-you shouldn't leave," she said. "Briar, don't let him leave. You should marry him, 'cause then you'd be a princess."

Briar blushed while Henry grinned in amusement. He knelt down to her level. "How would that make her a princess, little one?"

"Because that's what happens. When a girl marries a prince she becomes a princess." She looked up at Briar. Her innocent eyes wide; her best dress a plain cotton shift.

Her head filled with fairy tales. "Don't you want to be a princess?"

Briar shared an amused look with Henry. "That's not quite how it works," she said. She was about to explain the difference between last names and royalty, but Pansy's determined look quieted her. Let Pansy believe Henry could make Briar a princess if that helped her deal with his leaving. At that age, Briar would have thought the same thing and come up with some elaborately tragic love story. Now that she'd grown up, Briar knew that life was just tragic. Parents died. Children were orphaned. And older sisters failed at supporting their siblings properly.

Another group of well-wishers called Henry over to say good-bye, and Pansy, in that resilient way children have, put a smile back on her face and ran off to play in a new game of Red Rover.

Briar made polite conversation with the older ladies but kept her eye on Henry. She fingered the letter in her pocket, hoping he didn't think she was being ridiculous, sending him on a mission with odds as good as tossing a bottle into the ocean.

Finally, the folks said all they needed to, and the circle around Henry dwindled to his parents. They would say good-bye here, and then Henry and Briar would walk into town together. A Sunday afternoon ritual that Briar had never put much thought into before. Henry was always supposed to be there because he always had been.

Henry took all the attention in stride. He was a favorite in the valley and no one was about to let him go without saying their piece. Briar wondered if she were the one leaving, if anyone would notice. She hadn't the time to socialize like Henry seemed to. Too much work to do at the mill and then with the children. Speaking of... She searched the edges of the churchyard where the young ones tended to go—as far from the adults as they dared. One, two, three. All accounted for.

Briar hung back as Henry said good-bye to his parents. His mother adjusted his cloak, reiterated what she had packed for him. Touched his cheek. His dad stood with arms crossed, his face stoic.

"If it doesn't work, just come home. We'll continue what we've always done."

Briar jumped as Fanny touched her arm.

"Curiosity killed the cat," Fanny whispered.

Briar was about to protest that no, she wasn't listening in, but of course she was. Instead, realizing there was another way she could get information, Briar said, "Have you met the Prince family?" She stepped forward, grabbing Fanny by the arm so she had to follow. The woman stiffened at first, trying to avoid the introduction, but soon was face-to-face with the Princes.

"Hello, Mr. and Mrs. Prince," Briar said, studying their reactions to the newcomer. "Have you met Fanny? She's looking after the children until Nanny returns home."

With her usual warm smile, Mrs. Prince held out a gloved hand. "Welcome to Sunrise Valley. If you need anything, be sure to ask. On the weekends Henry is usually about the place—Oh!" She covered her mouth, and shook her head. "How could I forget? He's leaving tonight."

Henry busied himself with adjusting his small pack to avoid responding to his mother's outburst.

Well, Henry's mam didn't give any indication of knowing Fanny. Briar turned her attention to Mr. Prince, who stood stoically by until his wife's facade began to crack, and then he put an arm around her.

"Do you know where Nanny went?" Briar asked. "Do

you think she's gone to find homes for the children?"

All three Princes exchanged a look before Mrs. Prince answered. "Oh, no, don't think that. Not without telling you first."

Briar wasn't assured at all by Mrs. Prince's answer. Something was going on.

Mr. Prince nodded hello to Fanny. "We live in the farmhouse down the valley. You can get there by the lane, or, in the day, through the forest. Send the boys if there's an emergency; they know the way."

Fanny smiled. "We will be fine. After all, the trees grow without our help." At that, her eyes grew wide and she reached for Briar's arm. "Excuse us," she said.

Still trying to decipher the conversation, Briar was slow at noticing the twins. They were clear across the churchyard, having shimmied up the old oak, and perched themselves on a limb overhanging a group of older ladies. They were slowly releasing a string with a fishing hook at the end, getting closer and closer to Mrs. Clover's Sunday hat. It was a lovely hat, her pride and joy. Some said it made her too proud. It was covered in carnations and ribbons, but the centerpiece was a tiny bluebird sitting on a nest of eggs.

The boys had always been fascinated with Mrs. Clover's Sunday hat, and it looked like today was the day they were going to find out once and for all if the bird was a real trained pet (Benny's view) or a toy (Jack's view).

"Oh, no. I'm sorry, Fanny. They're generally good-hearted boys, although interested in everything." Briar ran over to intervene. *Too interested.* She waved her hands, trying to get their attention without arousing anyone else's suspicions. Mrs. Clover had suffered at the hands of the boys' curiosity before, and Briar couldn't take another incident.

"She's coming!" called the blacksmith's boy who stood

at the base of the tree as lookout. He took off running across the churchyard.

Instead of stopping what they were doing, the boys glanced up, judged the distance Briar had yet to go, and doubled their efforts to hook the bird. When the hook kept missing, they lowered it further to get the whole hat. They swung the hook once, twice, and hit their target.

"Mrs. Clover," Briar said as the boys pulled on the string. She reached up and caught the hat, deftly unhooking it. "Oh, look at that wind." Behind Mrs. Clover's back, Briar yanked the string out of the boys' hands, carefully balling it up and tucking the hook into her pocket before holding the prized hat in front of her. "I've always admired your Sunday hat. Where did you get it from?"

Mrs. Clover looked a little befuddled, especially with her hair out of sorts from the pull of the hat. "That's what I get for leaving home without stopping for my hatpin. Thank you, Briar. It is my favorite hat. It was given to me by my Matthew on our honeymoon."

Briar helped Mrs. Clover adjust her hair and her hat before turning around and looking for the boys. They had already scrambled out of the tree and were running for home. She was about to go after them when Fanny stepped in. "No, no. You go ahead with Henry. I'll just think of what Prudence would say, and say it twice. She's always been much better at reining in children."

Looking at Henry waiting with his cotton sack, then at the running feet of the twins, Briar felt pulled in two directions. She huffed. The boys would be here next weekend, and up to trouble again. She needn't worry about a missed opportunity to lecture them. Henry, on the other hand, was leaving. If she were to stop him, now was the time.

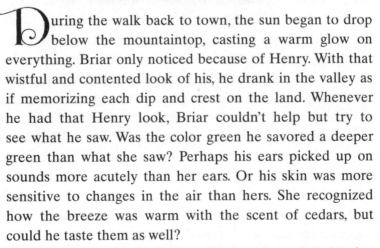

CHAPTER SEVEN

During the walk back to town, the sun began to drop below the mountaintop, casting a warm glow on everything. Briar only noticed because of Henry. With that wistful and contented look of his, he drank in the valley as if memorizing each dip and crest on the land. Whenever he had that Henry look, Briar couldn't help but try to see what he saw. Was the color green he savored a deeper green than what she saw? Perhaps his ears picked up on sounds more acutely than her ears. Or his skin was more sensitive to changes in the air than hers. She recognized how the breeze was warm with the scent of cedars, but could he taste them as well?

His cotton sack looked too empty for a boy leaving his home, as if he were leaving everything behind. It was filled with food his mother had put in for him. Briar knew because Mrs. Prince repeated what she had packed for him over and over: *cheese, bread, sausage, cheese, bread, sausage,* as if she couldn't find the words to tell him what she really meant: *Don't leave. I love you. You're my only son.*

"You think Fanny can keep an eye on those boys?" Henry asked, breaking the silence.

Briar groaned. "You saw?"

"I, myself, have been curious about Mrs. Clover's hat. I don't blame them at all for investigating."

"Well, Mrs. Clover would, had she known what they were doing."

"I had no idea you were so quick on your feet."

"With those boys? I have to be."

"I know you sacrifice a lot for them, Briar, but they won't be your responsibility forever. They'll grow up and you will be free to follow your own dreams."

"It might happen sooner than I like. Nanny only agreed to keep the children until I turned seventeen. That's this summer, and I don't know what I'm going to do. I'm afraid she's gone to find homes for them and Fanny is too nice to tell me."

"Nanny's *not* leaving you out of the decision making, Briar. She wouldn't do that."

"People do things you don't expect all the time." She gave him a playful shove, knocking him off-balance. "See? I never thought she'd leave without at least telling me. How well do you know her?"

He elbowed her back. "I've known her all my life, but I don't know her really well, just, you know, in the way that children know friends of their parents."

"So, like your family, she's always lived here?"

Henry smiled. "No. She moved in about the same time you moved here."

"Really? Good thing, that. No one else would take us."

"I know how just about every family ended up here. Or at least, my family used to keep track of that sort of thing before too many of the mills moved into town. Now it's a lot harder to notice the new people with all the comings and goings."

"So, your family keeps an eye on the valley?"

Henry laughed. "I guess it's a bit of a game with us. We are observers."

"Did you notice my family when we first moved here? You and I started the mill at the same time."

"Of course I noticed you."

"Lots of girls started work at the mill when I did."

"Ah, but no others were named Briar Jenny but you."

"So it's my name you noticed?"

"It caught my attention."

"And you were the one who introduced us to Nanny after Da died."

His jovial face grew serious. "With a name like yours, you needed protection. Nanny needed some life in her cottage. It was a good fit for everyone."

"What do you mean 'with a name like mine'?" Fanny had noted her name, too. But so many strange things had happened since yesterday, maybe this was just a coincidence. Henry never spoke of fairies like Fanny did, so he couldn't be teasing her about Sleeping Beauty, too. "Is it because I'm Irish and everyone assumes my da was a drunk and I'm a Catholic instead of a Protestant?"

Henry didn't answer. Perhaps she'd misunderstood him. He'd always said he liked her name, and now here she was assigning him bad motives.

"Speaking of names." Briar pulled out her letter. Flipped it over. Cleared her throat. "My mam had a sister who stayed behind. They lost touch and it was one of Mam's life regrets that the family never found out what happened to her." She gave him the letter labeled with as much of an address as Briar could remember, and he put it in his pocket.

"I don't expect you to find her. But if you have the letter with you and as you meet people on your way…could you… ask if they know her? She wouldn't want my mam's family to be split up. She might be our hope to stay together."

"Of course I'll try." He picked up an acorn and rolled it between his fingers. He handed it to her, like he did when they were kids and he collected them for her. "Is that where you plan to go when you leave the valley? Ireland? Even though you've never been there yourself?"

"Mam talked of it from morning till night: the green hills, the hunt for shamrocks, the music her da would play on the fiddle. She didn't want to leave in the first place, but her people were forced to. It was all she ever wanted to do, go back and find her older sister. But Da would always pipe in with how skewed her memories were. He'd say it wasn't as magical as she remembered. He focused on the potato famine that pushed both their families out. He only remembers starving." She paused, smiling at a memory. "Mam used to tell Da that it's easy to halve the potato where there's love. She always won that argument because Da did love her so. Had they lived, I'm sure he would have found a way to return home, since the famine is long past."

No matter how much Mam glossed over the lean years in Ireland, the stories of the potato famine scared Briar. Da spared no detail in telling how bad it got. How entire crops were destroyed by blight, a sick blackening of the plants and potatoes, leaving people with nothing to eat. How some were so desperate they ate grass and died anyway. How packs of dogs roamed looking for those not yet buried. And how much better things were for them in Sunrise Valley, despite the long hours and low wages. They ate. They were alive.

Until they weren't.

Weakened already from the famine, many died on the crossing, others after they'd arrived. Briar's immediate family was the only kin who survived the first full year in America.

She took a deep breath. "Mam had me promise that if I were able, I would set my feet on Irish soil. Try to find her sister who stayed behind with her husband."

After all the walks they'd had together, Briar had never told Henry this before. At least, not in so many words.

"Hope is a powerful thing." He looked at her with intense focus.

Henry was so earnest it broke Briar's heart. Not the way her heart hurt over Wheeler, but in a bittersweet kind of way. Why couldn't she be interested in Henry instead of Wheeler? Most of the time she couldn't take Henry seriously. If she were any other girl, not an orphan responsible for her siblings, maybe things could be different. She wouldn't feel like she was in a rush to settle with someone who was able to support an instant family. Besides, they were from two different communities. Some roots ran too deep to change.

He quirked a smile. "While I'm away, and if I were to do a feat of daring for you, what would you like? Take down a whale? Meet the queen? Build a railroad in honor of your upcoming birthday? I can do whatever you ask."

"Henry Prince, can you be serious for two minutes?"

He grinned. "Not around you, Briar. You fill my heart with too much joy I canna contain it." He attempted an Irish brogue that wasn't half bad.

There was a reason girls swooned around the young Irishmen working at the mill. That accent would weaken any girl's knees. Too bad Henry was such a flirt no girl could take him seriously.

As Briar looked up at the mountaintop, a strain of music settled into her mind. She had nothing else to give Henry but a proper Irish send-off. A peace offering, so he wouldn't leave thinking she didn't care.

She sang the notes of her da's fiddle. "Dum da dim diddle laddie, dumble da diddle dum." Starting off fast, she then repeated the song slowly and mournfully, ending twice as fast as she started.

"That was beautiful." He looked at her with gentle eyes. "What was it?"

"A farewell reel used in the leave-taking ceremony. Mam said when they left Ireland they held an American wake and that was the last song to send them off. A farewell to Ireland. They were being exiled to a foreign land." She paused. "And it's what Da sang to Mam as she passed on."

"Thank you. For sharing that with me."

Now that she'd done it, she was embarrassed she'd shared something so personal. "I hope you find whatever it is you're looking for," she said, turning the focus back to Henry. "What *are* you looking for?"

"First, I'm going to find me a sailing vessel and see if I can't convince some of my own family to take me in. We've much to catch up on." He swung his pack off his back and peered inside as if checking to make sure he had everything. The contents had shifted and Briar could see the corners of a boxy shape poking into the cloth.

"Perhaps you can live your dream through me until you can follow it yourself. I can send you letters detailing my great adventures," he said.

"In the Old Country."

"Yes."

"'Tis not the same." No, she couldn't ever live her dream

through Henry. She had to live it herself. "You've never talked about the Old Country before. You're not a family in exile like the Irish. Driven out by famine and ill treatment."

That shared family history was what had made her and Wheeler a good match, and what made their breakup hurt so much now. She had thought he was the one. How could she have been so mistaken? She could never trust her feelings again. Even more so, how was a girl to know the depth of a boy's feelings?

"I understand why you don't see my family that way. I've not talked about our home country to you. I didn't want to make you think of something that made you sad. But our family talks about it daily. Our past is as alive to us as a person living in our house, hovering in every room, listening in on all our conversations. My ancestors left things undone and I'm hoping I can fix that."

"And how—"

Henry held up his hand. "I don't want to talk about it. You won't understand what it's like to have something like this hanging over your family." He settled his bag back on his shoulder, leaning with the added weight.

Briar crossed her arms. Yes, she was familiar with a past that haunted the present. Her mam and da were always foremost in her mind. Her strongest memories were of Mam on her deathbed after birthing the twins, begging Briar to find a way to go home. Of Da on his deathbed as he lay stricken with consumption, admonishing her that she would have to look after the wee ones, and see the twins didn't hurt themselves. Neither one of them had spoken of finding happiness for their oldest daughter. They'd spoken only of duty.

She wasn't bitter, because she agreed with them. She

was the eldest Jenny left. It was up to her to raise the wee ones and keep them together. Given that she only made enough money to rent a shared bed in a company boardinghouse, she didn't know how she could make it work, but she had to try.

By this time they were nearing the edge of town and traffic had picked up. Carts and buggies and single riders driving into town pushed them to the side of the road. They passed the train station and Briar said again, "You don't have to walk me all the way to the boardinghouse. We can say good-bye here. I don't want you to miss your train."

"There'll be another one."

Henry was so stubborn. When he set his mind to something, there was no talking him out of it. If they said good-bye in front of all the other girls, Briar wouldn't be able to voice all that she was thinking. Not that she could pin down her thoughts yet. They swirled as fast as the threads winding on her spinning frame. Should they shake hands? Hug? They'd done neither in all their years growing up together. And why was this the foremost thought in her head now? It was just Henry. *Henry.* And he was leaving her.

They passed the mill and wandered down the row of boardinghouses. They all looked the same. Brown-brick, three-story affairs with stairs leading up to porches where, in nice weather, much socializing took place. Tonight, however, the front porch was blessedly empty of gossipy mill girls. Henry walked her to the front door and took a deep, shaking breath.

Is he nervous, too?

A sudden lump formed in her throat. The weekend trips home to the cottage were sure going to be lonely. She didn't know if she should admit that to Henry or not. He could get ideas. But if you can't count on a Prince, who can you count on?

The only way she'd be able to get through this was to stir up the anger she felt earlier. He was getting to do the thing she wanted to do most in the world. He didn't know how fortunate he was to have the choice to go. He had so many freedoms she didn't.

She stiffened her back. "Thank you for walking me home," she said. "I wish you safe travels." Her voice sounded overly formal, given their friendship.

He flashed a sheepish grin. "You could run away with me. See if we couldn't set your feet on Irish soil."

Incorrigible Henry Prince. "I'd better go inside," Briar said. Whether he acted it or not, he needed to catch that train. She reached out her hand to shake his at the same time he moved in to hug her.

They both laughed.

Before Briar could decide what to do next, Henry caught her hand and kissed it on that soft spot between first finger and thumb. There was something gentlemanly about the motion that raised her opinion of Henry another notch. When he held her hand longer than was proper, she let him, but then pulled away, clasping her hands together.

He opened the door and waited for her to turn around and wave before he nodded, shutting the door between them. The hallway darkened.

"Good-bye, Henry Prince," Briar said to the closed door. *Take care of the letter. And yourself.*

CHAPTER EIGHT

Briar hung her coat on a peg, and there was a rush of legs as the boarders in the house began dashing downstairs. Mim zipped by, pushing girls out of the way and squeezing into the parlor. Another room-mate, Ethel, followed slowly behind the other girls. Briar caught Ethel's arm as she was about to turn into the parlor. "What's the rush?"

"Miss Olive is finished with the latest Godey's Lady's book and is dividing it up. Mim wants the fashion section, of course. I'm vying for the conclusion to 'Loyal Foes' before Mary gets it. Want to help my odds?" She pulled Briar into the parlor.

"Actually, I'd rather have a look at the local paper," Briar said, observing the woman near the pianoforte carefully cutting pages out of the magazine while girls gathered around like little chicks about a mother hen. Her brown hair was put up in the fashion of the time, but her age was difficult to discern. She was old enough to be any of their mothers, for certain, but was she of grandmotherly age or not? Her hair had a touch of silver mixed in but was cleverly hidden with fancy combs placed just so. She had no family other than "her girls," as she called all the young women who came and went through the boardinghouse over the years.

Briar continued, whispering, "She's not going to save up much for herself if she keeps spending her earnings on us."

Ethel smiled. "You *have* been listening to my savings lectures. Don't worry about Miss Olive. She's a smart businesswoman—keeps her girls happy, educates us, and we all love her for it. If she were ever in need, we'd all pitch in to help."

"I think you are her star pupil."

"I have to be," Ethel said. "In this world a woman has to look out for herself. It is the woman's century, after all."

Ethel spotted an empty seat on the sofa and scooted the other girls over to make room for them.

Mim rolled her eyes at Ethel as she came back triumphant with the fashion section. "I'll show you the way out of the mill," she said. "Spend your money on frivolity such as these and catch the eye of a rich man. It's a whole lot less work and a lot more fun than what you've got planned."

"Make sure you pick the right man, Mim. You don't want just any rich man or you'll regret it the rest of your life," Ethel said.

"Oh, pooh. You're such a spoil sport." She wiggled her hips in between the two girls. "Let me show you, Briar. You've got such natural beauty buried under your plain garb. I can bring it out in a minute if you'd only spend your money on a trinket now and then."

Briar took one look at the fancy dress with leg-o'-

mutton sleeves ending in not one, but three ruffles of batiste lace. "I'll never be able to afford a silk dress trimmed in lace," she said.

Mim turned the page. "That's not the point. These pictures are for inspiration. You find what you like, then adapt it to what you have. Like this bonnet."

The bonnet in question was smaller than Briar's mam's, with an enormous bow on the front and a ribbon to tie under her chin. Such a flouncy thing would seem out of place with her plain calico frock.

"Wear this out walking with your Wheeler and what a handsome couple you would make. He would be proud to have you on his arm."

Briar did a quick check to see if Sadie heard. Thankfully, she was no longer in the room. "Keep your voice down," Briar chided. Having to live in the same boardinghouse as Sadie was hard enough, but to add Mim's cavalier comments about Wheeler made it oft unbearable. Mim was convinced Sadie was a passing fancy, the last wild oats of a young man nervous about marriage. She thought of Briar's time with him as an investment that needed protecting. However, after seeing him walking with Sadie yesterday, Briar wasn't so sure.

Briar spotted the newspaper and retrieved it, opening it to the want ads.

Mim flipped a couple of pages in her magazine section. "Or what about a scent? Give him a change from machinery grease. He'd become so intoxicated around you he'd follow after you like a puppy."

"Mim!" Briar fanned her face, trying to stop the blush from spreading and the gossips from noticing.

Ethel rose and went to get her story. "Now her," Mim said, pointing in Ethel's direction. "She's going to have a harder time catching a man than most. She's all points and corners. A man wants someone who is soft, welcoming. A sweet bun, not a horseradish."

Briar wanted to stick up for her friend, but Mim had a point. Ethel wasn't welcoming to any of the men who came around the house. She cut them off short before they could even get to know her. So if Briar was to take advice about men from anyone in the house, Mim was the most logical. She went walking out with someone every weekend, and this summer would likely have a picnic lunch planned for every Sunday. It wouldn't be long until Mim found the man who fit her list. She did have a way of getting their attention.

"How much does one of those cost?" Briar asked, pointing to the bonnet, knowing in her mind that a bonnet wasn't the reason she and Wheeler broke up, but her heart was interested anyway.

Mim must have noticed Briar's wary expression, because she followed up with: "We're industrious women. We'll spruce up the one you've got."

Briar focused back on the paper. Here wasn't much more hope than the bonnet. She scanned the want ads, looking for fancy housewives needing help with sewing.

Wanted: seamstress with skill. Fancywork a must. NINA.

Wanted: fast sewer for growing family. NINA

Wanted: smocking work. NINA

NINA. *No Irish Need Apply*. She only wanted to do their sewing, not nanny their children.

Mim read over her shoulder. "Ninnies. Remember, we have a deal."

Briar shook her head. "I couldn't. If we were caught you'd never be hired again."

Mim shrugged. "It'll be their loss."

Ethel came back triumphant with the story, followed by five other girls. "We're going to stay in the parlor and take turns reading it aloud. Did you want to listen?"

Happy to take her mind off her troubles for a moment, Briar stayed behind to listen to the serial while Mim pointed out that the fashion for colored underwear had passed, and most women now preferred white lingerie, hand-sewn and very fine.

They were nearing the climax of the tale when Miss Olive came in. "The curfew bell is about to sound. Be ready to end."

"Oh, but please let us conclude the matter! There was a shipwreck and innocent Arthur is alive after all. We must find out what happens when he sees his Millie again," said Mary.

"Please," begged the crowd of girls.

"Well, in that case." Miss Olive sat on the sofa's edge and waved Ethel on. "You'd better read quickly. We don't want to leave poor Millie in the dark about her love."

Minutes after the curfew bell rang, all the girls applauded Ethel's reading. Then they scattered, discussing the fate of the characters as they rushed off to bed.

By the time Briar got up to her room, Ania, the quiet Polish girl, was already in bed, having returned from her friend's boardinghouse. She hadn't learned much English yet, and preferred the company of her Polish friends to visiting with her housemates. It was no secret she wanted to change houses as soon as a bed opened up for her.

"I'll be sorry to see her go," Mim whispered, pointing to the sleeping form. "Best bed-mate I've ever had. She's hardly ever here and such a slip of a thing, I get more space."

"You mean since she doesn't own anything, you get her extra drawer space," said Ethel.

"Did you like the ending to your story, Ethel? Did you find it romantic, or was it overly sentimental?" Mim changed the subject, putting Ethel on the spot. "Do you think the wrong people ended up together?"

"I prefer the action sequences," Ethel retorted. "Briar? Be the voice of youth for us. What did you think? Your opinion should matter more than two old spinsters."

At this barb, Mim's eyes flashed, and Briar stepped between the two. "Neither of you are old spinsters and you know it. I liked the story just fine except for the shipwreck part." She sat in a heap on the bed. "Henry left on the train tonight. He plans to travel overseas. I'd hate for him to go missing for two years and have everyone think he was dead."

"A Prince is leaving the valley?" Mim said. "I predict a flurry of new rumors about the reclusive family. And that's a way to end the evening on a high note. Good night, all," Mim said. She clicked the valve to turn off the gas lamp, plunging the room into darkness.

Briar settled into her portion of the bed she shared with Ethel, and lay on her side.

After Mim had fallen asleep, Briar whispered, "Ethel? You awake?"

"Yes."

"I think Nanny has started making arrangements for the children."

"Why do you say that?"

"She knows my plans have changed and her deadline is coming up. She wasn't at the cottage this weekend. She sent a friend in her place while she takes care of some unnamed business that could go on for weeks."

"She could be doing something personal she can't share with you. Don't go jumping to conclusions just because it's foremost on your mind."

"I know, but that's not what my gut is telling me. I have to prepare for the worst."

"I'm sorry. And I'm sorry about Henry leaving," Ethel whispered before rolling over. "Are there more frames open on your floor? Could you take on another?"

Briar ran the figures in her mind. She was responsible for four frames. Eight sides with 136 spindles on each side meant 1,088 spindles in all, ten hours a day, six days a week. If number four would work properly, she could handle one more, two if everything ran perfectly, which it never did.

"Maybe. It would make for a busy day, but I'm there anyway."

Tomorrow she'd ask the overseer. Tonight she would fret over Henry.

CHAPTER NINE

And fret she did. All night long she imagined every possible tragedy that could befall Henry while he traveled for the first time, and so far away from home. Too soon the morning mill bells were clanging, signaling wake-up time. She thumped out of bed with the rest of her room-mates and dressed. Years of the same routine made it automatic.

While waiting for Ania to wash at the water basin, she stretched and yawned, trying to wake up. Mim was busy pinning her hair, peering at Godey's to mimic a new style. Ethel was already done and buttoning up her boots, her hair pinned tightly back, more concerned with safety than vanity.

Ania finished, and then nodded at her room-mates before scooting out the door. Briar quickly washed up, then gathered her items for laundry to add to the pile for Miss Olive. Meanwhile Ethel straightened out Briar's quilt while waiting for Mim to finish dressing. They all left together, Ethel leading the charge, and shooting glares at Mim for taking so long.

In all, a regular morning.

As if automated themselves, the boardinghouse doors all the way down the street opened to the dawning day as the operatives set off in a rush to the mill yard to make it through the gates before any stragglers were locked out. If seen above, it would look like a mass of ants streaming from their hills and marching out in formation.

"You two going to join me at the meeting later this week?" asked Ethel. "Mrs. Sarah Tuttle is coming all the way from Boston to talk to us."

"Oh, please," said Mim, scoffing. "No more of that vote-talk. I've got better things to do with my time."

Briar saw Ethel take a deep breath and knew she was going to start in on it. Mim knew just what to say to make Ethel mad. Miss Olive didn't know what she was doing pairing up these two in a room. Briar was always caught in the middle. No wonder Ania spent as little time with them as she did.

"I might," Briar said to defuse the fight before it started. A suffrage meeting sounded like a waste of time, but Ethel could be persuasive about her causes. And until Briar's nights were filled with sewing, she may as well hear about votes for women, however unlikely they seemed.

Ethel breathed out, then shot a triumphant look to Mim. "Excellent. Maybe you can talk some sense into that one."

"Hmm," Briar answered. Out of habit, she turned her attention to looking for Wheeler. They were passing his boardinghouse and she could usually spot him, since he was so tall.

"He's up ahead already," said Mim. She pointed, wiggling her gloved finger. Even going to work in the summer, Mim dressed as fine as she could.

"Oh, I'm not—"

"Please. I know you still look for him."

There was no use protesting to Mim, so instead she searched the crowd ahead. Wheeler used to wait for her and they would walk close together, bumping arms as everyone else hurried past. He must have already gone in.

They were at the mill gates now, not far from the outdoor wooden staircase they took to their respective floors. They were all pressed in, constricted by the hundreds of other workers all trying to get to their places on time.

They ascended the stairs together until the third floor where they parted. Briar waved good-bye and opened the door straight into the spinning room. Ethel and Mim would continue up another flight to the weaving room.

She stopped by the overseer's office and knocked on the door.

He waved her in, but returned his attention to the large account book in front of him.

"Excuse, me, sir. I'd like another frame, soon as one opens up," Briar said.

"Got a girl leaving at the end of the month. But you'll have to get all your frames up to peak production before then or it'll go to someone else." He looked at the time and stood.

Briar backed out the door. "Thank you, sir." She smiled. *Now, to make frame number four behave.*

As soon as she got to her frames, Briar performed a quick clean and oiling before stuffing cotton into her ears in preparation. When the next bell sounded, she threw the shipper handles on the first frame, wincing as the overhead leather belts began slapping into action, causing her spindles to whine as they twirled the thicker roving into thinner thread. She tapped the foot pedal to jog the rail until she was satisfied the threads were taut before moving on to the next frame.

The sound, or rather *noise*, was her least favorite part of the job. Some girls minded the close air. They had to keep the windows shut and the humidity high or the threads would break and they'd be run ragged on their feet all day mending the breaks. But Briar had gotten accustomed to a perspiring forehead, and the air did make for a natural greenhouse. At last count there were sixty potted plants in the spinning room alone, making the indoors pretend to be the outdoors.

The dinner bell rang at noon, and quick as anything, the girls all shut off their frames and scurried for the door. They had one hour to run home, get a bite to eat, and be back at their frames. Briar pulled the cotton out of her ears and stuffed it in her apron pocket for later. The silence was deafening after all that noise.

When Mim caught up to her from the weaving room, Briar could see from her quick pace and mischievous grin she had news.

"The overseer and agent were talking near my loom today and you'll never guess what they were saying."

"What?" Briar asked, wondering what would hold Mim's interest.

"They were talking about that new mill being built up in Burlington. They say they're bringing in more than seven hundred looms this summer. A new model that practically runs itself. They say a girl could operate sixteen all on her own."

"Sixteen? You're not thinking of moving, are you?" One friend leaving was enough. Briar didn't want it turning into an epidemic.

"No, silly, but I thought you might be interested, since that Wheeler boy of yours got hired by the Queen City Cotton Mills to help them set it all up. Of course, you could go as a spinner, too, since they're going to have thirty thousand spindles. I just thought you'd like to move up to a loom."

Briar stopped walking. Operatives zooming by in a hurry to eat jostled her, but she didn't care. Why would Wheeler move to another mill, in another town, no less, when he was waiting for a job at the shirtwaist factory?

"Oh. You didn't know? Not to worry, it's not until midsummer so you still have some time."

Briar was speechless, her mind gone numb. A push from behind made her start walking again.

"Did you hear me?" asked Mim. "It's a great opportunity. You can get a job with Queen City, too. I heard the town is beautiful, right on Lake Champlain. Pierre grew up across the border and told me all about it. You'll love it."

Briar drew in a breath. She had been hoping to move up to the weaving room because working the looms paid more and the job wasn't as tedious. But to move away from the children? It was what she was trying to prevent.

However, if she got a loom job, Nanny might agree to keep the children longer, knowing that Briar had a promotion and could send more money home.

Mim pinched Briar's arm, pulling Briar out of her reverie. "Ouch."

"Listen. My cousin was talking about taking a job there, too. He knows the agent and said he'd put in a word for me if I wanted to move closer to home, but I'd rather stay here. I like living away from my meddlesome family. He could put in a word for you, instead."

"Yes, please." By now they had reached home, and they

scooted up the stairs following the stream of their fellow hungry operatives.

"Please what?" asked Ethel, who had caught up with them as they made their way into the dining room.

"We're going to get Briar transferred to the new mill with Wheeler," explained Mim.

Briar cringed. *Why can't Mim ever whisper?* She quickly looked for Sadie and saw she was already seated at the far table, hopefully out of earshot. Briar wondered if Sadie would be upset when Wheeler left, or would she quickly move on to someone else? Briar didn't know her well enough to be sure how deep her feelings ran, though Mim was convinced they were as shallow as a butter dish.

"Mim overheard them talking about a new mill being built in Burlington. She thinks I could get a loom job there."

"Have you even thought this through?" said Ethel, steering Briar away from where Mim sat down. "Leaving everything behind is not a decision to be made quickly."

"Nothing has been decided. I have to consider every opportunity that comes my way."

There was no more time to talk as they gobbled down their dinner of cod and hash. On the rushed walk back to work, Briar kept a pace slightly ahead of Ethel so her room-mate couldn't tell her what to think before she had a chance to think it for herself.

Briar's mind kept wandering all day, imagining life in Burlington. It would be hard not to see the children regularly, but there would be more money for them, to ensure Pansy could keep going to school instead of working at the mill as soon as she was old enough.

Annie, the operative working the frames beside Briar's, nudged her arm and pointed at frame number four. Broken threads all over the place. Briar nodded her thanks and rushed to join the pieces before more damage was caused because of her daydreaming. She should have known with Henry gone she'd have to pay extra attention to her fourth frame. Seems she would just get it going again and before long all the threads were snapping and catching on one another. Constantly stalled equipment was no way to garner the right kind of attention, and the new doffer, Maribelle, was no help at all. Today was her first day on the job and the other doffers were doing their best to train her, but the girl was slow to learn.

Briar frowned as she fixed her threads. Maybe Henry was why she was out of sorts. The mill felt empty with him gone. His easy way, how he would swagger in and fix her frame, tapping that one corner as he said good-bye. She glanced at the corner and noticed an acorn sitting there. Where did that come from? She looked around but everyone else was busy at work.

She picked it up and examined it. A perfect acorn with a dark, variegated body and pale little cap like the ones she used as cups in her childhood fairy gardens. She smiled at the memory and placed the acorn in her pocket. Strange to find one sitting on her frame. She looked around again, expecting to see Henry jump out to surprise her, but he wasn't there.

CHAPTER TEN

It didn't take long for Briar to notice the big hole Henry Prince left behind. Aside from missing his mechanical skills with her spinning machine, the first time she walked the long road to the cottage by herself, she realized Henry was like the air—something you never really noticed because it was always there, but once it was gone, your chest felt like it was stuffed with cotton and left you struggling to breathe. She hadn't felt this way since Da passed, and was surprised to feel it now about Henry. Each quiet walk home reminded her of all she missed about him.

Fortunately, the children were getting on well with Fanny, who by now had found the bunny and made a big deal about the boys taking care of it without any help from her, and that it'd better not get into her garden. Although Briar had already caught Fanny out back hand-feeding the cute thing a piece of lettuce.

Jack said he thought Fanny was made of magic because she seemed to be everywhere at once. "She can fly," he said. "But not like a bird. She makes herself really tiny and then she can spy on us. That's how she found the bunny."

Briar laughed at how serious Jack was about his imagined theory. She was glad Fanny was keeping them on their toes. It helped ease her mind that the children were well cared for. It was never easy to leave them for the week.

As Briar turned the bend on her narrow path from the cottage back to the country road into town, there was a sudden change in humidity. A mist was creeping in, settling into the valley. The thick fog sent tendrils her way, wrapping around her ankles, penetrating to the bone, and pulling her faster into town.

It reminded her of the story Mam used to tell about the potato famine.

Late at night by the light of the fire, Mam would draw a wool blanket around her shoulders, get a far-off look in her eye, and begin the tale: "In the wee hours of the morn, a mist rose out of the sea and spread its spindly fingers across the land. It stayed for three days, thick as pease soup. A cry was heard across the moors that none could track as it came in all directions. A mournful sound. Then finally, when the mist lifted, we could see the tops of our potato plants and the blackness of blight that would change our lives forever."

Every time a fog seeped into the valley, Mam would stand in the doorway, her arms crossed, her eyes observant, watching. Listening. It unnerved Briar as a child, and even now she shivered with the thought and picked up her pace. She had a need to get off this empty stretch of road and catch up to others headed into town.

With each step, the fog grew thicker and thicker, becoming so dense Briar could only see inches in front of her. It was an odd feeling of white-blindness, viewing only her scuffed boots and a bit of the dirt path a foot in front.

She was so busy watching her feet that when she did meet up with another person, she was practically on top of him. The only warning she'd had was a jingle of the harness on the peddler's poor donkey.

"Oh, excuse me," said Briar, covering up her startled fright. "This fog makes it hard to see. I'm farther ahead than I thought if I've joined up the main road."

The peddler wore layers of rags with an odd assortment of accoutrements tied to his person. A scruffy beard, a too-floppy hat, and a cane completed his look. At his side, a sorry-looking donkey pulled an even sorrier-looking covered cart behind them.

If he at least had a donkey, he must have good things to trade. Out of curiosity, she examined the bundles hanging off the sides of the cart as she drew nearer. Saucepans, tin cups, a sewing machine, a hatchet, a birdcage, a dress form, a croquet mallet.

He saw her interest and stopped the donkey. "Whoa there," came the thin voice.

"Nay, sir," she called out, hurriedly. There was no point wasting his time. "I've no money to spend today." She smiled. "Thanks for pretending I did, though."

She glanced at her dirty hands and patched skirt. A good scrubbing hadn't gotten the oil out from under her fingernails, nor from the hem of her dress that dragged on the dirty spinning room floor when she bent down to reset the builder on the frames.

"You have no news to trade, then?" he asked. "It's been a long time since I've been to these parts. Would like to know what's what before I get to town."

"Don't know that I have news, either," she said. "Is there anything in particular you want to know?"

"The Prince family still in residence?"

She smiled. "Always." She thought of the youngest Prince and her smile dimmed. *I wonder where Henry is right now. Did he make it across the Atlantic already, or did his ship get caught in a storm? He's been gone several weeks; a letter should have arrived by now.*

The peddler nodded. "Just as I would have it."

His tone of voice threw Briar. It was like he wasn't glad the Princes were still here.

"And you?" he continued. "Is your family new here? You don't have features I recognize."

"Fairly new," she answered. She didn't like handing out personal information. A better set of questions would be to ask about the prosperity of the mill to find out if he could sell his wares here.

"Are you a spinner girl?" The peddler's eyes, a unique shade of blue, almost turquoise, bore into hers like he could read her thoughts and was daring her to lie to him.

"We have several prosperous mills in town," she said, avoiding the personal question. "How long was it since you passed through here last?"

"Long time. Before the mills."

"Before the mills? There wasn't much of a town here then. A few farms and a general store was about it from what I hear."

"And where, in particular, do you come from?" He studied her through narrow eyes. "Look more like a person who comes from the Emerald Isle with that fiery hair."

Briar didn't like the feeling she was getting from this peddler. He was too personal, in an odd way. Most peddlers tried to be complimentary to flatter a girl into spending her money. He was simply intrusive.

"I've been here since I was a child," she said dismissively. That was all he was getting out of her. She shouldn't have told him that much, for he was right about where she came from. She clamped her mouth shut and edged around his cart.

"And you are how old...sixteen, about to turn seven-teen?" He tapped the syllables with his cane when he said *sev-en-teen.*

Again, he was spot-on. Her birthday was in July, next month. Mere weeks to have a plan in place by the time Nanny came home. She squirmed under his intuitiveness. "Nice talking to you. I best get on."

He held out his cane to stop her path. "You've been so helpful; would you like to look at my wares? If anything I have wants to belong to you, you may have it as payment for your information. Never let it be said I don't take care of my debts."

Briar raised her eyebrows. *If anything wants to belong to me?* She was about to refuse, but a pretty piece of cloth waved at her in the breeze. Briar could ask Mim to teach her how to copy a fancy pattern. *It wouldn't hurt anything to look.*

The peddler removed the rough wool cloth hiding the majority of the goods he had for sale, and stood back to let Briar get as close as she liked.

Hesitantly she approached, drinking in the objects like her poor room-mate Ania always did with the candy peddler. Briar had a little money set aside as a cushion in case she fell ill or had to miss work for any reason, but he was offering her something for free. Ethel would advise her to get something practical. Mim would have her select something beautiful. Perhaps she could find something both practical and beautiful.

"May I make a suggestion?" the peddler said. "I've been studying you and think I have the item here in this box."

His unique turquoise eyes drew her in.

Curiosity piqued, Briar followed him back to the end of the cart where he pulled out an old wooden box. "Something from the Old Country. Something beautiful. Yet something practical."

Briar gasped then chewed her lip. Had she mumbled those words out loud?

He turned the box so the object would be facing her when he opened it. After clicking the lock, he lifted the lid to reveal a drop spindle nestled in a cloth of royal blue. It was unlike any spindle Briar had ever seen before. The whorl was carved with roses and the wooden shaft, stained a light brown, came to an unusually sharp point on the end.

"Well, spinner girl?" He tapped his fingers triumphantly along the edge of the box.

"It's beautiful. And practical."

"Even more, 'tis special." The peddler hiked his ragged boot up on the wagon wheel and leaned his arm against his knee. "That spindle is said to bring prosperity to the owner. Take that with you to your work and replace just one of your spindles on your frame with the shaft. Keep the whorl in your pocket and the wooden spindle will absorb the shock of the machine such that the threads will not break. You will finish your work quickly and easily ahead of all the other girls."

Briar eyed him sideways to show she wasn't believing his tale. Besides, if she got caught changing out a metal spindle for this wooden one, she'd be let go on the spot and given a dishonorable discharge. She looked more closely at a dark smudge on the whorl. "Has it been in a fire?"

"It's been through many a trial, an old spindle such as this, but it's proved its worth. Once belonged to kings and queens."

Briar let his words rush by. It was the habit of peddlers to create stories around their goods. An ax from a poor farmer became the ax used to forge a trail west by Daniel Boone.

"What is it made of, then, that it didn't burn? I don't recognize the wood."

"Looks to me like fairy wood," the peddler said. "A rare hardwood from the old German forests. If you believe it, legend says a fairy formed it out of briarwood from the Black Forest. Maybe she even imbued it with her magic."

Briar smiled indulgently at the peddler. "I've never heard of fairy wood, and I didn't know rose stalks could grow thick enough to make a spindle." She refused to even touch it. "I'm sorry, sir. It's worth too much for me to take just for giving you the news about town. You'll be able to sell that to an artisan. Don't waste it on me." She backed away and continued looking for something else. The peddler stood straight, closed the lid with a snap, and returned the box to the corner of the wagon.

She glanced up at the man and moved on. A doll with a real porcelain face stuck out of a box of toys. It would send Pansy to the moon and back, but then the twins would likely abscond with it and make Pansy cry. Besides, her mam always taught her: *If you buy what you don't need, you might have to sell what you do.* Even if she wasn't actually buying. Briar touched the doll's nose but kept looking. A plain and sturdy pot with only one dent lay on top of a box of kitchen items. Nanny could use it for her stews. What else did he have?

The peddler stood with his arms crossed.

"I'm sorry I'm taking so long, sir." She didn't want to waste her choice. It was like getting a wish.

His eyes followed her every move, making her feel like

she should take any old thing and let him move on.

"You already know what you want. Take it." He spoke so quietly Briar wasn't sure if the peddler actually said anything or if Briar made it up, because she really did know what she wanted.

The spindle.

She'd never seen anything like it. A spindle like that might be common in a royal's court, but not in out-of-the-way Sunrise Valley in the possession of a mere spinner girl. Already she felt guilty for wanting it.

"Use it in your spinning frame and let the fairy magic work for you. You'll be the best spinner in town."

She pictured the beautiful drop spindle lined up with the others, its beauty hidden with a bobbin. "No, thank you, sir. Sorry to have wasted your time. I have everything I need." With that, she turned her back and walked with the wind into town.

However, the farther away she walked, the greater the urge to turn around.

The spindle did want her. And she wanted the spindle.

So much it scared her.

CHAPTER ELEVEN

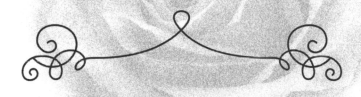

The next morning, the fog hovered among the buildings in town as if looking for something. Though the air was bright with the sun trying to burn through the mist, the fog held strong with feet dug in to stay. Briar raced from the boardinghouse to the mill, trying to shake the feeling that the mist was looking for her.

She'd slept in, making herself late, and her room-mates had gone on without her. Even after Ethel had woken her, she remained in bed, relishing a marvelous dream involving a magic spindle and reams and reams of cloth she'd woven on her very own looms. She'd never seen so much fabric, even more than the stacks in the warehouse, and she was quite heady with it.

The drink of water and two bites of breakfast she managed to gulp down helped to clear her thoughts and wake her up. The gates were still open when she got to the mill, but by the time she'd climbed the stairs, the bell had gone off, signaling the start to the day. Frustrated with herself, she yanked the door open and came face-to-face with a new overseer.

Her new boss stood with arm held aloft dangling a gold pocket watch from its chain. He was a slim man, not very tall, with a thick beard and mustache of the old style. His glasses had slid partially down his nose as if he didn't need them, and he peered at her through the dark lenses with a look that made the hair on Briar's neck prickle.

It was as if he had been waiting for her. He must have noticed a girl was missing and decided to welcome her.

Briar took a steadying breath.

If only she could see his eyes clearly. Mam said the eyes were a window to the soul, and you could tell a lot about a person by looking into their eyes. Something about him seemed familiar, yet at the same time, he was as out of place in their mill as a lit match. Perhaps she'd seen him in town before. At the bank? She paused to wait for the reprimand, but when he didn't say anything, she scooted past and got her machines up and running.

Beads of sweat dripped down her back as the day wore on. She couldn't shake the feeling she was being watched, but every time she looked up, no one was there. The other operatives were all focused on their frames. Intensely focused on their frames. There were no smiles or passing comments.

"Is there a problem?" came a shout in her ear over the roar of the machines.

Briar jumped. The overseer had come up from behind.

She shook her head and busied herself with checking threads that were perfectly fine. Then out of the corner of her eye, Briar witnessed a chain reaction of threads spinning wildly and catching onto neighboring spindles. She'd never seen the like of it. Her persnickety frame had decided to practically explode.

She raced to shut down all her frames so she could deal with the mess. The overseer stepped back and watched with a glare. Briar's face grew hotter the longer it took her to untangle the mess. Her fingers, normally nimble, were all thumbs as she fumbled her way through the strands. For once Briar was thankful for the raucous noise of the machines, or she was certain the overseer would be making disparaging comments. Of all days, this had to happen today.

When she finally had all the threads lined up and connected, the overseer glanced at his watch before walking away. He shut off the power to the spinning frames as the dinner bell went and the room fell silent.

Normally voices would rise to fill the void as the girls chatted on their way out of the room, but instead, the overseer called out, "Halt. You are all to come over here for a lesson."

By "over here" he meant Briar's frame. While waiting for the operatives to gather, he read the poems Briar had attached to her frame. At Ethel's prompting, several of the girls kept pieces of poetry stuck near the windows where the light was true, or small pieces on their frames so they could think on lovely thoughts whenever they were tempted to think only of the monotony or the drudgery of their work. Books were banned, since too many girls got engrossed in what they were reading and forgot to mind their frames, so these bits of paper were a nice compromise, and the old overseer hadn't minded.

She withered inside. If this lesson was long, they'd all miss dinner.

Once everyone had gathered, the overseer cleared his throat and spoke in a high, grating voice. "This operative is working at her lowest capacity. Her head is filled with silly notions of love." He ripped down the poem attached to her frame and held it up as evidence.

Briar looked at her feet.

The offending poem by Rosalie M. Janas was awfully sentimental and romantic, especially under the scrutiny of the new overseer. It was about a love being meant to be. At least, that was how Briar interpreted it. Youth who flirted with love thinking it was blind and wouldn't catch them missed that love was watching and waiting for the right moment to strike. She thought of Henry kissing her hand and her face warmed.

The overseer read the poem aloud in a mocking tone:

Rondeau

Love is not blind. Ah, no! Ah, no!
He only hides his eyes to show
A sweet unguarded mouth left free
To tempt his victims, while with glee
He works them thus confusion—woe.

For, sure as fate, rash youth will go
Too near that lovely Cupid's bow,
And none dare warn him, "Love can see!"
"Love is not blind!"

Then peeping stealthily below
His bandage, with sure aim and slow,
Love points his darts, and, one! two! three!
Straight to the heart of youth they flee
And never miss their mark. Ah, no!
Love is not blind.

The poem seemed pathetic and not romantic at all, as read by him. He crumbled the paper and let it drop to the floor with the bits of cotton to be swept up at the end of the day. He then strode about the room ripping down the bits of poetry and articles the operatives had posted. "We will have no more of this. I'm here to ensure this room increases production no matter what." He threw the crumpled scraps in the air. "Go!"

The operatives scurried for the door.

"Thanks, Briar," someone whispered as she hurried by.

It wasn't my fault. Their previous overseer hadn't had any problems with them tacking up poems. Briar glanced back at the new overseer, his eyes hidden behind tinted glasses. She had a suspicion there would be more unwelcome changes to come.

CHAPTER TWELVE

Briar passed several girls already coming down the porch steps as she arrived at the boardinghouse for dinner. Mim and Ethel were waiting for her in the dining room, having prepared a plate for her.

"What happened?" asked Mim.

"New overseer, and my frame pretty much exploded in front of him. Then he made an example out of me and tore down all our articles as frivolity." Briar gobbled up her sausage and potatoes.

Ethel crossed her arms. "This is just the thing I was talking about, Mim. You'll hear all about it at the meeting. We are treated terribly with no recourse. If we had women overseers, perhaps something like this wouldn't happen."

Mim turned her back slightly on Ethel. "You've got to get it together if you want to move on to Burlington. I heard your new overseer is here to pick out the best girls to train the others."

Briar didn't have time to think one way or the other on Burlington. The more pressing issues right now were her bad frame and the new overseer. She'd had so much downtime lately her pay would be docked, and surely the new overseer must think she was incompetent and therefore not deserving of an extra frame.

"I don't know how I can win anyone's favor if I'm stuck with that bad spinning frame."

"Are you sure there's not something you're doing to it?" Mim asked.

Briar huffed. "Of course not. I'm running three other successful frames, aren't I? No, it's that frame. Something's wrong with it. It's got a bad spindle." She paused. *A bad spindle.* The peddler had suggested she put the fairy wood spindle in her frame. If only the answer were that easy. "Henry always managed to keep it going, but ever since he left it's gotten worse."

"Henry? Haven't heard you mention that name in a while."

Mim's tone rankled Briar, so she retorted, "Haven't heard you mention Pierre much in a while, either." Pierre had been the latest beau, but he'd stopped coming around.

Mim closed her mouth and stood. The air between them was stretched with tension.

Miss Olive stood at the door, hands on hips and shaking her head as everyone left the house. "What has gotten into you all?" she asked. "Snippy, every one of you. Mim, Ethel, Briar, and Sadie, please come see me in the kitchen. I won't keep you long. Briar, you can bring your plate."

Briar checked with her room-mates to see if they knew what Miss Olive wanted them for, but they shrugged and followed the keeper down the hallway. *Maybe Sadie issued a complaint against us? Did she hear Mim talk about Wheeler and me one too many times?*

With a sick stomach, Briar followed the others into the kitchen where they all cast trepidatious looks at one another and the clock.

Miss Olive bustled about with empty platters. "Sorry, girls, I know you don't have much time, but I've got a new boarder arriving any minute and I need to be ready for her. A space opened up for Ania at her friends' place, so she is moving out tonight. Sadie, I know you wanted a change from your bedroom—the snoring and all that—so do you want Ania's place with these girls here?" She turned her back to lift the boiling water off the stove and pour it into her wash basin for the dishes.

Sadie's eyes brightened. "Do any of you snore?" she asked.

The three passed looks behind Miss Olive's back. No, they didn't, but Sadie and Briar in the same room?

"Great," said Sadie. "Even if one of you snores a little, it's got to be better than the elephant I'm living with now. Haven't had a decent night's sleep since I moved in, and what's worse is that she's such a sound sleeper I can't wake her up to tell her to stop. We'll be great chums in no time, you'll see." She linked her arms through Briar's and Ethel's but didn't seem to notice both girls go stiff with the familiarity of the move.

Mim just smiled and said, "Welcome to the family."

"Excellent," said Miss Olive, turning around. She fanned her face, now flushed with heat and exertion. "Now, off with the lot of you before you're late."

On the rush back to the mill, the mist was still so thick that Ethel's ghostly bonnet bobbed as if on an ocean. Briar would have pointed this out to Mim for a laugh, but when she turned to say something, Mim avoided her eyes. With a pang of guilt, Briar realized Pierre must have been more than the usual entertainment. Could Mim's heart be broken, too?

Well, if the past was an indicator of the future, Mim would soon have a new love to occupy her affections. Besides, Briar had something else on her mind. How was she going to share a room with Sadie? The last thing she wanted to hear about was Sadie mooning over Wheeler. What was Miss Olive thinking? Now she'd have a room with two sets of people at odds with one another.

"Terrible weather, ain't it?" asked Sadie.

Briar jumped. She'd almost forgotten they'd left at the same time.

"Sure is."

"It'll be fun being room-mates. Who did Ania share with?"

"Mim."

"Too bad. If we were together we could talk about Wheeler all night. You must be curious about him, aren't you?" She blinked innocent eyes at Briar, which weren't innocent at all. She was sending a message.

Briar slowed her pace, letting Sadie flounce ahead even if it meant Briar would end up late to her station for the second time that day. Her room-mates were the best part of working at the mill. The girl before Ania had been great fun to be around, too, until she got married. And now she had to room with Sadie?

That afternoon she worked as quickly and efficiently as possible, keeping track of her new doffer Maribelle, helping the young girl juggle the full bobbins that her little hands were too small to manage easily. Small hands were good for reaching in the frames to fix thread breaks and clean, but troublesome for keeping a grip on the full bobbins until they learned the proper balance.

The overseer continuously paced the floor, setting everyone on edge. Briar fumbled through keeping her frames going, which seemed to delight her new boss. Why would her becoming a trembling wreck be the only thing that pleased him? She'd heard about bad overseers before, those who looked down on the women they managed. He must be one of those.

As she worked, Briar's thoughts spun back to the peddler's cart and his solution for her problem. A wooden spindle. Could something so simple fix her frame? If only Henry were here, he would know. Plus, he wouldn't make fun of her idea, no matter how far-fetched it was.

She couldn't use the drop spindle by itself to earn a living. No one sold hand-spun thread anymore. Industrialization saw to that. She paced in front of her factory frames, noting there was nothing beautiful about them. They were made from impersonal metal, powered by the loud belts overhead transferring the might of the river and steam into her hands. They made the room alive with their motion, yet not alive. They were noisy and relentless and gave her headaches more often than not.

When she first started in the spinning room, she was fascinated how the thicker cotton strands called roving wound down to the bobbins below, pulled and twisted into thin but strong thread. The transformation happened so quickly compared to a hand spindle or even a spinning wheel. And all this by the thousands of spindles at the cotton mill. It was dizzying and exciting at first. But now, the job was monotonous. It left too much time for thinking.

Ethel told her the looms were more interesting to care for. Whether Briar moved up in this factory, or in the new one at Burlington, the change would be welcomed.

Briar got so caught up in her thoughts that she forgot

to keep on number four, and before she knew it, threads had snapped all over the place. *Not again*. Plus it was time for doffing and the girl was nowhere to be seen. Now all her frames were down as Briar quickly tied knots to fix the breaks before the overseer noticed.

By the time she'd worked her way to the last frame, Maribelle ran in, with an excited, flushed face. Evidently it had been a good game of tag outside. The fog probably made it easy to dart away and be hidden.

"Maribelle! Now look what you've done," she snapped. "You've got to pay attention. I need you in here every forty-five minutes." Even as she chastised Maribelle, Briar knew the words were meant for herself.

Maribelle bobbed her head, staring down at her own bare feet, splotchy-black with grease. "Yes, miss."

"What's going on?" The overseer was once again at Briar's elbow. He grabbed Maribelle by the ear and squeezed.

Maribelle went up on her toes as the overseer pulled her ear. Tears sprang to her eyes, but she didn't cry.

Briar instinctively reached to free Maribelle, but the overseer only squeezed harder, stepping between them. Briar's heart groaned for the wee thing, but she took a step back, hoping he'd let Maribelle go.

"It's that last frame. It's bad, is all. Let her go, please. She can help me tie the threads."

Maribelle caught her breath as the overseer gave her ear one last shake before releasing her. Briar fought the urge to rush to the girl's side in case the overseer would choose to inflict more punishment.

"You better do something about that frame or you're out of a job," he yelled over the other machines.

"Yes, sir." Briar quickly began tying threads, motioning to Maribelle to do so, too. Her heart was beating hard against her rib cage. It wasn't her place to fix the frame. She wished she could complain about the new overseer, but who could she tell who would care and be able to do something about it?

Once the overseer had gone, Briar mouthed, "I'm sorry," to the girl, and with a shaking hand stroked her hair comfortingly. The wee thing was taking on a big responsibility. If the girl's family didn't need the money, she'd be at school with the other children. Briar resolved to strengthen her mind to the task and be easier on her young doffer. Especially in front of the overseer.

"There now, we're back up and running. Off you go and have some fun," Briar said, choosing not to add another admonition to be back in time to swap out the bobbins. If she'd spoken to Pansy using the tone she'd used earlier with Maribelle, Pansy would have been blubbering tears. It didn't help that they had to yell at one another to be heard above the din, which made tempers sound harsher than what was meant. Never mind how Pansy would have reacted to being grabbed by the overseer. Maribelle was made of sterner stuff than Briar had thought.

Briar turned back to guard frame number four from any more mistakes when she noticed another token left in Henry's corner. This time it was a small, heart-shaped pebble. "Henry Prince," she whispered. "I know it's you. How are you doing it?" Grinning, Briar added the pebble to the acorn in her pocket.

Her whole mood changed with the latest gift. She couldn't stop from smiling until the final bell rang.

Instantly the girls shut down all their frames. But instead of the quiet ringing in their ears, murmurings spread like a wave through the operatives. Briar rushed to the door to find out what was going on.

"Didn't you hear?" asked Annie, the girl who manned the frames next to Briar's. "Grace's brother works in the countinghouse. He told her they're lowering our wages this week. Less money in our envelopes on payday. It's just like the panic last year. It's getting no better. Pretty soon our pay is going to equal our rent, and then where will we be?"

Briar closed her eyes and pressed her tongue to the roof of her mouth. After working so hard to make up for her bad frame, it didn't matter in the end. Going forward she would need four fully-working frames just to keep up her normal pay rate, never mind trying to impress anyone or earn a fifth frame. She sighed. However was a girl to get ahead in this world? She looked around at the other operatives' sullen faces. It was the same for all of them. Then her eyes settled on the overseer. He looked up with a scowl and met her gaze unblinking over his glasses, which slipped down his nose again.

Use the wooden spindle.

Briar sucked in a breath and looked away. *Where did that thought come from?*

Annie made a face. "Something about cotton cloth not selling as much as they expected and the train strike causing distribution problems. Say they have to trim expenses, but I don't see the agent cutting back on his expensive cravats. He was wearing a new one today. And look at our new overseer with a gold pocket watch! Bet his paycheck isn't getting shorted."

"It's not fair," said another girl. "There's nothing we can do about it. They'll want us to work as hard as before, but get paid less just because they say so, and we don't got no power to say no." By now they'd streamed out onto the staircase and began to mingle with the other levels of the factory.

Briar caught sight of Ethel. She couldn't hear her

friend over all the other voices, but Ethel was definitely passionate about what she was saying. Her arms were practically a blur as she no doubt weighed in her opinion on the pay reduction. Well, good. Ethel's passion would carry the conversation with their new room-mate tonight. Briar was drained from the day, and not looking forward to playing polite with someone new in the room.

If Henry were here she could ask his opinion about putting in a wooden spindle. He'd also know how to do it. Could she trust a peddler? One trained in saying anything to make a sale?

If the wooden spindle could absorb enough vibrations to keep her frame working, she'd at least be competing on even ground. After today, she was in danger of losing her job. Could a wooden spindle make all the difference? There was only one way to find out.

She had to find the peddler.

CHAPTER THIRTEEN

Ania had already cleared out her things by the time
supper was over. She must have slipped in while they
were eating, likely more eager to move in with her friends
than to worry about saying good-bye to her old room-
mates.

"Stay long enough to go over our expectations with us,"
said Ethel when Briar tried to leave after supper. Her eyes
were sympathetic, acknowledging how hard this was going
to be for Briar.

Ethel had no idea. To have a constant reminder of what
could have been with her ex-sweetheart was beyond what
Briar could handle. She pivoted in the doorway, weighing
the decision. She was eager to slip out of the house and
search for the peddler while it was still light out.

"It won't take long."

"Of course not." Briar sat down on her bed to wait for
Sadie. They'd learned to have the talk about expectations
early and straight out, so everyone would be comfortable
in voicing their concerns, and small irritants wouldn't grow

into big fights later on. They didn't spend a lot of time in their rooms, but they didn't want that time to be miserable, either.

Mim was already taking stock of her space, a look of concern as she eyed the places that should belong to a fourth girl, but that she had already taken over.

Ethel joined Briar on their bed. Soon, Sadie came in with more belongings than Ania would ever hope to have, and Mim willingly gave up more space to her.

"Are you sure you only need that much room under the bed?" asked Mim. "I can stack some of my things up in the corner here. Just let me know."

It was more than Briar could take. It was as if Mim was being extra friendly to punish Briar for her comment about Pierre. Briar stood and put a shawl around her shoulder. "I'll be back before curfew." Ethel was really the one who cared about the rules anyway.

"Stay with us," said Sadie sweetly. "We're just starting to get to know each other."

"And the rules…" said Ethel.

Briar waved her hand above her head on the way out the door. Two steps outside and she was able to take a deep breath. Her churning stomach was sufficient motivation to find the peddler. Briar couldn't tell if she didn't like Sadie because she was seeing Wheeler, or if she didn't like Sadie because of Sadie herself.

She wrapped her shawl tighter around her shoulders to guard against the evening chill. The damp vapors seeped through to her skin and on any other night would have made her retreat to her room. The fog hung heavy, creating softly glowing balls of light around the lampposts turned on early because of the strange mist.

Up and down the street, various peddlers' carts parked

in front of the boardinghouses, but with the mist she couldn't tell one apart from the other. She ran to the edge of the road where her peddler had been. She started to walk out of town, but quickly decided that was a bad idea. It was already growing dark and the curfew bell would go soon. Besides, he was a transient and had probably moved on to the next town.

He'd wanted to give her a gift. Why had she fought taking the spindle?

Her mood shifting with the mist, she returned down the long row of boardinghouses, eyeing the carts as she passed. No sign of an overpacked cart pulled by a rough-and-tumble old donkey.

She drudged home, letting the long day weigh on her. It was not meant to be.

At her boardinghouse, a peddler cart had pulled up last minute to catch all the girls leaving from visiting, and going back to their homes. Several girls had crowded around so she couldn't get a good look at it. *Could it be?*

She pushed her way through. "Excuse me," Briar said. But it was only Jolly Jim at the helm of his cart, a regular who never had anything of interest for her. Cheap goods that broke as soon as he left town. Disappointed, she squeezed through the mob again and started up the stairs.

"Seems to me the girl changed her mind," came a voice out of the shadows on the porch.

The peddler!

"Where is your cart?" asked Briar, both eager and frightened at the same time. Something about this man sent shivers down her neck, and she found herself wishing Ethel were here to help her keep a level head.

"I don't need my cart. Only this box." He looked down at the bench.

Briar blinked. She didn't remember a box being there a second ago, although with the shadows it was hard to tell.

"Is that…?"

He nodded. "I was about to leave town and I still had it in my cart. I know to whom it belongs, so I couldn't leave without bringing it to you. Remember what I said, but keep it hidden. Someone might try to take it from you."

He used his cane to push himself off the bench and stood close to Briar. "Be careful. The end is sharp." She took a step back. He tipped his floppy hat at her, and was down the stairs and up the street before Briar found her voice.

"What's that?" asked Lizbeth, a girl who lived on the first floor. She made a move toward the bench.

"It's mine," said Briar hurriedly. She scooped up the narrow box and, hugging it to her chest, rushed into the house. Not even stopping to see who was in the parlor, she raced up the wooden staircase to the third floor.

The door to her room was closed. That either meant no one was there, or her room-mates didn't want to be bothered. She held her ear to the door and didn't hear anything. Opening the door, she prepared an answer to explain what she was carrying. But the room was empty. Good. She had time.

She set the package down on the mattress she shared with Ethel. Their double bed was covered in a dull patchwork quilt that Briar had brought from home. Some prints were so faded you couldn't tell what the original color was, though Briar could remember each one from her childhood. Ethel didn't care if their bed was fancy or not, so she welcomed the quilt. In fact, when Ethel came to town the only thing she came with was a bag full of hope.

Thinking that Ethel wouldn't approve of the fancy

spindle, Briar glanced over at Mim's bed. Mim would approve. Her bed had a quilt with lace sewn all the way around. The lace was patchwork, constructed of pieces Mim had acquired over the years that weren't fit for dresses but serviceable for a quilt. The lace seemed extravagant to Briar, but it was important for Mim.

A stuffed rabbit had been added to Sadie's side of the bed, and the top of the dresser looked a bit more crowded with Mim's relocated cosmetics.

She needed to hurry if she were to get a look at the spindle before the others returned. She quickly opened the box. It was as she remembered it. No, better. The intricately carved roses were even more delicate. The variations in the wood more pronounced. Her heart ached with how beautiful it was. It would be a shame to take it apart to put in her frame.

She hadn't touched it when the peddler showed it to her, and she was hesitant to grasp it now. Before, she didn't get too close because she didn't want to become attached. Now it was hers, and it was the prettiest thing she owned. Even if the spindle didn't work in her spinning frame, she could use it to teach Pansy. They could practice with wool from the Princes' sheep. Mrs. Prince, with no daughter of her own, had taken a shine to Pansy and would no doubt let her have as much wool as she could handle.

"Where'd ya get that, eh?" a girl named Mary asked, pushing her way into the room. Mary was friends with Sadie, likely coming by to see her.

Briar automatically closed the lid. She was sure she had closed the door all the way. The other girls were usually good about keeping to their own rooms. There wasn't enough privacy to go around in a boardinghouse.

Mary jumped onto the bed. "Don't hide it, I only

wanted a look." She pawed at the box, and Briar pulled it away when Mim walked in.

"What's going on?"

"I only wanted to see what Briar has. She never buys anything. I wanted to see what was so special." Mary left in a huff.

Mim eyed the box. "Best go to the privy if you want absolute privacy, though you have to close the door fast on that one." She flicked her thumb toward the door. "Besides, the bell's about to go and Sadie's on her way up with Ethel." The mill bell clanged and Mim shrugged.

The halls filled with noise as all the girls made the climb up to their rooms for the night. A chase erupted over a hairbrush, and an argument from across the hall broke out over someone leaving crumbs on the shared bureau. Before anyone else came into the room, Briar stashed the spindle under her bed.

When Ethel opened the door, she eyed the two of them, her gaze shifting back and forth. "You look like you're up to something." Sadie followed in at her heels.

"Nothing you'd be interested in," said Mim, taking first rotation at the wash basin to brush her teeth.

"Now that we're all here," said Ethel, looking pointedly at Briar, "let's go over the rules."

Sadie flounced onto her new bed and rolled her eyes at Briar.

Briar ignored the look and turned her attention to Ethel, like listening to her talk about the rules was the most important thing in the world.

"No one is allowed to be messy. We each take care of our own things, but common areas like the dresser tops, the water basin, and the desktop, are to be kept orderly at all times. We take turns with the wastewater, the trash, the sweeping, the dusting. No food is to be left out to rot. If any is found, we are allowed to toss it in the kitchen trash so the room doesn't stink or attract mice."

"Next," called Mim, backing away from the water basin.

Sadie made a dash for the basin. After they'd all cycled through, the rules were done, and Ethel had started in on inviting Sadie to the next suffrage meeting. "Given what the mill wants to do to our wages, it's time for us to band together again like they did a few years ago when the operatives went on strike. But we need the vote if we're to make any lasting changes."

"No more suffrage talk, please." Mim turned off the light. "I want pleasant dreams."

Soon the gentle shuffles of everyone settling in for the night shifted to the quiet sounds of room-mates sleeping. Briar stared up into the dark, wide awake despite her aching feet and sore shoulders. She was as exhausted as the others but couldn't shut down her mind. Fanny's constant talk of fairies was working its way into her thoughts and she was trying to keep separate the ideas of fairies and fairy wood. The spindle under her bed may be made of something called fairy wood, but that didn't mean it was magical.

CHAPTER FOURTEEN

Finally, the fog began to lift, and with it the ill tempers. Briar had hoped to get a good look at the spindle, but with all her room-mates in the room, there was no time.

When she got to her station at work, she examined her frames to check their suitability for a wooden spindle. She'd never paid much heed to the inner workings, keeping her eyes on the thread itself. Now she noted the rows of spindles and how they attached to the machine. When she had to shut down one of the frames, she used the time to lift a bobbin out of the way and measure the size of the spindles. She tried unscrewing the bolt on one but it held fast. It wouldn't be easy to twist off.

As the dinner bell rang and everyone shut down, Briar quickly checked out her fourth frame. She'd watched Henry attend to the frame so many times applying the oil, which got all over the doffers' feet and the hem of Briar's skirts.

His theory was that one spindle in particular was causing the most trouble with her frame. He could never get it perfectly straight. So, if she could find that crooked one, she was confident she could get it off and replace it. All she'd need was a tool to apply enough force. If she swapped them out near the end of her shift when all the frames were running, the noise of the machines would cover up any banging she made. The overseer couldn't watch her all the time. At some point he'd be called to the far corner of the room to either help or berate another operative, and Briar would have a chance to act.

She walked the length of the frame, lifting up bobbins until she found the offending spindle. There it was, near the end on number four.

"Oh, hello, Briar," Sadie said.

Briar dropped the bobbin and stood, heat rising to her face. "Hello. What are you doing in the spinning room?"

Sadie pointed to the agent in charge of the mill, who was walking away. "I'm moving up here today. When I told him we were room-mates, he said you could show me what to do."

"I thought the frames were opening up at the end of the month. Whose frames are you taking over?"

"Whoever had those ones." She pointed to the next row over where a girl named Ruth had worked only yesterday.

Ruth had been at the mill for several years and had developed the same racking cough Mam had had after breathing in too much cotton dust. They all knew the risks to their lungs from breathing in the cotton floating in the room, but what were they to do? Hope and pray they didn't have to spend too many years in the spinning room.

"What happened to her?" Briar asked. Ruth had said nothing about leaving, so this was unexpected.

"Guess she found other work or went back home. Don't care."

Briar took in a calming breath. "Fine. After dinner. We'd better hurry back to the house before all the food's gone." If nothing else, it was a chance for Briar to prove herself, that she could train someone. Hopefully Sadie learned quickly and well, because she'd be learning on Briar's frames. If Sadie messed up, Briar's pay would get docked. And Sadie, she wouldn't get paid anything until she had her own frames.

Sadie walked on ahead, and Briar, in exasperation, briefly closed her eyes and tilted her head up. A drop of water from the ceiling hoses landed on her cheek. The water sprayed on the frames to help keep the cotton from breaking as it was pulled and twisted into thread. Well, maybe now her emotional threads wouldn't break. She wiped off the water drop. Nothing so simple would help to hold her together if she lost the children.

"Heard you've got a new spinner," Mim said, her eyes wide. She and Briar were walking up to the room after supper to work on two baby dresses Mim had brought in over the weekend.

Briar mimicked Mim's wide eyes. "It was a surprise." They both laughed at the understatement. "She's actually a quick learner, for which I'm glad. She shadowed me for a couple of hours and then I had her work one of her own frames for the rest of the day. She'll do all right." Briar was glad she hadn't tried to swap out the spindle yet, or Sadie would have seen.

"And did the overseer get a good look at you teaching? You'll need his recommendation for Burlington."

"All he does is watch us. The old overseer used to spend most of his time in the office. This one paces all day and makes us nervous."

"Gather 'round ladies," Miss Olive said, calling up the stairs to those who had already escaped. "Everyone. It's an all-house meeting and I've got your mail captive to make sure you come."

Mim groaned. "Not again. How much improving does she think we need?"

Miss Olive believed it was her duty as keeper of the boardinghouse to instruct her girls in the ways of the world and she took her role very seriously. There were several activities the girls in the mills were required to participate in: work and church, and they were to avoid any activity meant to destroy one's moral character.

Mim plunked down in the most comfortable chair in the parlor and crossed her arms in annoyance. She was of the opinion that these meetings were generally a waste of time. She received the majority of her information from Godey's Lady's Book and would rather practice her man-catching skills than sit about in improvement circles.

Miss Olive stood in front of the fireplace and began calling out names, handing out letters. The stack was down to a handful when she called out, "Briar."

"Me?" She never got mail. Everyone she knew was right here. Except Nanny and Henry. She took a deep breath, unsure of who she'd rather receive a letter from.

New York City
May 25, 1894.
Sweet Briar Rose,
I made it all the way to the Atlantic Ocean. My ship leaves tomorrow, so by the time you read this I may already

be halfway to England. (A stone's throw from Ireland.) From there I'm off to Germany to see if I look like any of my relatives. Hope number four is working for you.

Yours,

Henry.

"May twenty-fifth? That was more than three weeks ago. Where did he mail it from? Germany?" Mim said, reading the date upside down.

Smiling, Briar folded up the paper, imagining Henry penning his letter, thinking of her.

Ethel looked from the letter to Briar and smiled herself. "Good news, I take it?"

Briar felt heat rising in her neck. She shrugged it off. "He's started his adventure."

Miss Olive had finished handing out the mail and now stood, hands clasped, waiting for everyone to settle in. She had a big smile, which meant she was more excited than usual about today's topic.

"I will begin with a recitation from last September's *Outing* Magazine, a poem from Madeline S. Bridges:

> *The maiden with her wheel of old*
> *Sat by the fire to spin,*
> *While lightly through her careful hold*
> *The flax slid out and in.*
> *To-day her distaff, rock and reel*
> *Far out of sight are hurled,*
> *For now the maiden with her wheel*
> *Goes spinning round the world.*

Miss Olive gestured to the parlor door.

The mill girls looked questioningly at one another, then simultaneously turned to the door as a woman in reform clothes strode in with a bicycle.

Gasps sounded, followed by excited voices.

Miss Olive raised her voice above the others. "Today is a new day for you girls. I've managed to make a little purchase for us to share, and I've invited a guest to teach us how to use the new safety bicycle."

Murmured excitement continued to spread through the room. Briar sat up eagerly. She'd always wanted to try riding a bicycle.

"Hush, hush, we'll all get a turn. First, let Miss Spence give us the basics of being a wheel woman, then we'll take the vehicle outside and give it a try."

Mim stood, hands on hips. "No way. You can make me come to these meetings, but I'm not riding that thing." She held out her full skirt as if to emphasize the ridiculousness of the notion.

"You need yourself some bloomers!" called out Hettie, a sharp-witted weaver. She peeled with laughter at Mim's shocked face.

"Never," said Mim. "You'll never see me out in public in bloomers." She sat down in a huff and said to the room, "You won't either if you want husbands. Men don't like women who push their freedom."

Ethel reached across Mary and pinched Mim.

"Ouch. What did you do that for?" Mim rubbed her arm, which was already turning red.

"If you don't know, I should've done it harder. Be polite and listen up. You might learn something," she whispered.

Miss Spence continued on as if nothing had happened. "Bicycling will not only improve your health, but you will also come to recognize it as a freedom machine. I've recently come from Massachusetts, where I witnessed with my own eyes Annie Londonderry setting out on her bicycle to wheel around the world. Like Nellie Bly, who only a few short years ago traveled around the world unaccompanied, Annie Londonderry is demonstrating what the new woman is capable of achieving."

Heads nodded around the room. The male operatives had told them how much they like cycling. You didn't have to ask permission to take the horse out, or spend so much time walking.

"I will teach you first to get on the seat, to pedal, to turn, and to dismount. A bicycle is not as expensive as a horse. It is within reach of all of you, especially these new safety bicycles. They even have skirt guards on the back tire, although if you are serious about wheeling, I suggest reform clothes."

Everyone couldn't help but look at Mim. She gave them all a grimace.

The bicycle looked fun. If Briar had one of those, she could go back and forth to the cottage every night instead of living in the boardinghouse. She added the idea of purchasing a bicycle to her list of possible ways to keep the family together.

"Susan B. Anthony says herself that the bicycle 'has done more to emancipate women than anything else in the world. It gives them a feeling of freedom and self-reliance.' Furthermore, 'The moment she takes her seat she knows she can't get into harm unless she gets off her bicycle, and away she goes, the picture of free, untrammeled womanhood.'"

Miss Spence slapped the seat. "And even Frances Willard promotes riding the bicycle to help women to a wider world." She paused and smiled at them one by one. "That is what you want, isn't it?"

Miss Spence's sermon over, she clapped her hands. "Who wants to go first?"

"If I'm to teach the girls, I'd better learn first," Miss Olive said.

In all eagerness, the mill girls filed out of the house and lined up along the porch. The sun had gone behind the mountains and the lamplighter had already started turning on the gas street lamps, creating scattered puddles of pale yellow on the dirt road.

With Miss Spence holding the bicycle, Miss Olive gathered her skirts and hoisted herself onto the seat with a giggle.

"Do as I demonstrated earlier," admonished Miss Spence. "Your body's natural sense of balance will take over if you do not hesitate. Push and don't stop pedaling. The pedals turn with the back wheel so your feet will keep rotating with the wheel. If you need a rest, or you feel your skirts are getting twisted in the pedals, put your feet up on these coaster brackets."

And with that, the two women set off, Miss Olive laughing loud, and Miss Spence running to keep up.

"She's doing it!" called the mill girls encouragingly. "Keep going, Miss Olive!"

Neighbors opened their doors to see what was going on, and soon it looked like a parade with people lined up on the street watching. Miss Spence was coaching Miss Olive on how to turn when the front wheel began to wobble. The girls held their collective breaths and watched. She straightened out and began cycling back confidently, breaking away from the attentions of Miss Spence.

Suddenly she shrieked. "Look out, girls!" She drove through the middle of the crowd, the girls parting like the Red Sea as she plowed straight into the hedge at the side of the house with a crash.

Miss Spence followed close behind. "Are you all right?"

She leaned over the bicycle and the bush and pulled Miss Olive out of the greenery. She completed a quick inventory of Miss Olive's condition, plucking a twig out of her hair before Miss Olive brushed her aside.

"I'm fine. Really, I am. Girls, the wheel is marvelous. Who is next? I've shown you how not to stop, so now you can do what you are supposed to."

Several of the girls took a step back, looking for someone else to try first.

Briar and Ethel looked at each other. "You go, Briar. I'll catch you when you circle around."

Eager to try, despite Miss Olive's mishap, Briar stepped forward.

"Good for you," said Miss Spence. She held the bicycle aloft.

"Be careful," Mim warned, "or you'll fall and break your wrist and then where will you be? Unable to work." She adjusted her hat and smiled at a gentleman walking by, who eyed the group warily.

Briar copied how Miss Olive gathered her long skirts and arranged one foot on a pedal. She took a big breath and pushed off, leaning heavily toward Miss Spence. "Whoa."

"Straighten up, that's it," Miss Spence said encouragingly, holding Briar upright. "Steady now."

Briar concentrated on keeping her balance so she wouldn't fall on Miss Spence. A few pedals in and she'd found her balance. Miss Spence let her go. "You're doing it!" she called.

Briar grinned as she rode down the road under her own power. What a marvel. She was getting the rhythm down and it wasn't at all as hard as she thought it was going to be.

Until she road past Wheeler.

He stood amid a group of boys who had all stopped what they were doing to watch her attempt the bicycle. His jaw opened wide at the sight of her. Did he not approve or was he impressed? She had started to raise a hand to wave when her front tire hit a rock and the handlebars yanked her other arm sharply. It was all she could do to maintain her balance.

"Briar, is that really you?" Wheeler called out.

"Yes, but let me concentrate!" Riding under the scrutiny of the pack of boys made her nervous. She rode farther than she needed to so they couldn't watch as she took a wide turn. She rode back to the boardinghouse without mishap and without giving the boys another glance.

Her legs were shaking as she got off, but she couldn't stop herself from smiling. "Who's next?" she asked. Riding a bicycle was one of the most exhilarating things she'd ever done.

Once Lizbeth was off, wiggling down the road, Briar searched the sidewalks for Wheeler. Now she had just the excuse to talk to him and find out about his move to Burlington. Only, he had disappeared. She'd have thought he'd want to tease her about the bicycle, as it was something they'd discussed before.

"We ought to form a wheel women's club," Mary said.

"Why?" Mim said. "We've only got one to share amongst the lot of us." She brushed her hands like she was brushing off the dirt of the whole affair and marched back inside.

Mim might not be able to see it, but Briar and the small cluster of mill girls eager to try the bicycle saw potential in those two wheels.

While Briar watched the next girl ride off down the street, she imagined how the same conversation she had with Wheeler would have gone with Henry: "Briar, is that really you?" Henry would have called. She would have looked over at his grinning face.

"What are you doing here?" she would have said before snapping her attention back to the road, wobbling under the distraction. "Go away, Henry Prince. I need to concentrate."

"Oh, do I distract you?" he would have asked with a wink.

She'd be able to feel his grin without even checking to confirm it, and would set her lips in a line, trying to ignore him. If only she could ignore him now. Henry had gone and left the valley; he should leave her thoughts as well. But she kept finding him there. She touched the letter in her pocket, wishing she knew where he was so she could send a reply. *Henry. Are you well? How long before you send another?*

CHAPTER FIFTEEN

Had it been a regular spindle, Briar wouldn't have felt the need to keep it a secret. But the beauty of it and the manner in which she acquired it made her want to protect it. She was nervous leaving it unattended.

For the past few nights under Mim's careful eye, Briar had sat on her bed, sewing delicate blue and yellow stitches into the tiny pleats of a little girl's dress to make a pretty pattern. It was Briar's first smocking job that Mim had shared with her, and they both needed it to be perfect.

With the spindle under the bed, she felt like a bird sitting on an egg, keeping predators at bay. She didn't know how long she could go on like this. She was beginning to feel anxious and nervous all the time, afraid someone would take the spindle while she was gone. Just as she was anxious and nervous all the time at work, teaching Sadie and feeling pressured by the overseer to increase her production. Not to mention each day brought her closer and closer to her birthday and Nanny's deadline for Briar to have a home for the children.

Something had to give, soon.

The house bell rang, interrupting Briar's thoughts.

"Meeting time! Come on down!" called Miss Olive.

Ethel stood, pulling Briar with her. "This talk will be good for you. You're a single woman who's taken on the role of provider for your family, yet the law limits you."

Mim harrumphed. "You overstate. Briar is doing a fine job with the little ones. She doesn't need your lectures."

"You need the lecture, too, Mim. Maybe you'll have your eyes opened."

"You have your strategy and I have mine. I'm going to find a husband who is rich enough so I don't have to work anymore." Mim took a step closer to Ethel.

"And if you marry a drunkard? What recourse have you?" Ethel closed the gap between the two, raising her voice so that the others passing the room stopped and stared.

"I shan't marry a drunkard," Mim said, eyes flashing. "Why would I do that?"

"No woman sets out to marry a drunkard," Lizbeth said quietly from the hallway. It was well known in the house that Lizbeth's father garnished her wages to feed his habit while her mother struggled to keep food in the house for all the siblings Lizbeth left behind.

That small declaration took the fight right out of Ethel and Mim. "No, I guess she doesn't," Mim said. "I'll work on your reform clothes while you ladies are at the meeting."

Briar followed Ethel to the parlor. "She might try to put lace on your bloomers," Briar warned, attempting to reconcile. She did hate to see them being contentious with each other.

"Ha! She might." Ethel laughed as they found seats. "But if anyone can figure out how to sew my trousers without turning my figure into a man's, it's Mim. If she does a good job, she'll have extra work for as long as she needs it. So many of us are keen on having the proper clothing for exercise but aren't sure about the pattern."

"She only relented because she saw the bloomers in a magazine. If it's not in *Godey's* or *Good Housekeeping*, she'll have none of it."

The two shared a laugh while waiting for everyone to get settled.

The woman who had come to speak to them that night was Mrs. Sarah Tuttle. Briar didn't know what she expected, a larger-than-life figure perhaps, but Mrs. Tuttle was average in every way: brown hair, brown eyes, average height. Her clothing didn't call attention to herself, either. And she was married! The way the newspapers reported on suffragettes you'd think they were all single, angry, man-hating women.

Mrs. Tuttle continued to defy Briar's expectations when she began speaking. Her voice was strong and clear, and she spoke with conviction. No wonder Ethel liked to come to these meetings.

"Thank you, mill women, for having me speak to you. What a wonderful effect has been caused by you operatives coming together *en masse* to live and work and educate yourselves. Much has changed since those early days, but we have much left to do. No one suspected back when Mr. Lowell built his first mill over in Massachusetts and invited rural farm girls to move to his boardinghouses that women's lives would never be the same. For the first time, those industrious farm girls got paid for their work."

Applause broke out across the room.

"They could take their paychecks, send some money home, put some in savings, and spend a little on themselves.

They gained independence. They gained choices."

More cheering.

"These weren't silly or rebellious girls. They loved their families, but they wanted more opportunities. Many a girl put her brother through school with her earnings, and then as educational institutions opened up for women, she could go on to put herself through school, too."

Briar joined in the applause.

"Even though we were getting paid, it was still less than what the men were getting paid. And then, management wanted us to work faster, and for less money. What was once freeing for women became shackles. You all know the song:

> *Oh! isn't it a pity, such a pretty girl as I-*
> *Should be sent to the factory to pine away and die?*
> *Oh! I cannot be a slave,*
> *I will not be a slave,*
> *For I'm so fond of liberty*
> *That I cannot be a slave."*

By the end of the song, the entire room had joined in; they all knew the words. They knew how those mills under Mr. Lowell had been better places to work than they were now. How he didn't want his mills to be like those in England that Charles Dickens wrote sad tales about.

In fact, the first mill girls were proud when Mr. Dickens came to visit and pronounced them well dressed, healthy in appearance, well mannered, and none in need of rescuing from the mill. If Mr. Lowell hadn't died so young, conditions may have stayed the same across all the mills, but they would never know.

"Thank those operatives before you for their efforts in bringing in the ten-hour workday. If it were not for them, you would still be standing at your machines toiling until dark."

Murmurs spread around the room. Briar's feet were sore enough after ten hours of standing.

"We've seen what can be done if we band together. We ladies possess a stronger power when we work together, and we need your help in attaining a voice for women everywhere. Already, we have school suffrage for women in twenty states, but not Vermont. School suffrage allows women to vote in school-board decisions that affect their children.

"Let's make Vermont next. Know what you are fighting for. You must be educated. Search out a subject and ponder it. Believe you have something to say and a right to say it. Have an opinion, ladies, and express it winsomely."

She pulled out a well-worn notebook and turned to a bookmarked page. "Listen to how Elizabeth Cady Stanton speaks to the assemblies on our behalf:

'To throw obstacles in the way of a complete education is like putting out the eyes; to deny the rights of property, like cutting off the hands. To deny political equality is to rob the ostracized of all self-respect.'

"Mrs. Stanton gives them facts to touch the intellect, and then illustrates with examples to touch their hearts. She tells them of a girl of sixteen thrown on the world to support herself, like many of you."

Mrs. Tuttle caught Briar's eye. "You who must maintain your spotless integrity but with so many temptations and trials to pull you down you feel like you are swimming upstream when all you want to do is rest a moment. You long to drift with the current, but you risk losing all you have gained only because you are weary of the struggle."

Mrs. Tuttle paused. She shook her head slowly, allowing the operatives time to imagine a girl giving up and giving in to the baser ways of surviving when you are young and alone.

"'*She* knows the bitter solitude of self.'"

Briar felt a tightening in her gut. She was that girl of sixteen trying to support herself. And it was hard. She worked tirelessly to keep a home for her little sister and the boys. They were blessed to have Nanny to shelter them for as long as she was willing. The old woman shared what little charity she had for the sake of the children. If only Nanny could hold on a few more years.

Nanny never asked for more than Briar offered to pay, which never did seem enough, but somehow, with the food baskets from the Prince family, they were surviving. Briar's solitude wasn't bitter, but it was burdensome.

She glanced at Ethel, who was leaning into the speech, nodding along with every point Mrs. Tuttle made. Ethel never talked much about herself, never told her story. But she sure was drinking in all that Mrs. Tuttle was saying.

Likely every girl in the boardinghouse knew what it was to feel alone. All together, yet still alone. They should help carry one another's burdens more. Briar smiled when Ethel looked her way. Yes, Briar resolved to be ready to help her fellow mill girl when the opportunity presented itself. They needed each other.

"We are told to stay in our sphere, the home. But what if a woman can't stay in the home—either through widowhood, or an abusive husband, or no husband at all?" Mrs. Tuttle put her hand on her hip. "If the woman's place is in a good home, where are all the good husbands?"

She paused to allow for laughter from all the single women. It was a question the mill girls batted around in their parlor on a nightly basis.

"Your sphere goes beyond the home to include whatever work you are able to do. At the Chicago World's Fair last year, Lucy Stone, God rest her soul, pointed out that 'the tools belonged to those who could use them; that the possession of a power presupposed a right to its use.' Use your God-given tools, ladies. As she would say, 'Make the world better.'"

Mrs. Tuttle smiled demurely as she received a standing ovation.

"Well? Isn't she marvelous?" Ethel leaned over and grasped Briar's hand. "Tell me all your thoughts."

Briar took a deep breath to take time to compose herself. "She described my situation almost exactly." Her voice cracked. "I feel like I'm constantly trying to swim upstream but getting nowhere."

Ethel squeezed her hand. "You are getting further than you think you are. Next, you'll have to come to a temperance meeting. We're making real progress bringing the issue of drunkenness to light. We'll be marching through town Saturday night, which you would miss, but you can help with the signs. And then we need to make the white ribbons for the WCTU rally."

Briar turned to the door, about to excuse herself. "Thank you for inviting me, Ethel. I do mean it, but I'm going to turn in early tonight." The lecture had given her much to think about, and she wanted to be alone to think through her next steps.

"I know it's overwhelming to take in all at once. I'll come up with you." Ethel started to follow Briar out of the room.

"No, no. You stay and talk with Mrs. Tuttle."

Ethel looked relieved, like she had really wanted to stay. "Is there anything you'd like me to ask her?"

Briar shook her head. "No, I already know what I need to do."

Ethel's eyebrows shot up. "You do? Oh, Briar, I'm so

glad. I hoped she would inspire you in the right direction."

Ethel couldn't possibly know what Briar was planning, but Mrs. Tuttle had given her the push she needed to take a risk, to use the tools she had, even if that wasn't exactly what the lecture was about.

Tomorrow she would do a quick spindle swap, and if it didn't change anything, a quick swap back. She could do it all in one shift, if the overseer got distracted enough. At least then she would know, and if it didn't work, she could move on to another plan. She didn't want to become the girl who stopped fighting and allowed the current to sweep her away.

All she had to do was get to the spinning room tomorrow morning before the overseer.

CHAPTER SIXTEEN

The room was still dark when Briar woke. Ethel was facing away from her, but Briar noted the steady rise and fall of her shoulder as she slept. With as little movement to the bed as possible, Briar slipped out. She quickly changed into her work clothes, forgoing washing.

As she tied her apron, there was a familiar bump of the small book against her thigh, the one that reminded her she never completed her education. She pulled the book out of her pocket and slid it under her pillow. Maybe one day she'd finish reading it; mark a new chapter in her life by finishing the old.

After checking and rechecking that the girls were all asleep—Sadie snoring, and Mim with her pillow over her ears—Briar knelt down to retrieve the spindle from under the bed. She slid out the box, cringing as wood scraped against wood. She paused. Listened. Then opened the box.

There was just enough light to see the spindle against the silk cloth. With only a slight hesitation, Briar reached in with an old cloth handkerchief and scooped up the spindle, silk and all.

She quickly wrapped everything securely, pausing only to lament that she still hadn't gotten a good look at it, or even touched it yet. Her fingers were itching to glide over the roses. The shaft was long and stuck out of her pocket, but wrapped in her handkerchief people might think she had hastily jabbed the cloth into her apron.

Now, even if the girls woke early, she was ready. She buttoned up her boots, and still no one woke. She allowed herself a small smile as she gently opened the door and stepped out. At the click of the doorknob, the first mill bell of the day began to clang. *Drat.* She rested her forehead on the doorframe. She wasn't as early as she'd hoped.

Standing tall, she took a step and bumped smack into Miss Olive. "Oh! Excuse me," Briar said. A stir of guilt pricked her conscience. Why was she feeling guilty? She'd done nothing wrong. The peddler gave her the spindle.

Miss Olive's brow furrowed and she sniffed in the air.

"Is everything okay?" Briar asked as the bedroom doors flew open. Girls streamed out, racing one another to the outside privies, and jostling Briar and Miss Olive in the process.

"Yes, oh, yes. I was merely tracking down an unusual scent." She breathed again, a look of confusion crossing her face. "Seem to have lost it now amongst all the handcreams and other concoctions up here." She waved her hand. "No bother, it was probably my nose playing tricks on me. Something I haven't smelled in years." She sniffed once more at Briar before heading back downstairs.

By this time, Mim had opened their bedroom door and stood in the open space. "What was that about? I didn't think Miss Olive ever came up here until we were gone, and she was collecting our laundry."

Ethel stumbled out next, yawning wide. "You're up early," she said to Briar. "Or am I late?" She dashed back into the room and banged out drawers in her hurry to dress.

Mim laughed. "Ha! Haven't seen that one ruffled in a while. I've got to fix my hair yet. I'll see you at breakfast."

Briar didn't wait for her room-mates. She skittered to the kitchen to find Miss Olive. The boardinghouse keeper was up to her elbows in dough as she kneaded the daily bread.

"May I borrow a tool from the box?" Briar asked.

"Yes," Miss Olive answered distractedly. "Make sure you return it tonight."

Leaving Miss Olive sniffing the air again, Briar opened the utility closet and located a wrench. Hopefully it would do the job. She stopped by the dining room on the way out to grab a flapjack and was on her way.

Alone at last, Briar stepped outside, self-consciously trying to hide the spindle end, and now a wrench poking out the top of her apron pocket. Had the season been winter, the morning darkness would have helped, but this early sunrise exposed all.

"Morning," another mill girl called in passing. Briar nodded back and then waved at another friendly mill girl.

When Briar reached the mill, the gates were open, but only a few people were going inside the yard. Most waited for the bell to call them there, which was what Briar was counting on. She needed to be alone with her spinning frame.

She'd never been the first one in and hoped the overseer wasn't an early bird.

"Hello?" she called out. Silence. "Anyone here?"

She let out a breath of relief. The spinning room was empty, the machines looking like hulking, sleeping monsters. If she got too close to one it might reach out and snatch her.

Briar had been fortunate to have had no accidents

in the years she'd worked there. Others had gotten their clothing pulled in, or had their fingers mashed. No one in her mill had been scalped, but there were stories, and thankfully they'd avoided any fires in their mill. After the hullabaloo at the World's Fair in Chicago where electric lights were on display, the owners of the mill got on a list to have their mills lit up with incandescent bulbs instead of gas lights. With the floating bits of cotton and the grease-soaked floors, fires were a constant fear.

Her footfalls were loud on the wooden floor without all the noise to dull them. Her frames stood silent, waiting for her, as familiar to her as her own hands. With set lips, she marched to frame number four and located the crooked spindle. She lifted the bobbin and bent low to get a good look at how the connection was made.

She fitted the wrench around the bottom and tried to give it a good twist. It held firm.

"Well, aren't you the early one?" Annie said as she took up her place at the frames beside Briar's.

Briar inhaled sharply and her heart began to race. She immediately let go of the bobbin. As it dropped back into place she pocketed the wrench and pasted on a smile. "Was up and wanted some time to myself."

"I know what you mean. You've discovered my secret. I'm usually the first one here. Gives me time to water the plants and quiet my mind." She held up a watering can. "I'm certainly not here early because of the pay. Especially not today, since it's the day we get less in our envelopes. Being early quitting time, I was hoping to spend a little in town tonight—"

"Don't let me keep you from the plants," Briar interrupted, hoping to send her on.

"They're fine. I probably overwater them anyway." Annie

rambled on about their pay until the overseer came in.

There went any hope of swapping out the spindle before the day began.

He walked the length of the floor, pausing when he saw Briar and Annie. Briar self-consciously held her hands in front of her pocket. He gave them a thoughtful expression before continuing on, not saying anything. Briar couldn't tell what that look was about. It was almost as if he was pleased she was there early.

Next, a steady stream of girls filed in and lined up near their frames. The overseer took his place by the pull cord. Like an automaton, Briar lined herself up with the lever on frame number one, ready to go through the motions. The spindle bumped against her thigh, reminding her of what she needed to do. She would not give up and let the current pull her downstream. Today, she would stay alert for the right moment, and then be quick about changing out the spindles.

When the bell clanged, the overseer pulled the rope that connected the electricity to the leather bands. The girls simultaneously threw the shipping handles on their machines and the room roared to life. Briar could never decide what her body felt first. Was it the thrumming of the vibrations on the floor buzzing her feet, or the flapping of the leather bands pounding her ears?

The spindles spun like rows of tiny dancers, stretching and winding the roving into thread. It was a routine that woke her up and energized her. By quitting time, she'd be dragging her feet, but for now, it was a fresh new day. She glanced at that corner of frame number four. Like Henry, she was going to try something new to change the future for her family.

Chapter Seventeen

For the first time, the overseer stayed in his room the entire morning. Briar kept checking over her shoulder for him, jumping at the slightest movement of the operatives around her. *Odd.* After days of hovering, he was letting everyone work. It was almost more off-putting than his hovering. The operatives kept casting looks and shrugging at one another until they got used to his absence.

Near the end of the shift, before the dinner bell, Briar checked on Sadie to see if she needed anything. Sadie shook her head. She was now able to handle two frames on her own, and next week would take on a third.

Briar waited for her doffer to work down to the farthest frame away from pesky number four. With her big cart of bobbins and quick movements, the girl would draw attention, and Briar could do what she needed to do.

Because her task was dangerous, Briar couldn't just set the spindle break on the chosen spindle to turn it off and make the switch. She had to shut down the entire frame or risk injuring her hands. This meant she had to work fast before the overseer left his office and noticed her stalled frame. Taking a deep breath, she pulled the lever and set to work.

She drew off the bobbin and set it aside. Then, using the wrench, she attacked the bolster case...or was it the lock...or the bearing? Who knew? Henry had tried to talk to her about the parts of the frame so she could keep it running better, but at the time all she cared about was him getting her frame up and running again. Sweet Henry. She'd only gotten that one letter from him. Surely he would have had time to write another by now. Let her know he was okay and if he was able to do anything about the letter to her aunt. She looked at that place on the frame where she'd been getting the little tokens, but it was empty.

Briar wiped the sweat off her hands to get a better grip on the wrench. Already, the room was unbearably hot and muggy. She leaned into the frame, using all her strength. If she could only loosen this bit, the shaft should slip out. Like that. She grinned. Ha! She did it. But when she pulled the bent spindle out of the frame, she realized it wasn't simply a shaft. It had its own version of the whorl molded to it. But the whorl on the wooden spindle was way too big. Now what?

She glanced up to see where everyone was. No sign of the overseer, which meant he was likely at the far side of the room. Maribelle was on the first frame, working her way closer.

Now what could she use to make a smaller whorl? There was no way she'd whittle down the rose-carved one it came with. It was too beautiful to destroy like that.

Quickly, Briar took the bundle out of her pocket. But before she could unwrap it, the bell rang, and she shoved it back out of sight. The noise in the room fell silent as everyone shut down their frames and the overseer emerged from the office to turn off the power. He caught Briar's eye, nodded once, and left the building.

Briar cocked her head, wondering about the change in the overseer. Perhaps he had recommended she be sent to Burlington so she was no longer his responsibility?

"Aren't you coming?" asked Annie.

Briar shook her head. "In a minute. I'm having some trouble with my frame, as usual." She stood in front of it, hands behind her back and blocking Annie's view.

Annie frowned in sympathy. "That frame never has worked right. Don't be too long or you'll miss out."

Briar waved and then turned back to analyze the metal spindle to see if she could take the whorl off.

Maribelle stood at her elbow. "Can I help you with something, miss?"

Briar nearly jumped out of her skin. "Go have your dinner. I'll adjust this spindle and be off myself."

Maribelle nodded, her eyes darting to the metal spindle in Briar's hand before skipping away.

Panic welled up inside. What was she going to do? She didn't want to give up so easily. She kept her eyes on the operatives headed out to dinner while she felt the wooden spindle through her apron until the whorl separated from the shaft and dropped to the bottom of her pocket.

Before doing anything else, she would measure the spindle to see if it even fit. Keeping the wooden spindle hidden in the handkerchief, she lowered the shaft into the gap-toothed sneer of the frame. Perfect match. So if she could figure out a way to make a smaller whorl for the spindle, it just might work.

She pulled the wooden spindle away, but all that came loose was handkerchief and silk cloth. The spindle had caught in the frame.

Briar glanced over her shoulder. No one but the shadowy machines watching her. She reached back in with the cloth, trying to keep the spindle hidden.

She wiggled the shaft, but it held fast.

She bent down to see what the spindle had caught on. Nothing. She peered closer. The wood had grown a new whorl in the exact shape and size it needed. She gasped and pulled her hand away. Then she took a step back. What was this thing the peddler had given her?

Fairy wood.

Impossible. Fairy tales were stories her mother made up to help them live through the hunger. They were tales. Not real.

With trembling fingers, Briar tested the strength of the bond again. It was even more solid than before. Hardly daring to breathe, she replaced the bobbin then stuffed the royal blue cloth back in her pocket. She hid the metal spindle in a little hollow at the base of the frame, hoping that it wouldn't roll out with the vibrations when the machine started up again. She didn't want to take it back to the boardinghouse in case she needed it again or in case someone saw it in her pocket and asked questions.

Letting her feet carry her back to the boardinghouse in a daze, she left the building to join her mill sisters for dinner. So befuddled, she barely noticed she was going against the tide as everyone was jostling their way back to the mill.

"Briar!" called Ethel. "You're late. Here, I slipped out some food for you." Ethel handed her a sausage wrapped in a flapjack, then turned Briar around to go back to the mill. "Don't tell Miss Olive. You okay? You've been acting strange ever since the meeting last night. I didn't scare you off, did I? I don't expect you to plunge right into a campaign. I just want you to realize your potential. We can get tied up in our work, becoming machines ourselves if we're not careful."

Ethel preached on and on until they climbed the stairs and had to part ways. Briar had mindlessly nodded to keep Ethel going while she tried to understand what had happened to her frame and the spindle. She put her hand in her pocket and felt the whorl with its carved roses. It was buzzing, the way the floor in the spinning room felt when all the machines were on and the vibrations worked their way up her body. She yanked her hand out.

What had she done? Had she fought further upstream like Elizabeth Cady Stanton encouraged, or was this an example of giving in to temptation? This was no normal spindle. By placing it in the frame it was as if she had turned it on the way the overseer turned on the power each morning.

When she stepped into the room, she was afraid to even look at the spinning frame. What if it had started to grow like Jack's beanstalk and taken over the room? She glanced down her row. Her frame looked as it always had. An inanimate object waiting for Briar to turn it on and set its spindles to spinning. She laughed nervously. Her anxiety over getting caught had given her an imagination as wild as the twins'.

There had to be some rational explanation for how the spindle stuck in the frame. The wood swelling from the high humidity in the room, for example. And the whorl didn't start its buzzing until she crossed the threshold. It might have been reacting to the looms above, which were turned on and off in shifts and could be felt below.

The bell sounded and the machines around her roared

to life as the girls threw their shipper handles. Maribelle, who had come to finish the doffing she'd started before the bell, pointed to Briar's silent machines. "Aren't you gonna start?" the girl yelled over the din.

Briar shook herself out of her musings and rushed to get all four machines up and going. When she turned on the power for number four and the spindles began to whirl, she sucked in a breath and waited for something bad to happen.

Little Maribelle, after finishing her doffing, wandered off to find someone to play with. Briar paced up and down her frames, fixing the odd broken thread on numbers one, two, and three, but keeping her distance from number four. She didn't want to get too close, and she didn't have to.

For the first time ever, the threads never broke. Just as the peddler said.

Soon, Maribelle joined her to exchange the bobbins again. She started with frame number one. For a moment, Briar wondered if she should volunteer to take care of the work, but that would raise suspicion if the other spinners happened to notice what she was doing. Instead, while biting her lip, she watched Maribelle lift up a bobbin, drop it in her cart, and load an empty one in its place. Over and over as she worked her way toward the fairy-wood spindle.

CHAPTER EIGHTEEN

Maribelle was one spindle away now. Briar watched, bouncing on the balls of her feet, ready to step in if there was a problem. She didn't want to call attention to the new spindle, but she didn't trust that small piece of fairy wood. It did something unexpected and that made her almost as worried as getting caught.

Maribelle's chubby hand reached for the bobbin atop the wooden spindle. Briar's heart beat against her chest. She rushed over and reached for the same bobbin. "This one is tricky," she yelled over the noise of the machines. "I'll help you with it."

Maribelle shook her head, clasping the bobbin before Briar could get to it. "I can do it. I don't need help anymore. Honest."

Briar thought of Pansy as she looked into Maribelle's earnest eyes. The girl was trying to show how grown-up she was. Fine. Briar wouldn't take the burgeoning pride away from her, but she would stick close.

Grinning, Maribelle zipped off the bobbin, an empty

one ready to replace it. A slight hesitation was the only indication that she'd noticed something amiss. She dropped the new bobbin and moved on.

Briar lowered her hands and backed away. Maribelle, with her tongue sticking out in concentration, finished the line, pushing her cart as she went. The full cart took all her strength, and again Briar was tempted to help her. But the girl was determined, and she made steady progress.

Briar breathed out her tension. So far so good. As long as the spindle held, everything should be fine. It would be fine. Better than fine.

All the same, Briar remained on edge. Frame number four never left the corner of her eye. She stayed attuned to it even more than usual, but for a different reason now. She wasn't worried the threads would snap; she was worried they wouldn't. Others would surely notice the change in routine and question her.

The day continued with Briar both hovering over frame number four and staying as far away from it as she could. Not once did her persnickety frame break down. Not once.

Not only that, the bobbins were filling up faster than usual. By the time Maribelle had gone down the entire line, frame number four was ready for doffing again.

Finally, near the end of the day, the overseer stopped by to see what was going on. "Frame cooperating today?" he said.

Was that suspicion in his voice? Briar nodded and kept working.

For the first time since being assigned these frames, she was ahead of all the other girls in production numbers. Even though it was Saturday and they'd be ending early, she'd made a full day's production.

The spindle was working.

When the bell rang out signaling the end of the day, Maribelle was at her elbow to help clean the frames. Briar and her doffer worked together to get the stray bits of cotton out of the frames, either sticking the bits in their apron pockets or dropping them on the floor for the boys to sweep up. It was messy work and they came away with cotton fluff stuck to their clothes and hair, but it was worth it to go home early and, for Briar, to ride out on the bicycle to the cottage to see the children.

"Thank you, Maribelle," Briar said as they finished up the last frame. *The* frame. "You did some good work today. Tell your mama I said so."

Maribelle beamed. Then she turned her rosy face up to Briar and asked, "What happened to the spindle on this frame? Before dinner it was metal; now it's wood."

Briar searched for what to say. "It's working better than it ever has before. Don't trouble yourself over it."

"It's pretty. Do we oil it like the others?"

Briar hesitated. "No, leave it be. If it sticks we can oil it then."

Nodding, Maribelle waved and was off with a speed only the young doffers could manage at the end of a long work week.

Briar turned back to her frame and noticed a sprig of Solomon's Seal sitting innocently in that corner spot where an acorn and the heart-shaped rock had been previously.

"Henry?" she whispered as she reached out for it. The little white bells shook in her hand as she lifted it to smell the sweet scent. What was going on? How were all these little remembrances of him cropping up?

She carried the sprig with her to the payment line, trying to make sense of all that had happened that day. The spindle had worked even better than she had hoped, but her spirit was unsettled, and she began to question herself. *It grew its own whorl*. Humidity aside, how was that even possible?

The paymaster had already started distributions. Girls were receiving their envelopes, glancing inside, then passing wide-eyed looks to those behind them in line. No one dared complain outright in front of the overseer, but tonight in the parlors, tongues would be wagging.

Briar waited patiently for her turn. When the girl in front of her looked inside her envelope and then gave Briar a twisted smile, Briar responded with a knowing frown. She handed her payment number to the paymaster and he flipped through his box of envelopes until he found hers. She grabbed it and stuffed it in her pocket without looking.

After a final glance at her frame with the new wooden spindle, she escaped the spinning room, her legs trembling. What would happen while she was gone? Would someone find out what she had done? It was far too late to ask permission, but the overseer *had* told her to fix her frame. And fix it she did.

CHAPTER NINETEEN

Descending the outside stairs, Briar inhaled the summer air. The temperature inside the mill and outside was about the same now, but at least outside you could smell the fragrance of summer. The cedars warming in the sun, the wildflowers blooming. She breathed deeply to steady her racing heartbeat.

Everything would be okay. Once all the operatives left the building, the door would be shut, the gate locked, and no one would step foot into the spinning room until Monday, when she would be the first one in.

She skirted around the groups of operatives gathering to complain at the base of the stairs. Half of the money she earned had already been taken out to pay for room and board at the company boardinghouse. With what little was left, she'd give the majority to Fanny for the children, but she made sure to deposit a little, no matter how small, into her savings account. Ethel had taught her that much.

Ethel had been the one to take Briar to the bank and open an account. They continued to go together every payday, meeting just outside the mill gates if they didn't see each other earlier. Briar waved. Ethel was waiting for her now.

"Shorted?" Ethel asked.

"Haven't looked," Briar said. She self-consciously covered her pocket, hiding Miss Olive's wrench and the whorl as they walked down the street.

The bank was beyond the row of boardinghouses, in the center of town. The streets were always busy on payday. They reached a crossroads and waited for a horse and wagon to go by before continuing. The driver raised his hat and called out, "Lola! Oi, is that you?"

The man was looking right at them, so Briar shook her head.

Ethel lowered her hat and pulled Briar to go around the wagon. "All us operatives look alike, don't we?" she said.

"From Stowe," the man persisted, stopping his vehicle and turning around in his seat.

"He's likely a confidence man, thinking he can fool us into some scheme." Ethel pressed on. "Don't look. He'll keep talking to you."

"Seems like he's just moved to town," Briar said, noticing the wagon filled with an assortment of boxes, chairs, a table lamp, and more. "You can check at the boardinghouses if you're looking for a factory girl," she called to him, seeing as though Ethel wasn't going to tell him.

People were moving in all the time as the mills prospered. The storefront they were passing used to be where the blacksmith worked, but he and the stables had been pushed out to the edge of town to make way for another general store stocked with ribbons and perfume and small trinkets. Anything to tempt a mill girl from her hard-earned money.

After they'd walked a bit farther, Briar asked, "Where *are* you from?" Even though they had shared a room for over a year, it suddenly struck Briar she didn't know much about Ethel's personal life.

"Not Stowe." She looped her arm through Briar's. "Tell me in your heart of hearts you want to leave Sunrise Valley, the children, and your room-mates to go to Burlington."

Briar smiled. "I don't think I'll have to. My persnickety frame is fixed. Worked like a dream today. I think I can pull my production up and even take on another frame." *As long as everything holds*.

Ethel brightened. "Really? I've been so worried for you. Will it be enough?"

She thought of how fast the frame was working. It was hard to tell, but it seemed to be getting slightly faster with each doffing. Next week she'd pay attention to see how often Maribelle had to work the frame. "I don't know yet."

They'd reached the bank, and as always there was a line on payday. They queued up to wait. The people in line were also grumbling about their pay, so it wasn't only the spinning and the loom girls who had theirs cut.

When it was her turn, Briar opened her envelope to count out how much was there. She frowned. A disappointing amount. She hoped what she could bring Fanny would be enough. Quickly, she separated the money for deposit then filled out her deposit slip. The amount was so pitiful it seemed a waste of paper, but it was important to stay consistent and build up her emergency funds. Putting even the smallest amounts into an account like this kept her from spending it on a whim. She'd watched Mim buy too many things on impulse and later regret her decisions. Not that Mim would ever admit it to Ethel.

Deposits made, they rushed back to the boardinghouse. The wrench in Briar's pocket thumped against her thigh, reminding her that she had one more thing to do before leaving for home.

It had been a long time since she'd felt so hopeful, and it made her not want to talk to the disgruntled mill girls today. Fortunately, avoiding eye contact on a Saturday was not unusual behavior for Briar. Everyone knew she was in a hurry to leave, so no one stopped her as she waved good-bye to Ethel and barreled through the front door, not stopping until she was at the utility closet. She bent down to drop the wrench into the toolbox, and upon straightening, bumped into Miss Olive again.

"Oh, I'm sorry," Briar said. Miss Olive sure seemed to be hovering over her lately.

"Shouldn't you be on your way?" Miss Olive asked.

"Yes, leaving now."

"That's a pretty fabric," remarked Miss Olive, eying Briar's apron.

Face burning, Briar shoved the royal blue cloth back into her pocket. "I got it from a peddler."

Miss Olive smiled. "Dearie, it's okay to splurge now and then. You work so hard. Have you ever thought about why I placed you, Ethel, and Mim together? And now Sadie?"

"I thought we were placed where you had open beds."

"True, but I like to put girls together who go together."

Briar frowned. She'd never considered Ethel and Mim as two persons who went together. They were at sword points more often than not. And Sadie? Did Miss Olive not know the dynamics between them?

"Think on it," Miss Olive added before Briar could

finish forming her thoughts. "Iron sharpens iron. Have a good time at the cottage."

Briar rubbed the base of her head, anticipating a headache more than answers. "I will. Are you sure it's okay for me to take the bicycle? Some of the others might want a turn on the weekends."

The others did want a turn. Briar had overheard the whispered grumbles as they complained that Briar was getting preferential treatment. She also overheard Mim reminding them that the bicycle belonged to Miss Olive and shame on them for being so greedy, wanting a pleasure ride around town while Briar had that long walk to the countryside to care for her poor orphaned siblings. Mim did know how to word things.

"Of course you may take the bicycle. It's meant to be ridden. And that reminds me. Mim left something for you upstairs."

Sweets for the children. Briar raced up to their room, wishing Mim had given them to her earlier. She was wasting time. But the gift wasn't sweets for the children. There on Briar's side of the bed was a pair of tan bloomers. *Mim!*

Briar's eyes filled with tears at the thoughtful gift. She'd thought Mim was making them for Ethel. She shouldn't have. Briar had planned to eventually get around to making herself a pair.

Eagerly, Briar undid the buttons on her skirt and slipped on the bloomers. The cool fabric closed in around her legs. She strutted about the room like she'd seen the men do walking down the street. Laughter bubbled up inside. Blessed Mim. A perfect fit, and she even included a man's trouser pocket. Briar transferred the whorl to her new pocket and set off.

Energized, Briar pulled the bicycle out from the shed in back and pushed it to the street. Enough girls had taken it out for a spin that it no longer caused groups of young mill workers to gather out front of the boardinghouses to watch, but her bloomers might revive the interest.

She kicked off and pedaled down the street toward the mill, reveling in the ease of the bloomers. As she passed the mill, she tried to figure out which window was closest to her frames. Not that she'd be able to see the spindle if she looked. She had the prettiest part of it in her pocket anyway, the whorl with its decorative carvings. When she got to the cottage she'd take it out and really look at it.

If only there was someone she could talk to about the spindle. She could go out and search for the peddler, but since she'd never seen him before the other day and he talked like he traveled far and wide, she doubted she'd find him. Mim wouldn't ever believe her. Ethel could get mad at her for messing with her frame. Miss Olive would be obliged to tell the corporation. The children would blab it everywhere. Nanny and Henry were both gone, and Fanny, well, Fanny would find anything that seemed like fairy magic delightful, not understanding how dreadful it felt at the same time.

Briar continued to steer her way through the streets, avoiding the horses and carriages. She wasn't that confident of either her steering or stopping abilities, so she pedaled slowly and carefully. But once she got out of town and started down the road to home, she let loose and pedaled as fast as she could. Her legs were strong, and the wind in her hair felt like freedom. Who knew a bicycle could be balm for the worker's soul?

The town well behind her now, she bumped over the dirt roads, which became progressively bumpier the farther away she rode. In some places she had to stand up on the pedals to get enough force to keep the wheels moving, which she could never do so easily in her skirts.

The jangle of reins signaled someone was coming up behind her. Briar angled toward the side of the road and stopped. She didn't like the idea of hitting a rut in the road and ending up under a horse's hooves.

She looked over her shoulder as a pair of horses passed, and Mr. and Mrs. Prince pulled up beside her in their wagon. Briar's heart lifted, hoping they had news of Henry, but then it plummeted just as quickly. The expression on Mrs. Prince's face revealed a mother worried about her son. What if the news was bad?

Chapter Twenty

he Princes were the last people Briar expected to meet on the road. Maybe with Henry gone, they were forced to venture farther from home. They might not have news of him at all; they could just be on their way back from running an errand. She waited for them to offer any clue.

Mrs. Prince broke her worried look with a smile. "Care for a ride?"

"Oh," Briar said. They'd caught her by surprise, and she didn't know how to answer. On the one hand, she had been enjoying being by herself. She was rarely alone. Living in a boardinghouse filled with girls granted no privacy. But on the other hand, a ride would get her home in a few minutes and she'd be rested up to play with the children before bed. The horses stamped their impatience while Briar decided what to do.

Nodding at the Princes, she said, "Yes, thank you." She wheeled her bicycle to the side of the wagon and handed it to Mr. Prince, who had hopped into the back. Briar had never ridden in their wagon. She'd never actually spent any time alone with the reclusive Princes. Though she knew Henry as well as she knew this dirt road home, his parents were more like the mountains. A steady presence in the background.

The Princes weren't rich by any standards, and their wagon looked like it had seen better days. Boards had been repaired, giving the vehicle a patchwork look of its own, although Briar could tell it was sturdy, rebuilt by a fine craftsman. *Henry or his dad?*

She climbed up the side of the wagon and sat beside Mrs. Prince.

After loading the bicycle in the back, Mr. Prince returned to his seat and clicked the horses forward.

"How are you, Briar?" asked Mrs. Prince. "We haven't really spoken since Henry…since Henry left."

Briar smiled. "I'm well, thank you."

"Do you enjoy riding the safety bicycle?" Mrs. Prince craned her neck to look at it. "I've never tried one, but I can see the possibilities for a young girl such as yourself."

"It's easy once you practice and don't have an audience of mill boys watching you and giving you their thoughts."

Mr. Prince laughed.

"You look positively radiant with the exercise," Mrs. Prince said. "Doesn't she, darling?"

Mr. Prince nodded.

"Miss Olive encourages us to take care of our health."

"She is a wise woman."

They rode on in silence, and Briar suddenly wished she'd stayed on the bicycle. The *clip-clop* of the horses not in a hurry made her wonder if she was saving any time at all.

"How is your work at the mill?" asked Mrs. Prince.

Briar stopped fiddling with her bloomers, glad for

something to talk about. "I've got a new little doffer named Maribelle. She's not as fast as Henry was, but she's a sweet thing and is learning. Fortunately, my spinning frames have finally started to cooperate, which makes life easier for all of us."

"Even that frame Henry had such a time with?"

"He told you?" Briar shouldn't be surprised. Henry was so open and honest, he probably told his folks everything.

"Yes. He says it's the only frame like it in the whole building. Says the company should just replace it and start over. He thinks there is something wrong with it at its base. A crooked frame or something."

Mrs. Prince cleared her throat. "But you say it's working now? What made the difference?"

Briar's face grew warm. "Maybe they changed the humidity in the room, so the threads aren't breaking so much." She wiped her hands on her knees. "Have you heard from Henry?" she asked, changing the subject. She wanted to hear he'd made it to Germany.

"That's why we went to town," Mrs. Prince said. "We were hoping for news. We got a letter from when he was in New York telling us he'd found a ship, but that's the last we've heard."

"Oh," Briar said, her voice falling. "That was weeks ago. Did he say anything else?"

"No, it was a pretty short letter. I suspect the railroad strike might be slowing delivery."

She sounded as disappointed and hungry for more news as Briar was.

"I don't understand why he left," Briar said. "He loves it here."

Mrs. Prince sighed. "Yes, he does. But sometimes in life we make choices thinking we are doing the right thing, don't we?"

Briar nodded. She was working hard to secure the children's future and fulfill her mother's dying wish. But the tone in Mrs. Prince's voice suggested she didn't approve of Henry's leaving.

"Do you think he's not doing the right thing?" Briar asked.

Mr. Prince grunted, and his wife patted his leg.

"We don't know, Briar. He is trying something no one else in the family has done in a long time. His dad is a farmer, his grandfather was a farmer, his great-grandfather, you get the idea. They've all done the same thing. Tradition. Playing it safe. He was the first to get a mill job, so he has different ideas than past generations." Again, she patted her husband's leg. "Henry wanted to try something new. See if he could change the course for the Prince family even more."

"I see," Briar answered, even though she didn't. More than anyone she knew, Henry was the one she least expected to go away. Seems like Mr. Prince should be the one to go to change the family's lot. "What exactly is he doing? He didn't really say."

"He'll tell us all about his adventure when he returns," Mrs. Prince said.

"He was kind of vague about that as well," Briar said. "You sound like he'll be returning soon. Doesn't it take years to make your fortune?"

"Ha!" Mrs. Prince laughed. "Being mysterious, was he? Likely trying to keep your interest, Briar. I'll probably embarrass him for saying this, but he's taken a fancy to you lately. He's always favored you over his other playmates, but now that he's looking toward the future, I suspect a lot of what he is doing has to do with you. You're turning seventeen soon, aren't you?"

Briar nodded but didn't say anything. Mrs. Prince was confusing her. Briar was still an Irish spinner girl, and not who Mrs. Prince wanted her son involved with, wasn't she? What had changed Mrs. Prince's mind?

"Seventeen is such a stable age. Once you reach seventeen, you can breathe a sigh of relief and look forward to your future, don't you think?"

"Darlin', you've gone and embarrassed the girl." Mr. Prince cleared his throat. "Henry wasn't seeking his fortune. He won't need years to do what he is doing. Besides, I think he'd be afraid to leave you unaccompanied for too long."

"Look who's doing the embarrassing now?" Mrs. Prince put her arm around Briar. "Don't mind us, but we're missing Henry, and you're the next best thing."

Again, Briar was confused. They'd never shown such concern over her before.

Mrs. Prince pointed to the cloth poking out of Briar's pocket. "That's a lovely piece of silk," she said. She cocked her head as if examining it closer. "Did Henry give that to you?"

Briar shook her head. "No. No, I got this from a peddler in town."

"Oh. May I see it? We used to have one that color. Did you buy anything else from the peddler?"

Reluctantly, Briar slipped out the silk handkerchief, careful to shake free the whorl first, and handed it to Mrs. Prince. Briar hadn't the chance to examine the silk piece, since her attention had always been on the spindle itself. "No, I didn't buy anything else from him." *It was all a gift.*

Mrs. Prince grasped the silk piece by two corners and held it up to the light. "Oh. How lovely," she said. "Darling, look at this."

Mr. Prince glanced over. "Nice," he said, turning his attention back to the road.

Briar held back a laugh. Mr. Prince obviously had not the care for pretty cloth as his wife had.

"No, honey, look at it," Mrs. Prince insisted, her voice tense. "You can see the faint pattern in the silk when you hold it up. It's certainly unique. Not made in the mills here, that's for sure."

Again Mr. Prince glanced over, but then he took a second look. "Briar," he said. "Do you remember which peddler you got that from?"

"He was passing through. Said he knew you, though." Briar bounced in her seat as the wagon hit a rut.

Mr. Prince was taken aback. "Knew me, you say?"

"Of your family, anyway. But lots of people in the valley know your family, since you've been here so long."

The Princes exchanged a glance.

"Was he a seller of cloth?"

"No, he had all sorts of items. Pots and pans, a wash bin, a crate full of candles, and some, uh, sewing things."

"When was this?" Mr. Prince pressed on.

"A few weeks back, not long after Henry left. I don't know if he had any more of these."

"The silk is lovely." Mrs. Prince spread it out over her heavy cotton skirt. "Imagine if this was used to line a bassinet. What a royal baby that would be."

Briar squirmed. She hoped Mrs. Prince wasn't hinting that Briar and Henry should…

Mrs. Prince handed the cloth back, clasping Briar's hand with both of hers. "I think you should keep it always in your pocket. It would be a nice comfort to feel it and know that there are such pretty things in this world. I know working in the mills can be hard."

"Yes. It can. But Henry made it fun. I miss that."

Mrs. Prince looked off to the forest. "Henry does

enjoy life. I hope he's okay." She smiled tentatively at her husband. "He sounded fine in that one letter, didn't he, honey? Told us not to worry."

Mr. Prince held his wife's gaze. "That is what he said. Hard not to worry, though, isn't it?"

CHAPTER TWENTY-ONE

"**B**riar, Briar!" the boys called when they heard the wagon jingle into their yard. They ran from the back of the house, their fresh faces grinning. "We got a goat," Benny said.

"A goat?" Briar jumped down. *Fresh milk.* But how could they afford a goat?

"An' a chicken!" said Jack.

Eggs. She touched the coins at the bottom of her pocket. Her meager contribution to their upkeep wasn't enough for such luxuries. Fanny must be spending her own money on them. The boys would be crushed when Nanny came back and the animals had to go.

Pansy came around the corner, hugging the chicken to her thin body like it was a doll. *Oh dear.*

"Hello, children," called Mrs. Prince from the wagon. "Are you enjoying the animals?"

"Oh, yes," Pansy said. "Thank you ever so much. We're taking great care of them." The chicken came to life and flapped its wings in Pansy's face. She dropped it with a yelp and the boys began to chase it into the backyard with Pansy at their heels.

Oh dear. Oh dear.

Meanwhile, Mr. Prince had hopped out of the wagon and had taken out Briar's borrowed bicycle.

She looked questioningly at the Princes. So the animals were theirs? "Thank you for the ride," Briar started, thinking of a way to graciously decline their generous gifts without offending them.

"It was our pleasure, Briar. All of it. See you later."

Mr. Prince avoided eye contact, clicking his tongue at the horses and leading them out of the yard. Mrs. Prince waved as if she were the queen in a parade, a big smile showing her pleasure.

Briar sighed. For the children. She could swallow her pride for them.

"Is that the Prince family?" asked Fanny from the doorway. "Didn't stop to say hello?"

"They saw me on the road and gave me a ride in," Briar said. "Are those their animals?"

"I thought you were early. Those are Henry's. He sent a note asking the boys to look after them 'til he's home."

Fanny's face held a look of concern. Maybe she thought one bunny was enough for the children to look after.

"You got a letter from Henry?" Briar said. "The Princes went to town, hoping they'd have one there."

"The children did. Came this week, but it only had directions for them regarding the animals. No news. I suspect he wrote it same time as yours, but it just got here this week."

Without a brother or sister of his own, he'd sort of adopted Briar's younger siblings. Coming from Henry it didn't feel like they were receiving too much charity.

She wished she'd gotten another letter so she knew what he was doing, but at least she was getting the small gifts left on her spinning machine that reminded her of him. They were almost as good as a letter. She absently pulled out the Solomon's Seal.

"What's that?" asked Fanny, a big grin on her face. "A love token?"

Briar looked up. "Oh, no. It's just something I picked up at work today."

"Well, come in, come in. Put your feet up a spell." Fanny waved her inside, her smile disappearing, replaced by a furrowed brow.

Uh oh. What did the boys do this week?

Briar stepped over the fresh primrose petals that were littered outside the front of the door. Since spring, Fanny had somehow managed to find primroses while she waited for hers to take in the garden and routinely scattered the petals about the windowsills and doorway.

"The children are fine being out in the fresh air. I'll fix you some tea and you can tell me all about your week."

Not all *about my week. How to explain a fairy-wood spindle fixing my frame so perfectly?*

"Here you are, dearie," Fanny said, setting a teacup on the table and sitting opposite.

"You're still putting down the petals," Briar said. "I thought you told Pansy it was only in the spring that you spread the petals to keep the bad fairies away."

"Yes, well, now Pansy insists we keep up the practice." Fanny absently picked at her fingernail.

"Fanny has a trick," Pansy yelled as she ran by the open door. "She makes rose petals."

"Pfff. I don't *make* rose petals." Fanny waved her hand.

Briar bit back some of her irritation. Fanny obviously wasn't used to being around children and didn't think about how they had a hard time deciphering imagination from reality.

"Pansy insists because you scared her half to death, Fanny. What were you thinking telling a child there were bad fairies? She believes everything you tell her." As she spoke, Briar's volume and intensity tapered off and her gaze dropped to her teacup. The weight of the whorl in her pocket had reminded her there were things in this world she didn't know how to explain, either.

Fanny shrugged. "It hurts no one to have the petals strewn about. The scent is lovely. Besides, you can't protect the children from every bump in the road, as much as you'd like to. They know there's evil in the world, but what they need to know is it can be overcome."

They were both quiet, staring at the teacups.

"What do you know of fairy wood?" Briar asked quietly, testing Fanny's response.

Fanny examined Briar over her teacup. "A better question is, what do *you* know about fairy wood?"

Briar slowly swirled her spoon in her tea. "I know it exists, but I've never heard of it growing in our forest and wondered what it was."

"The mere act of growing is not what makes fairy wood." Fanny slowly traced a crack in the table as if measuring her words. "It takes a fairy." She quickly rose, her chair legs scraping the floor, and took her empty cup to the sink.

Briar's skin tingled with anticipation. With fear? "You talk about fairies like my mother used to. She would tuck us into bed with a fairy story, but Pansy was too young to remember them now."

"What stories did your mother tell you?"

"About fairies in Ireland. All her stories were about the Old Country."

"Paw, Irish fairies," Fanny said, scrunching her nose. "Flighty lot they are. Can't count on them for a straight answer even if you've got their feet tied and threaten them with a good dunking in the lake."

"Excuse me?"

Fanny waved her hand again. "They don't like water. So I've heard. What else did your mother know about fairies?"

"Oh, I don't know. She kept a fairy garden in the wood close to a little brook. She said it was a tradition for all the girls in our family. We planted flowers and set up paths with pebbles, that sort of thing."

"A grand idea. Pansy would so enjoy one. I've been trying to think of something special for her. Those boys take up so much of my energy I'm afraid there's not much left over for the girl. Sweet thing, she is. So willing to be a help."

Briar glowed with the praise for Pansy, but wouldn't be put off. "About that fairy wood," she said, bringing the conversation back to where it had veered.

"More tea?" Fanny asked. She bustled over to the stove and moved the kettle back to the burner.

"No, thank you. I want to know about fairy wood." If only to find out why Fanny was dodging the question.

Fanny wrung her hands as her eyes darted about the kitchen. "Biscuit? You must be hungry from your long day." She opened the little cupboard the children called the magic cupboard and pulled out a shortbread, one of Briar's favorites.

"Yes, please." No wonder the children called it a magic cupboard. Fanny had a way of keeping everyone's favorite foods in stock. Then she raised her eyebrows questioningly. Fanny was a master at changing the subject, but Briar wasn't going to let her get away with it tonight.

Fanny rifled through the pile of vegetables from the garden. "Where did you hear of fairy wood? Cucumbers for supper?"

"Cucumbers are fine; I'll cut them." Briar joined Fanny in the kitchen. "Fairy wood?"

Fanny stepped aside to let Briar have room at the small counter. "It's rare. Yet not rare. It can be made out of any kind of wood. The secret is how a fairy fashions it to her liking."

"What do you mean to her liking?" Briar's tingling skin gave way to a worrisome churning deep inside. She expected to get a fanciful answer from Fanny, but this conversation felt different. This felt…electric, like an invisible veil was about to be lifted. Like her whole day was leading to this moment.

"Posh, the fairies aren't going to tell their secrets, now are they?" Fanny crossed her arms and stood closer to Briar. "Now, what can a girl in far-off Sunrise Valley know about fairy wood?" She stared straight into Briar's eyes as if trying to read her mind. "Have you seen something made of fairy wood? *Touched* something made of fairy wood?"

Briar shrugged, forcing herself to look calm, but inside she was taut as the roving line on her machine. She held her breath, waiting for a reaction from Fanny to know how to proceed.

It was odd how protective she felt about the spindle. As if she sensed people would take it away from her if they knew about it. As if someone like her shouldn't own anything so beautiful. Or they would want her to sell it to help pay for the children's care. Thoughts she'd already wrestled with herself, and she couldn't bear to think of others judging her the same way.

Fanny stood and began pacing around the room. She walked to the window, looked out. Walked back, muttering. "I want you to know that you can come to me for anything. Anything at all. At home. At work. Anything odd going on?"

Briar studied Fanny. There was a tension between them, and Briar was sure Fanny felt it, too. What did she suspect? "Henry is gone. That's pretty odd. Nanny hasn't been in touch. That's odd. You…being here is odd."

They shared a smile.

"Suppose you're right. From your perspective there are several odd things going on."

"You know more than you're telling me. Why not share with me? The children are my responsibility." Briar leaned forward. "How can I plan for them when I feel like plans are being made in secret?"

Fanny shook her head and took a deep breath. "Prudence will have a fit."

"I need to know," Briar said, her pulse quickening.

Fanny let out her breath. "I shouldn't do this. One more mark against me."

"How bad can it be? Just tell me."

Fanny closed her eyes tight and said, "I'm a fairy." She opened her eyes. "There it is. You know my secret. A true-to-life real fairy."

CHAPTER TWENTY-TWO

Briar gaped at Fanny. This was not the revelation she was expecting. *Is she daft?* Sure, Fanny was diminutive, and had a cute pixie face. But a fairy? Fanny was nothing like the fairies Mam talked about. The fairy gardens they made in the woods were for tiny little creatures. Miniature doorways. Bitty pathways. Small tree-bark tables. Now if she could produce wings, Briar might consider believing her. Speechless, Briar continued gaping at Fanny for several uncomfortable seconds.

"You're not a fairy. Not a real one." The fear swirling in her gut took hold and began to spread. Fanny couldn't be a real fairy, because if she was, that meant that the spindle could, in fact, be magical. And everything Briar had heard in the stories about fairies said that some were good and some were wicked. The question would then be, which fairy made her spindle?

Fanny tossed her hands in the air. "You want to see proof, don't you?" She shook her head. "They all do." She turned. "Follow me outside. My abilities are still somewhat, er, hindered at the moment." She glanced over her shoulder. "Long story. But I can show you this."

After they went outside, Fanny picked up one of the dried rose petals strewn about the ground and breathed on it. The petal filled with a soft pink color and became silky smooth again.

Briar took a step back. How was this possible? She didn't know if she should be impressed or scared. Her hand shook when she held it out, wanting to touch the petal to see if it was real.

"See?" Fanny held out the lush petal, inviting Briar to touch it.

Briar took another step back. "Who are you and what are you really doing here?" She strained her ears to pinpoint where the children were in case she had to flee with them. "What do you want with the children?"

Fanny dropped the petal and put her hands on her hips. "I'm disappointed you would ask. I love those wee babes. I'm here to watch over them while Prudence is…is gone. I can assure you they are safe with me." She blinked rapidly as moisture flooded her eyes.

"Does Nanny know what you are?"

"Yes."

"And it doesn't concern her that you're a…a…?" Briar couldn't even say it. *Fairy*.

"I have no secrets with your Nanny. She accepts me the way I am, though I suspect she wishes I were a touch more responsible, among other things."

"What else can you do?"

"I'm not about to perform tricks for you, if that's what you're asking." Fanny scowled. "I'm a fairy, not a circus act."

Briar didn't know how to process this information. "How am I to go back to town tomorrow, knowing what I do now?"

Fanny frowned. "I've been here for weeks. You see how the children are happy? Fed? Growing like flowers themselves? Be off with you like normal and be content that I am managing them well."

Her tone had gone from wounded to irritated. But it didn't matter how Fanny felt. What mattered was the children and their well-being. How could Briar leave them with a creature known for its unpredictability?

Briar blinked. A creature? Fanny, in the flesh, standing in front of her with arms crossed and foot tapping, waiting for Briar to make up her mind.

What were those fairy stories Mam told? Mostly ones of mischief, the likes of games little boys played. Some older folks talked of the potato famine as being a fairy curse, even though the true source was found.

Laughter floated in on the wind, cutting into Briar's thoughts. Benny giggling. Pansy shrieking good-naturedly. Obviously, the children were very happy with Fanny taking care of them. "You haven't—" Briar waved her hands over the rose petals. "In front of the children?"

"Oh, no. Of course not. I freshen things up when they're sleeping. They haven't seen a thing, the dears, though they would love it. Prudence made me promise not to do anything in front of them. I don't know why, though. The children have no problem with fairies, it's always the grown-ups." She rose up on her toes and looked guiltily to the side.

Briar twisted her lips. Fanny may not have purposely shown the children magic, but she knew they had still seen. "How long until Prudence gets back?"

Fanny shifted her feet. "I thought she'd be back by now. I suppose she's slowing down in her old age. Or there was a problem. But a problem for Prudence would be highly unlikely, don't you agree? She's practically perfect. Her friendship with someone like me stretches her very being. I am a bit of a rarity."

Fanny's description of herself was an understatement. "Can't you tell me what Prudence is doing? It has to be serious if she sent…you…to take her place. Is it her family?"

Fanny paused. "Does she talk about her family?"

"She's mentioned her sisters. Is that where she's gone?"

Fanny let out a deep breath. "Yes. One of her sisters got into trouble and she's helping. See, you don't have to be worried about the children. It'll all work out."

Briar closed her eyes. She'd seen two strange things today that she couldn't explain. First the spindle fitting itself into her spinning frame, and now Fanny claiming to be a real-live fairy and restoring a rose petal to full bloom.

Fanny smiled and clapped once. "Why don't we let you think on this for tonight and we'll talk again in the morning. In case there's something you'd like to tell me. About your interest in fairy wood—or anything else." She left Briar gaping in the doorway while she went to round up the children for supper.

All night Briar's attention was glued to Fanny while the children told her about the silly antics of the new animals. They'd named them all, of course, and fought over who got to visit the chicken (named Betty) in the morning to see if there was an egg. Briar studied every motion, every breath. But nothing revealed who or what Fanny claimed to be. And how did ever-practical Nanny make room for the presence of fairies in her life? She didn't even like flowers.

"Why are you going to sleep at the same time as us?" asked Pansy. She was lying on her pallet, head cradled in her hands and watching Briar toss and turn.

"I'm tired." Briar's whole body was weary and she

hoped sleep would take all the strangeness away for a time. She'd be better able to think things through in the morning.

"You don't act sleepy," said Jack.

"Sorry, I'll settle in a minute." Briar flipped over one last time so she could watch Fanny bustle about the cottage. A real fairy?

Once the children's breaths relaxed into the regular pattern of sleep, Briar pulled out the whorl from her pocket, keeping it under the sheet. She ran her fingers over the carved roses. It was so smooth; someone had taken great care when carving the wood. When Fanny slipped outside, Briar peeked under the sheet to study the whorl. A faint scorch mark marred one of the roses. Briar wondered what had happened to it. Where exactly had this spindle come from?

When Fanny returned, Briar whispered, "What does it mean that you're here now, at this time?" She was afraid to ask the question but needed to. Her mind was forming a picture she didn't want to see. A magic spindle. A girl named Briar. A fairy. Was the Sleeping Beauty fairy tale a warning? A prophecy? A coincidence?

Fanny padded softly over and sat on the edge of the bed. "Hopefully it means nothing, dearie. I've told you too much already. Miss Prudence will have my head if nothing comes of it and I've told you what I have."

"Comes of what?"

"You tell me. Is there anything on your mind? You seem to be having trouble falling asleep."

Briar stopped a laugh. "You think I can sleep after finding out you're a fairy?"

Fanny shared a grin. "No, I suppose not. I wanted to tell you earlier but couldn't risk Prudence's wrath. She can have a temper." Fanny pulled herself up tall, forming her expression into a pretty good impression of Nanny.

"So why did you tell me now?"

She looked intently into Briar's eyes. "I won't force you, dearie. But if you and I are going to share secrets, we need to share everything."

Briar bit her lip. What would happen if she told Fanny about the spindle? The fairy would try to stop her from using it, that's what. It didn't seem like something Fanny would approve of, a human using a fairy tool for her own good. Briar shook her head. "I've nothing to say."

"In that case, neither do I. We haven't had any problems all these years. Miss Prudence will likely be home tomorrow. You'll continue on as before and I can go back to where I'm supposed to be." She patted Briar's arm.

Briar frowned. Fanny had been saying for weeks that Prudence would likely be back soon, with nothing to show for her optimism. "But that's just it. She only agreed to watch the children until I turn seventeen. That's in two weeks. Will she really send them away after that if I can't care for them?"

"Hmm. Miss Prudence is punctual about things," Fanny said with a frown. "She's like a clock, grinding things out. Doesn't like change. If she said that's what was going to happen, you can be sure it is."

CHAPTER TWENTY-THREE

In the morning, Briar found Miss Fanny outside with Whitey Hoppers, the bunny. A warm glow lit up the trees and the wind blew in a sweet smell of dewy earth.

Miss Fanny straightened, putting her hands in the crook of her back, and stretched. "'Morning. You look like a girl with something on her mind."

Briar offered up a half smile. "There is a lot on my mind."

"The weight of the world on your shoulders, dearie. It can weigh you down if you don't share your burdens." She handed Briar the bunny.

The animal quivered until Briar flipped it onto its back and then it relaxed, nestling its warm fur into Briar's palms. "You said I could trust you. Can I trust you not to share with anyone what I tell you?"

Fanny took a deep breath and let it out. She squinted against the sun. "I don't like to make promises like that."

Briar waited, taking comfort from the warm bundle in her hands. She wasn't going to go any further without a promise.

Fanny appeared to grow uncomfortable with the silence. "Fine. I won't tell anyone your secrets. You can trust me." Fanny twisted her lips like she wasn't happy about the agreement.

"I did something this week that both excites and scares me. A peddler gave me a drop spindle. He said I should put the shaft in my frame at the mill and it would fix my problem and increase my production."

Miss Fanny narrowed her eyes. "Why does a spindle from a peddler scare you?"

Briar set the bunny down. It hopped two hops and sat. "Because he said it was made from fairy wood."

Miss Fanny raised an eyebrow. "Go on."

"I thought he was selling me; you know how peddlers exaggerate. I never imagined the spindle contained real fairy magic. I didn't put it into the frame until yesterday. I was desperate. My frame was worse than ever and they cut our pay. My new overseer threatened to fire me. I need that frame to work or I'll lose the children for sure."

"What happened when you put the spindle in the machine?"

"I wouldn't have believed it if I hadn't seen it. But it grew like it was alive and it attached itself to the frame. I can't get it off."

Fanny didn't look surprised. It was as if she already knew.

Briar remembered Jack telling her Fanny was magic, that she could make herself really tiny and spy on them. Could Fanny have been in the spinning room?

"Oh dearie. You have no idea what you've done, do you? Well thank heaven you didn't hurt yourself. I don't know how it happened, but you've found the spindle. *The* spindle. The one that made Aurora sleep for almost a hundred years."

Briar paused, processing yet more unbelievable information. "But that was a fairy tale."

Fanny took a bow. "And I'm a fairy."

Briar leaned against a garden post, needing the support. Aurora was a real person. The spindle was real. She was talking to a fairy who knew these things. How was any of this even possible? "Is the spindle dangerous?"

"The curse on it is old, potentially weakening, but yes. The spindle is still very dangerous. Very, very dangerous." Fanny waggled her finger with emphasis.

"What would the spindle be doing in a peddler's cart?" Briar asked.

"Bah. Peddler. Describe the woman."

"It wasn't a woman. He was an old man with a beard and a canc…"

"Turquoise eyes?"

Briar nodded.

Fanny clenched her hands. "Isodora. Of course. Can't turn your back for a minute."

"Who?"

"The fairy who cursed the spindle in the first place. Spiteful thing she is. I didn't know she had enough power to transform into another look."

"I thought she was dead. At the end of the fairy tale she dies."

"Dead? We've made that mistake before. No, she's very much alive. Don't believe everything you read. Well, that's it, then. I'll have to tell—" She caught Briar's expression and stopped. "No one."

"I don't understand why Isodora would bring the spindle here. Sunrise Valley is the middle of nowhere. There aren't any kings and queens in America. No princesses to…" Briar thought about her name. "Am I related to the original

Sleeping Beauty? Is this about revenge because she didn't die and now Isodora wants to kill me?"

Fanny shook her head. "For one, I don't know how Isodora got hold of the spindle." She cleared her throat uncomfortably. "Two, no, you are not Aurora's descendant. It is, however, unfortunate that your mother's family liked flower names, because Isodora is after revenge. Revenge on me, and your name just makes that revenge taste better. Innocents often do get caught up in these trials."

"I don't understand. Why would killing a spinner girl satisfy her revenge?"

"It doesn't have to be a spinner girl, specifically. She is after a young girl to fulfill her curse so she can have her full power back. Right now her power is tied up in the unfulfilled curse of the spindle."

A slight smile played at her lips. "I'm the one who stopped her, which is why she and I are in this battle of wills and she wants out. She knows my role is to protect the girls who cross my path and killing one would be devastating to me. Death is against everything I hold dear. The original curse was that Aurora would prick her finger on a spindle and die before her seventeenth birthday. I softened it so that she would only sleep for a lifetime and then awaken with true love's kiss—my personal touch. The others thought it excessive. They thought the sleeping was enough, but where's the romance in that? My way, she woke to someone who loved her. I think it was necessary after all that time."

"But if the curse was for Aurora, then the curse won't ever be fulfilled."

Fanny scratched her nose. "I wish it were that simple. It's the way Isodora made the curse. She was enraged at the time, making herself a bit sloppy. Make no mistake.

That spindle can kill you."

Briar's heart skipped a beat. "Can't you stop the curse again?"

"Not this time. The curse must run its course. We've held it off as long as we can. Isodora will not be satisfied until a girl dies, and she's chosen you. I can only hope that my blessing over Aurora and the spindle carries over to another girl, but I don't know if it will. We've never followed a curse as old as this one before. We've been watching it very carefully."

Of all the things to be chosen for. Death.

What would happen to the children then? No one would be watching out for them, trying to keep them together. They'd be put on that orphan train, separated into three different families in three different states. She couldn't let that happen.

"I'm not going to prick my finger. I know what it truly is now, so I'll stay away from it." Seemed like an easy solution.

Fanny looked doubtful. "You don't feel an overwhelming need to touch it?"

Briar closed her eyes, trying to name what she felt about the spindle. "I feel possessive of it, like I don't want anyone else to have it. I haven't wanted to touch the tip."

"Yet," Fanny said. "We need to get it out of there right away."

"It won't come off. It's as solid as if it were built with the frame."

"I'll see what I can do." Fanny rubbed her hands together. "Then I should try to find Isodora, now that I know she's here. Can you take the children today?"

"Of course," Briar said. "Earlier, you hesitated over promising not to tell my secret. Who were you going to tell?"

Fanny shrugged. "I was going to tell Prudence. She's my overseer."

Briar's mouth went dry. "Is she a fairy, too?"

Fanny scrunched up her face, then nodded.

Briar felt like she'd been punched in the gut. She quickly searched her memories for any hint of unusual behavior from Nanny and couldn't think of a one. "We've been under the care of a fairy all this time?" It was like waking up to find out a knife had been dangling over her bed the whole night and the only thing stopping it from hurting her was someone watching it. Briar would have rather been told about the danger so she could have prepared for it.

"Oh, I'm breaking so many rules. Prudence is diligent about keeping herself a secret. But since she's gone to find Isodora, I must contact her to tell her that Isodora is here."

"No, please don't. You promised." Briar grabbed Fanny's hands as she pleaded. The first time she'd touched her since finding out what she was.

"But Briar, now that you know the significance of the spindle, surely you would want to tell Prudence."

Briar dropped Fanny's hands. "No."

"The whole reason she left was to find Isodora—now we know she'll never find her out there. She needs to come back to the valley."

Briar shook her head. "I don't want to upset her. I'm trying to keep the children together and if she finds out what I've done she might not wait until my birthday to send them away. You're a fairy, too. Can't you handle it?"

Fanny plucked a dandelion puff and breathed on it. The dainty white puff shrank and became a yellow flower again. "I understand wanting to fix your own mistake. I've been fixing mine for years. Together, then. We'll do it together.

But if my best isn't good enough, I'll have to tell Prudence. Your life is more important than our pride."

Briar felt a prick of conscience but brushed it aside. With Fanny's help, they'd figure it out. "Why did Prudence take us in in the first place? She doesn't take to children naturally."

"Your name is Briar Rose, our name for the princess when we were protecting Aurora. You live in a city of spindles. It was a precaution. She thought the temptation for Isodora would be too great if she found out about you... and apparently she did."

What world was this that Briar had fallen into? Fairies and magical spindles and her name bringing them together. She remembered another conversation with a certain wistful boy who was setting out on an adventure across the sea. "Henry said I needed protecting because of my name. Does he have anything to do with this?"

Fanny's expression went from shock to panic to resignation in a matter of seconds. "Some parts of this story are not mine to tell."

"The Princes seem worried that they hadn't heard from him in a while. Did something bad happen to him?"

Fanny shrugged sadly. "I don't know. I can tell you that what he set out to do, he has not accomplished."

Briar swallowed hard. "Should we be worried about him?"

"We have to wait and see if a letter gets through. These rail strikes are slowing everything down. If it were an emergency, he would send his parents a cable. He may already be on his way home. Don't worry until you have something to worry about. Time will tell."

"Speaking of time, that's why Nanny set the deadline at my seventeenth birthday, isn't it? She's only concerned about me pricking my finger and then she'll be off to watch over some other girl named Briar?"

"Prudence doesn't tell me her plans, but that sounds like a fair assessment."

"Morning, Briar," called Pansy, up before the boys for once. She had a basket with her and was headed for the garden.

"Sweet Pea, could you start the twins' breakfast?" asked Fanny. "Briar and I are having a little talk."

"About boys, I bet." Pansy made a face.

Briar laughed nervously. "We'll be in to help you in a bit." She reached for the basket and then followed Fanny to the strawberry patch.

Once Pansy had gone back into the house, Briar continued the conversation. "I have so many questions I can't get them out fast enough."

"The question now is what do we do about the spindle if I can't remove it? We can't just leave you working at the mill with a cursed spindle. Too risky."

Briar shook her head. "If I left, another girl would take my place. That's risky, too. I'm the one who put it in there. Now what?"

"I suppose you're right. We are certainly in a pickle. It'll be up to you to make sure no one under seventeen goes near the spindle. You must become part of the story, dearie. *You* watch over the spindle."

CHAPTER TWENTY-FOUR

At church, Briar thanked the Princes again for giving her a ride and for sharing Henry's animals, then she asked them to check in on them once in a while to make sure the children were caring for them properly. And to surreptitiously check on Fanny at the same time.

Before Briar could leave the cottage Sunday afternoon, the children made her say good-bye to each of the animals in their growing collection. Last thing she did was hug each child tight, to the point of making the boys squirm. "You be good. I'll see you next week."

Pansy poked at Briar's bloomers. "Can Miss Mim make me these, too?"

"I can copy her pattern and we can make a pair together, how about that?"

"Okay. Bye!" Pansy scampered off in her dress after the boys.

Fanny walked with Briar and the bicycle down the lane.

"I did everything I could to dislodge the spindle while you and the children were at church, but you're right. It is firmly attached. I wish you hadn't made me promise not to tell anyone, but I know what it is to want to fix your own mess. We'll do this together. You and me. But you need to do everything I tell you. Let's just make it till the end of your birthday. Once the danger for you has passed, then we can attack the problem without fear."

"Thank you." Briar spoke with relief. She was more worried about Prudence finding out than the spindle causing harm. The way it was positioned in her frame, it should be easy to avoid the tip.

"The most important thing is, never touch the spindle. Ever." Fanny raised her eyebrows. "Ever."

"I understand." Briar hopped on the bicycle and rode back to town, her mind cycling as fast as the wheels she was riding on. If only Mam were here to talk to. She would help Briar make sense of all this, because she didn't understand. Not at all.

Back in town, Briar eyed the mill warily, wondering what a magic spindle did when no one was around. Lie in wait for its next victim?

She zoomed down the row of boardinghouses, savoring her last few minutes of freedom. She slowed to a stop by the porch, turning heads of the girls sitting outside. "I'm back! Anyone want to use the bicycle before I put it away?" She slid off the seat. Her legs wobbled a little, not yet accustomed to cycling such a distance.

Met by blank stares, she assumed no one was interested, and so she parked the bicycle back in the shed. When she climbed the porch stairs, one of the girls she didn't know very well leaped up from the bench and said in an exaggerated deep voice, "Miss Jenny increased her production today. Let her be an example of what you can accomplish with focus and hard work."

Another mocking voice joined in. "Work more quickly, and like Miss Jenny, your next paycheck might go up."

"What do you mean?" she asked.

"That's what the overseer told everyone in line after you left on Saturday. He thinks we're slow and lazy, and because you were suddenly working faster you've made us all look bad. Thanks a lot. We're working as fast as we can."

"I'm sorry. I don't know why he would say that." Briar was mortified. "I know you work hard. It's just my bad frame started working better is all." She searched the faces of the girls on the porch. They didn't look convinced.

Briar sighed and went directly to her room to freshen up. She was hot and sweaty after cycling. The room was empty, so she splashed some water on her face then lay down for a rest before supper. She'd not had a restful time at the cottage, nor a welcome greeting back at the boardinghouse.

When she came down to eat, there was a hush in the dining room, followed by more quiet whispers and looks directed her way. Ethel squeezed her hand encouragingly, and Mim gave her a wink. Their support was just enough to see her through until she could go back to the room.

Later, she asked her room-mates upstairs, "Why are they so angry with me? *I* didn't lower their wages."

"They're not angry at you exactly, they're frustrated that our wages were cut again and we have no recourse." Ethel paced between the beds. "Where else are we going to work? The next mill over? They offer the same wage. Our working conditions keep getting worse and worse, our pay lower and lower, and our rents, paid back to the mills, are staying the same. We're going to have to walk out to get their attention."

"For once I agree with Ethel," said Mim, blocking Ethel's path to stop her pacing. "The other operatives will forget about it by morning. Don't you worry."

"But what about our wages?" asked Ethel, hands on hips. "Do you finally agree with me that we're getting a bad deal?"

"Of course I do, I'm just not as loud about it," retorted Mim. "But the bosses are going to do what they're going to do. They can pay us more, but then have to fire some of us to make up the difference. Is that what you want?"

"If you believe what they're telling us. I still see the agent driving up in his new buggy, wearing his fine tailored clothes. They used to treat us operatives better. Like Mrs. Tuttle said about Charles Dickens's report on the Lowell girls. He said conditions weren't like those in the factories in England, but here and now we are already halfway to workhouse conditions like those in *Oliver Twist*."

And with that, Briar's troubles with the other operatives were forgotten as more and more girls wandered in to watch Ethel and Mim go at it. There were operatives sitting on the beds, the floor, and spilling out the hallway. At the bell, they all cleared out, not having solved anyone's problems, but feeling better for letting off steam.

"That was exciting," said Sadie, squeezing her way back in. "Couldn't even get into my own room."

Briar hoped everyone had put their anger back on the company and off her. She'd quietly go about her business, keeping her frames running as best she could and staying away from the spindle until she turned seventeen. She didn't want to be the focus of anyone's attention anymore.

Not the other operatives, nor the overseer or agent. She hoped the girls wouldn't walk out until after she and Fanny had figured out how to get rid of the spindle. She didn't want to have to choose between supporting the operatives and keeping her job so she could protect everyone from a cursed spindle.

The next morning, Briar tried to leave by herself again, but Sadie also woke up early, and followed her all the way to the mill, asking questions about Ethel and Mim, and finally getting around to the real questions she wanted to know.

Twisting her fingers nervously, she asked, "Do you think Wheeler's parents would accept a girl who's not Irish? I haven't met them yet, even though they live right here in town. He keeps telling me he is waiting for the right moment to invite me over."

Briar stood up from resetting the builder on frame number one. She was surprised Wheeler hadn't had her to their home yet. Briar had been invited right from the start. She hid a smile as she answered. "His parents are very nice. His da plays a mean fiddle, so as long as you tap your feet, you'll win him over."

"And his mother?"

Briar walked over to frame number two and checked the lines of thread. "She is a little more particular."

"That's what I was afraid of." Sadie kept walking past frame number three until she was in line with number four. "Mmmm, smells like apples over here, Briar. How do you get your area to smell so good? Mine stinks like machine oil. Can't get the smell out of my hair, even. Girls, come here. Briar's hidden an apple pie on us."

Briar looked up to see the morning rush of girls coming in to set up their frames.

"I haven't hidden any pie. My area doesn't smell any different from yours." *Leave it be, Sadie.*

Annie and several others started walking over, and Briar began to panic. She didn't need all the girls coming over and making a fuss about her frame, even if they were all older than seventeen and the spindle posed no risk for them. "A summer breeze must be slipping through the cracks or something." She tried to shoo the others away.

"No, there is something here. I'm getting closer." Sadie sniffed her way down frame number four.

The overseer marched past. "To your frames," he called. The girls scattered and Briar let out a breath of relief. She thought of the Sleeping Beauty story and how Aurora couldn't help but touch the tip of the spindle. Could the spindle be drawing the girls close to it? If so, why didn't it have that affect on her?

When the machines were up and running, she wandered by number four and sniffed. Apple pie? Maybe. To her it smelled more like spoiled apples, not pleasant at all.

Shortly into the morning shift, Maribelle came bouncing in with the other doffers.

Maribelle! How could Briar have forgotten about her young doffer? She was a girl under seventeen. Briar couldn't let her near the spindle.

"I'm going to doff frame number four from now on," Briar yelled above the noise. "I figured out just how to handle it properly."

Maribelle's face fell.

"It's nothing you did," Briar was quick to assure her. But the girl's pride had clearly taken a hit. She worked with less enthusiasm and avoided eye contact each time she came up to doff. Briar wished she could let Maribelle doff all the frames, but keeping her away from the spindle was for her own protection.

When doffing the wooden spindle, Briar was careful each time to keep her fingers far away from the tip of the spindle. As the day wore on and she wasn't once tempted to touch the spindle, as Fanny had feared, Briar began to doubt it was cursed at all.

So far the spindle had done nothing but good for Briar. Even though she was taking the time to doff her own frame, her production increased. The effect of the spindle was spreading to her other frames, evidenced by how frequently Maribelle had to come up to replace the bobbins.

Briar avoided the curious looks of the other operatives. What else could she do? She couldn't go any slower unless she periodically shut down her frames.

After the dinner bell rang Annie went over to Briar. "Why are your frames working so well now? Did you know I used to have this frame before you came along, and was I ever glad to be rid of it, but if it's working again, I might ask for it back." She continued to examine frame number four.

"We're going to miss dinner if we don't hurry," warned Briar, putting herself between Annie and the frame. Even though Annie lived at a different boardinghouse, everyone knew she was fond of eating, and Briar hoped the prompt would get the girl moving.

"Don't worry about me, you go on and get your food."

Briar crossed her arms. "Not with you poking around my frame I won't. I'll call the overseer first and tell him you're causing trouble." As Briar raised her voice, other girls walking past turned to see what was going on. They stayed to watch.

Annie leaned forward and peered around Briar, into the frame. "It's this here spindle. Why have you got a wooden spindle in your frame?" She took a deep breath. "Smells heavenly. Must be all that spinning rubbing the scent off the wood."

As quick as lightning, Annie slipped around Briar and lifted the bobbin.

"No!" Briar dodged too late to stop her. "It's sharp. Don't touch it."

Annie ran her finger along the length of the spindle, just shy of the tip, and rubbed her fingers together. "It's a bit sticky."

Briar's cry faded when she realized Annie hadn't pricked her finger. With relief, Briar pulled her away only to have Sadie come along from behind and touch the spindle also.

"Stop it. Please," Briar cried desperately, wedging herself between them and her frame.

Sadie sniffed the tip of her finger then licked it. "Tastes like syrup. I want one for my frame. Where did you get it?"

Annie wiped her hand on her apron. "Ew, I'm not going to taste it."

"It was a fix for a broken spindle, now would you all leave my frame alone?" Her voice rose in pitch.

She watched helplessly as one by one the girls trotted past, trying to smell the spindle. "Maybe you aren't working hard enough if you've got time to come by and bother me," she said, knowing it wouldn't make her any more popular, but she had to keep them away. They didn't understand the risk. At least none of them pricked their fingers—this time. They were all so intrigued by the spindle. How was she going to keep them away?

CHAPTER TWENTY-FIVE

Shuffling out onto the porch after dinner, Sadie held her hand to her forehead. "The spinning room is giving me such a headache. I don't know that I can last. I thought a move up to spinning would be better than the carding room, but today I'm regretting the move."

"It is better than the carding room for your lungs," Ethel said, clomping down the stairs. "And if you know what's good for you, you'll pull yourself up and be back at those frames. Too many others waiting to take your spot."

Sadie glanced at Briar. "Don't I know it."

Somehow, after all that had happened in the last few days, the thought of Wheeler and Sadie didn't cause her any pain or jealousy. The current problems in her life so eclipsed any others that it was possible her heart was preparing to move on. She even walked beside Sadie all the way back to the mill without any churning bitterness in her stomach.

No one bothered to come back to Briar's frames that afternoon, for which Briar was relieved. She was enjoying the new efficiency of her frames and didn't want anyone getting in the way of it. But midway through the afternoon, there was a commotion on the other side of the room. Maribelle was busy doffing the far frame, so Briar moved down the aisles to see what was going on.

Sadie had collapsed next to her frames, lying like a lump of cotton on the greasy wood floor. Annie was hunched over her, yelling for the overseer. The call for help was carried on down the line over the pulsing noise of the machines.

Briar ran to see what she could do.

"She's burning up," said Annie, fanning the air over Sadie's face with her hands. "We've got to get her out of this heat."

"Back to work, everyone," said the overseer, arriving on the spot. "Which house is she at?"

"Miss Olive's," answered Briar.

"Get someone to cover your frames and walk her home, then," he said.

"Me?" She couldn't leave the spindle unguarded.

"Would you rather I fired you so you could take the time?"

"No, I'll do it."

Briar raced back to her frames and got three other girls to each cover one. The bosses liked to see the frames running at all times, and when a girl was sick, the nearby operatives pitched in to help so she wouldn't lose her wages. It was the only insurance they had. Helping each other.

She'd let frame number four stay off and hope the overseer didn't notice. Briar wasn't thrilled about leaving curious Annie alone with her frames, but gave her number one. Although, Annie didn't look well, either.

"Are you okay?" Briar yelled above the noise. "You look flushed."

Annie waved her away.

The girls who had gathered around Sadie were half-heartedly walking back to their frames when Briar returned. The overseer had gotten Sadie to sit up, and with Briar's help she was standing. After looping the girl's arm around Briar's neck, Briar hoisted her up by the waist. She felt like a life-size rag doll stuffed with heavy cotton. "Can you walk?" Briar asked.

Sadie nodded. Slowly, they made their way through the room and out the door. Briar worried about descending the stairs. "Let me know if you need a break," she said. "I don't want us to fall."

It took several minutes to descend the first flight, and several more for the next two. "Good thing we weren't on the top floor," Briar joked. There was no response from Sadie, and Briar worried the bright sun would make her fever worse. The girl was having trouble moving her feet now.

As they were inching their way across the yard, Briar spotted Wheeler coming out of one of the outbuildings. "Wheeler!" she called.

He took two seconds to register that Briar was having trouble keeping Sadie standing and sprinted over.

"Sadie." He scooped her up in his arms and she rested her head on his chest. "What happened?"

"She fainted. I'm to bring her home. I think she'll need a doctor. She's getting worse by the second."

He nodded toward the building he came out of. "Would you go tell my boss I'm helping you? He'll need to unlock the gate anyway."

Briar ran and got Wheeler's boss, who opened the gate for them.

Wheeler's long legs strode purposefully toward the boardinghouse while Briar almost had to jog to keep up.

"I won't be able to stay," Wheeler said as he took the

porch stairs two at a time. "I've got to get back to work."

Briar opened the door, calling out, "Miss Olive! Sadie's taken ill."

Miss Olive stepped into the hallway, wiping her wet hands on her apron. "This way to the isolation room." She led the way to the first floor, to the room they kept open for any of the operatives who were sick. Wheeler gently lowered Sadie to the bed and then ran out the door.

"He's in a hurry," remarked Miss Olive. "Don't you need to get back, too?"

"I should. Is she going to be okay?"

Miss Olive felt Sadie's forehead. "That's some fever. I'll see what I can do to get it down. Meanwhile, I'll send someone for the doctor. Don't you worry."

Sadie's face had turned deathly pale, her breathing shallow.

"Shoo. Away with you." Miss Olive shoved Briar out the door. "There's nothing you can do for her, so go relieve the girls working your own frames."

Briar glanced over Miss Olive's shoulder. The paleness of Sadie's face reminded Briar of how her mother looked after the boys were born. Near death. She ran out of the room.

Intermittently throughout the rest of the day, the girls kept checking themselves and others to see if they, too, had fevers. Briar touched her own forehead and thought it was warm, but it was a hard thing to tell, given the stifling air on their floor anyway. By the end of the day Annie was also complaining about a piercing headache. The operatives passed worried looks behind her back.

When Briar got home, she found Miss Olive coming out of the isolation room. "Doctor's been and says he'll know more in the morning. I've got to stay here with her; do you think you girls can serve yourselves? Food's ready."

"Of course," Briar said. "Do you want me to get anything started for breakfast?"

"Kind of you, but there is nothing to do tonight. Check with me in the morning."

The mood was somber around the table that night. The rumor, whether exaggerated or not, had spread that Sadie was on the verge of death. When one of the girls told a joke, those around her laughed, but the laughter died quickly under withering gazes of the others.

"What happened to her?" asked Mim from the floor of their bedroom. She refused to sleep in the same bed Sadie had slept in, and Ethel wouldn't let her squeeze in with her and Briar. "I heard she fell and cracked her head open on her frame. And I also heard that she licked the grease on the spindles? Why would she do such a thing? That would make anybody sick."

The spindle! Briar's heart sank. Could the spindle have made Sadie sick, even if she didn't prick her finger?

"She didn't hit her head, but she did faint." Briar searched her memory for the chain of events. "I've never felt someone with such a fever. She couldn't even walk back to the house. Wheeler had to carry her here." *But that's not dying and it's not falling asleep for a hundred years. It could be a coincidence. A summer flu, perhaps.*

"Well, I better not get it," said Mim. "Wish we still had Ania living with us."

In the morning, Ethel checked in on Sadie first thing and reported back. "Oh, girls. She's in an awful state. Worse than yesterday. Miss Olive is pacing, waiting for the doctor. I've never seen her so worried before."

On the way to work, they peeked down the hallway on the first floor, but the door to the isolation room was closed. Maybe the doctor was in there now.

They looked at each other grimly. Maybe there would be news at dinner. Until then, they'd better hustle to be through the mill gate before it closed.

When Briar got to her station, she noticed immediately that Annie wasn't at work, either. The overseer assigned Briar and two others to cover for the missing operatives before he started the pulleys. The spinning machines whirled to life and the girls were too busy covering the extra frames to gossip about anything.

Briar's fourth frame hummed along perfectly all morning, giving her plenty of time to wonder how Annie was doing, and if she had the same fever Sadie had.

At the dinner bell, Briar shut down her machines and sought out one of Annie's friends.

"She's feelin' real bad," the girl said. "Last night she was moanin' so loud she woke up the whole house. Doc's coming by today."

"Tell her I hope she feels better soon. We're tending her frames for her." Briar waved to the girl, then turned and raced home to find the doctor still in with Sadie.

In the dining room, the girls ate in silence, which wasn't that unusual, since they were always in such a hurry, but a pall hung over the table as everyone's thoughts were with Sadie. None of them were strangers to illness. In fact, family illness was often the very reason girls like Briar were working in the mills.

The doctor walked past the dining room, his face grim. After Miss Olive had seen him out the front door, the girls gathered round, risking being late and having their pay docked.

"What did he say?"

"He has narrowed it down to one of two things but is still not clear. It's either a bad case of rheumatic fever or something called poliomyelitis. Let's hope it's rheumatic." Miss Olive looked meaningfully at the girls. "The doctor heard of two cases of polio down in Rutland: a farm boy who is paralyzed and won't walk again; another, well, they're still waiting to see if he recovers. His infection attacked the muscles used in swallowing and breathing. Very serious."

"When will the doctor know about Sadie?" Briar asked, relieved the illness was confirmed to be a case of something going around and not from the spindle.

Before Miss Olive could answer, Mim said, "We share a bed. And Briar helped carry her here. Is it catchy? Are we going to get it, too?"

"How are you feeling, Mim? Briar? Any symptoms?"

They both shook their heads.

"We'll keep an eye on everyone who has been in contact with Sadie for the last few days; it's all we can do for you. Meanwhile, we'll watch her and see how the illness progresses. Within a day or two we should know what she has. The symptoms of rheumatic fever and polio are similar to start with, but if it is polio, it may or may not permanently affect her limbs."

"Poliomyelitis?" Mary asked. "What is that?"

"Isn't polio the sleeping sickness?" Mim asked. "We've never had that in the valley before."

The sleeping sickness.

It had to be a coincidence. Sadie wasn't sleeping under a curse, she was ill. A doctor had visited and noted the symptoms. It couldn't be the spindle. It *couldn't*.

Chapter Twenty-Six

Briar sped out the door and flew down the stairs when a movement on the porch caught her eye and made her stop. She turned around to see Wheeler standing near the bench, his hands shoved in his pockets. She retraced her steps, noting his furrowed brow. With a pang, she wondered if he had ever worried about her like that.

The front door continued to open and close behind them as the mill girls rushed past in a hurry to get back to work. They pushed Briar aside and she stumbled toward Wheeler.

"Hi," Briar said. "The doctor's been to see Sadie. The news isn't good." She started to reach out to touch his arm but quickly stopped herself.

"I figured that was him leaving. What did he say?" His voice came out even, controlled.

"He thinks it's either rheumatic fever or polio. We'll know for certain in a few days, but he's leaning toward polio." Briar paused. "There've been two other cases reported."

Wheeler nodded, his expression unreadable. Then he rubbed his neck and sat down on the bench. "Polio? That's serious. One of the mechanics told me his cousin had it. Now the kid can barely walk. Sadie could be paralyzed for life or...or die."

"I'm sorry." It was all she could think of to say. Ethel said Sadie was in a lot of pain, but she didn't want to tell Wheeler that. There was nothing he could do to help Sadie anyway. "They're keeping her comfortable, best they can, and Miss Olive is a good nursemaid."

He nodded again then slid over to make room for her. Briar sat tentatively on the edge of the bench, trying not to think about the nickname the girls had for this seat. *The courting bench.* She also tried to ignore the curious looks the girls were giving as they rushed by on the street on the way back to work.

"We had good times, didn't we?" he said, smiling at her.

"We did." Briar couldn't smile back. This wasn't exactly how she wanted to become friends again with Wheeler—because Sadie fell ill. Why did life have to be so complicated sometimes?

"You're a sweet girl, Briar. My mam was gunning for us to be wed. Being you're Irish and all."

He kept looking straight ahead and Briar still couldn't read his expression. *What is he feeling?*

"Seems like I messed that up, didn't I?" he said. And then, "Do you think Sadie will get better?"

"Of course she will," Briar said, not knowing what else to say. "Give her a few days."

"But what if she's paralyzed?"

"Well, she'll work around it, then. That's what people do." Briar didn't want to think about what would happen if Sadie didn't recover.

"I guess." He didn't look convinced. "I'm leaving soon, for Burlington. Don't know if you heard they want me to help get the new mill up and running over there. Sadie's going to stay here."

Oh. "I-I had heard something about that. Congratulations. You're onto a new step in your plan."

He squinted at her. "You remember that?"

"It was my plan, too," she said quietly.

"Right."

That reminder seemed to stir something up in Wheeler. He slapped his hands on his knees, then stood. "I best be going. The bell will be ringing soon." The way he said it made Briar think he wanted to walk alone back to work. She watched him jog down the steps and out onto the street without a glance behind.

Briar let her head fall back against the brick wall and closed her eyes. She couldn't tell what she felt about Wheeler anymore. At least he showed some signs of regret that things hadn't worked out between them. It hadn't all been in her mind.

She felt someone take her hand, and she opened her eyes. It was Ethel. "Come on. We have to run or we'll be late."

Briar smiled. "Thanks for waiting."

"No problem. How did he take the news?" She cocked her head and arched her eyebrows.

Briar didn't like Ethel's judgmental tone. "He's worried," she said defensively. "He's concerned if it's polio that her legs could be permanently affected, or that she could die."

"Or that he'd be stuck with a cripple?"

"Ethel! How could you say that?"

After too long a pause, Ethel said, "You're right. I'm

sorry. It's a shock for him and I'm sure he'll be there for Sadie no matter the outcome of her illness."

Briar doubted Ethel's sincerity. Or was it that Briar had doubts herself?

The bell rang, giving them ten minutes to get to their stations. They looked at each other and broke into a run, arriving out of breath but on time.

The rest of the day was somber. Not only were the operatives still grumbling about the pay cut, now they were worried they'd get sick, too. Briar kept her focus on her frames. Deftly tying up threads on Annie's frames, adjusting tension, and keeping an eye on her young doffer.

By the end of the day, another girl on Briar's floor complained she wasn't feeling well. The operatives cast worried glances around, and encouraged her to quit early and go home.

Briar couldn't help but note that all the girls who were falling ill were the girls who had come over to poke around her frame. But if the spindle were the source of the illness, Briar should have been the first to fall sick, since she'd been around it the longest. Although she'd never actually touched it, since she'd always kept it covered with the blue silk.

In the fairy tale, Aurora pricked her finger and fell asleep. None of the girls had pricked a finger, and they were all very much awake. No, the source of the illness had to be from somewhere else. Especially since it wasn't only the mill girls who were coming down with polio symptoms. Briar was just overly sensitive about the spindle, and she was reading into things that weren't there.

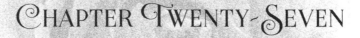

CHAPTER TWENTY-SEVEN

When Briar walked down the stairwell, she saw Wheeler standing at the bottom, waiting for her like he used to. She drew in a breath. Met his eyes. Smiled.

"Hi," he said when she reached the bottom of the stairs.

"Hi," she said shyly. She remembered the first time he'd waited for her there. That was the day she knew he was interested in her, when he braved all the female operatives pouring out of the building. Why was he here waiting for her again? Had things changed that much with Sadie?

"I hear you're the top producer in the spinning room now."

She nodded.

"They need someone to move to Burlington to teach the new girls to spin." He smiled at her and her heart skipped a beat. *Oh, that grin.* It used to be just for her. She pulled up the memory of him and Sadie trying to find her pond, and she could almost hear Henry whisper in her ear to be careful, don't get hurt again.

"Will you be stopping by tonight to see Sadie?" she

asked, putting up a wall that needed to stay between them.

"Will Miss Olive let me past the parlor?"

"I don't know. She might."

"I'll come anyway. To check up on Sadie." He held Briar's gaze a little too long and Briar felt her face grow warm. She looked away, hoping he didn't notice the effect he still had on her. He needed to figure out his intentions toward Sadie before renewing any plans with Briar. She refused to be a stopgap until Sadie got better.

"No visitors yet." Miss Olive blocked Briar from entering the room. The diagnosis was in. Polio. Everyone was to stay away. "Get yourself ready for supper."

Lost in thought, Briar climbed the stairs to her room and bumped into Ethel, who was carrying up a big box of leaflets and white ribbons. The box tipped and fell, scattering temperance material about the stairwell.

"Briar!" Ethel set down the box and started gathering the papers.

"Oh, I'm so sorry. I was distracted and didn't see you." Briar started to help stack the leaflets but paused to skim one. A WCTU meeting. It was hard to keep track of all Ethel's meetings. "What's this one about?"

With mounting enthusiasm, Ethel filled Briar in on the latest news in women's suffrage. "If women have the vote, we can change the laws, so we are taken care of instead of taken advantage of. We can vote the saloons away and have our husbands back."

"Are you already planning on having a husband who frequents the saloons?" Briar teased.

Ethel scowled and snatched the leaflet from Briar. "The WCTU, the Woman's Christian Temperance Union, is sending a representative to speak to us this week. You should come and learn about how unfair the laws are for us women and what we can do to change that. Mrs. Tuttle's speech helped you, didn't it?"

"Yes, her speech encouraged me to fight harder, and not let myself get swept away." But Briar pushed back a little. "The laws are already in place for our vote. When we marry, we are supposed to work as a unit. My vote will be cast through my husband."

Ethel scoffed. "Weren't you listening the other night? Where are all these good husbands we keep hearing about?" She opened her arms wide, indicating all the single women in the house. "You're the youngest here, Briar. The rest of us are over eighteen. And even if we do marry, what of the bad husbands? What recourse do we have when the one we marry turns out not to be a good man?"

Mim came up the stairs in time to catch the end of the conversation. "I plan to marry a good man. I'm very thorough with my process. That's why I haven't settled down yet."

"You have to be asked, first," Ethel said, irritated.

"Maybe I have been asked, but I turned him down." Mim leaned against the wall.

This is news. "Who asked you?"

Mim waved her hand like it was of little consequence. "There was this boy back home. It was a setup really between our parents, but I didn't like him. He wasn't the sort for me, so that's when I left and came here."

"You ran away from home?" asked Briar.

Mim chortled. "I suppose I did. And I'm not going back in defeat. Not until I've found a man on my own." She scooped up a bunch of white ribbons and piled them into the box. "What about you, Briar? I heard you were outside with Wheeler, on the courting bench no less."

Briar gasped. "Is that what they're saying? I had to tell him about Sadie, that's all. I-I'm the one who knows him best."

"Tut-tut. Don't you worry what those gossips say. Once you leave this mill, you won't care one hoot what they think. Concentrate on your future. Do what you need to survive. Even you have to agree with that advice, don't you, Ethel?"

Ethel shrugged. "I suppose. We've got to be smart. Children are orphaned," she said and looked at Briar. "Or they try to force you into a match you don't want." She pointed to Mim. "You can't always control what happens to you, but you can choose how you respond."

"And what about you, Ethel?" asked Briar. "Has anything happened to you?"

"You know why I'm here. The mill is a stepping-stone to earn money for college and a better life."

"Yes, but we don't know what brought you here."

Ethel picked up the box and led the way to their room.

Mim looped her arm through Briar's. "Better give up, Briar. She's keeping it to herself. That's why she's so annoyed with me. I poked her too hard about it when she first moved in. I suppose she's entitled to her secrets."

Ethel stuck out her tongue before putting the box on their bed. "Mark my words. One day we'll have the vote and you'll see what a difference it will make. We could use your help, though." She held out stacks of leaflets. "You can come with me tonight to hand these out."

Mim picked a leaflet from the box. "WCTU? Aren't they for prohibition? I'm not sure I want to push for that."

Ethel frowned. "What, it's not like you go out to the saloons every weekend."

"No, but I like to think I could if I wanted to."

Ethel snatched the leaflet away. "You wouldn't be caught dead in a saloon and you know it." She turned to Briar. "And you? Do you think the cause is more important than keeping open the *option* to do something you don't do anyway?"

Briar sighed. "I don't know what I think anymore. Sure, I'll come with you to hand out leaflets." She would consider it penance in case it really was her fault the mill girls were getting sick.

CHAPTER TWENTY-EIGHT

Ethel marched purposefully down the street with Briar double-timing it, trying to keep up. "We're going to be late," said Ethel. "Hurry up."

"How many are we meeting?" Briar asked.

"Only a handful tonight. It's the factory girls taking this side of town. Some ladies' auxiliaries are canvassing other districts. Sunrise keeps growing and growing. We want to make sure it grows in the right way. Fewer saloons, more schools."

The gathering was held outside another boardinghouse. Briar didn't know the other operatives, as they were mostly older, and Ethel said they worked in the weaving rooms or in the new shirtwaist factory.

"A new recruit," said a woman in a crisp shirtwaist and long cotton skirt. "I'm Miss Ellison. Welcome to our group." She shook Briar's hand.

"Now that we're all here, let's divide up the leaflets. We'll start with our own street then work our way into town. Give them to whoever makes eye contact but focus on the women. Remind them we have strength in numbers."

Briar and Ethel took their allotment and started on the boardinghouses on the right-hand side of the street. At this time of night, most of the operatives not on the town would be in their parlors.

The first house they entered was Annie's. About a dozen girls sat around, playing various parlor games or reading.

While Ethel worked the room, Briar spoke with one of Annie's friends. "How is she tonight?"

"Worse. The doctor's really worried. They've called in her parents. Her dad will be here tomorrow to take her home. She was the oldest of twelve. I don't know how they're going to manage having her back at home without her wages."

"They'll manage just fine," piped up another girl. "It's Annie who'll have the hard time when she gets better and finds herself playing nursemaid to all her siblings again."

Ethel returned to Briar's side. "Hand them each a leaflet," she whispered.

Briar thrust a paper into each girl's hand. "Tell Annie I'm sorry."

They continued down the row of boardinghouses, Ethel chatting up the cause with anyone who would listen, Briar thinking about Annie and Sadie.

She felt terrible that the two had gotten so sick. What if the cause was the spindle? She wouldn't be able to tell anyone; no one would believe her. If she started talking about a fairy-wood spindle that could make girls ill they'd think she'd lost her mind, then she'd lose her job, and then where would the children be? Hopefully Miss Fanny would come up with a way to get the spindle off the frame.

One thought niggled the back of her mind, though.

Henry. What role did he play in all this? He had been at her side for as long as she was in Sunrise Valley and then practically overnight he was gone. A fairy had appeared, and a magic spindle was now in her spinning frame. She couldn't figure out how everything was connected.

Next house was their own. A loud burst of laughter came out of the parlor as they opened the front door. A heated game of progressive Tiddledy Winks was going on, and Wheeler, a master at flipping the winks, had worked his way up to the head table.

Briar froze in the doorway. She'd forgotten he was stopping in. It was so strange to see him here. He and Sadie usually went out instead of hanging around the parlor where he and Briar once spent all their time. Ethel started right in, passing out the leaflets while Briar stood in the doorway. Wheeler looked up and waved before concentrating back on the game.

Ethel was quick to pass out the leaflets as she'd already spoken to each of the girls about the WCTU before. She saw who Briar was fixated on, then stood in her way. "Let's go."

Once outside, Ethel marched to the next house. Then she stopped. "You're not thinking about Wheeler again, are you?"

"No," she was quick to answer back. Too quick.

Ethel cocked her head. "What if I told you Sadie was going back home to her parents? Would you still not be thinking about Wheeler?"

"She is?"

"They want her to recuperate on the farm. Wheeler's moving north; she's moving south. They're never going to see each other again."

"Oh." Briar's heart took the news with mixed emotions.

As long as Sadie was still around, it meant she didn't have to decide on her true feelings about Wheeler. She'd been trying so hard to move on and in that process had noticed things about Wheeler and her that she didn't necessarily like. Not that she was comparing him to Henry, but Henry was so steady. She always knew where she stood with him, and that accounted for a lot. Could she ever trust Wheeler again?

Ethel led the way up the walk. "This is our last house. Why don't you do the talking this time? You've heard me plenty."

"But I couldn't. I'd get all tongue-tied."

"You have to start somewhere, Briar. If you're afraid to try, you won't get anywhere. Weren't you scared when you first applied at the mill? Yet you still did it."

"I had no choice," she said. It was easy to do something when it was for the children.

"Consider this your first lesson in proactivity. I know you want to keep your family together, but to do so, you're going to have to learn to advocate for others. It's not about you, it's about them. Tell these operatives how meetings like these can help us all. We can go from feeling helpless and powerless to hopeful and powerful."

Briar gave Ethel a skeptical look.

"Baby steps. You're still finding your voice. Read the leaflet out loud and invite them to come."

"I can do that."

Ethel held back, making Briar open the door. The parlor was half-empty and when Briar stepped in she had everyone's attention. They were all clearly looking for some excitement to walk through the door.

Briar gave them a shaky smile. "I'm distributing leaflets for the WCTU meeting this week." She thrust a paper at the closest girl. "We have a special speaker coming in to teach us all how we can band together to make a difference." She continued around the room, handing out the leaflets while Ethel stood quietly by the door. Briar answered a few questions, checking with Ethel for accuracy, then said good-bye.

Outside, Briar breathed a sigh of relief.

"Wasn't so bad, was it?" asked Ethel. "It won't always be so easy. These ladies weren't carrying rotten vegetables to hurl at us."

"People do that?" Briar asked, aghast.

Ethel nodded. "Not often. But you should be prepared."

All their leaflets were gone with half an hour to spare before the curfew bell. When they returned home, the parlor games were still going on. The group was pushing chairs into a circle around the room, setting up for another game.

"Got a new one," called Lizbeth as they entered the room. "Join us. It's called Crossed and Uncrossed."

Once everyone was settled, Briar between Ethel and Wheeler, Nell supervised as they passed a pair of scissors to their neighbor, and said either crossed or uncrossed. Nell would then tell you if you were correct. The purpose was to discover the secret about what made the pass a crossed or uncrossed pass.

Briar was among the first to figure it out and tried to give Wheeler hints. Each time she spoke was like a test, asking *can we go back to the way we were?*

By the end of the night, all the girls knew the trick but several of the boys left the game baffled. And Wheeler hadn't answered her silent test.

"I don't understand," said a new boy named George, shaking his head and grinning. "But I'm determined to figure out if I'm crossed or uncrossed. Tomorrow night?"

"Yes, yes!" Lizbeth said. "Everyone, let's meet here again tomorrow night. No telling the secret."

"I'm going to get it out of Briar by then," joked Wheeler.

She shook her head. "Only hints. You've got to figure it out yourself." Her words held a double meaning. He did need to figure out what he wanted. And so did she.

Nell and Lizbeth, the spontaneous organizers, stood at the door to the parlor saying good-bye to everyone.

Mim slipped in just before the curfew bell sounded, and she gave Briar a wave on her way to the stairs. George paused in the doorway and watched Mim pass.

Briar smiled. Another one smitten. He'd be back for sure, hoping Mim would join in the games. "Good night, all," Briar said.

She missed nights like this: fun and carefree, like a few months ago when her deepest concern was getting to work on time. Back when her seventeenth birthday felt so far away and it looked like she knew where her future was going. Suddenly her birthday was looming and her future was tied to a fairy-tale spindle and an evil fairy who wanted her dead.

CHAPTER TWENTY-NINE

"Why are you in such a kerfuffle?" asked Mim after supper the next night when the room-mates gathered back in their room. A third girl had taken ill on the spinning floor, but she was one who worked on the far side of the room, giving Briar hope that her spindle wasn't the cause. The overseer, instead of getting upset by another operative down, spent the day in his office with his feet up on his desk.

"Wheeler is stopping by," Briar admitted. The thought had been playing out in her mind all day.

"Interesting." Mim burst into a grin.

"To play parlor games of course." Briar anxiously squeezed her fingertips.

Mim leaned against the desk. "Don't waste your chance. You can remind Wheeler what you once had. If you want to."

What she wanted was to know if they could go forward, not back. To decide, she needed to spend time with him again. It wouldn't take long. She'd know pretty quickly if the old feelings were still there.

"Don't go putting such thoughts into her head," Ethel said, stepping into the room to grab her box of leaflets. "Come with me again tonight, Briar. They want to hand out more leaflets. Not everyone finished their lot."

Mim ignored Ethel and got out her cosmetics. "With my help, you can't go wrong. We'll sweep your hair up into a pompadour and turn you into a Gibson girl."

Ethel cocked her head and put her hands on her hips. "You don't want a man who doesn't want you," she said, cutting straight to the heart. "And what about Henry? Are you sure he's only a friend to you? I've seen you reading that letter he sent. Surely it's memorized by now."

"Ethel! Spying on me?" Briar tried not to blush, but she could feel her face heating up. Henry was still as unlikely a beau as before—an insincere flirt. Of course Briar was missing him. They were friends. Didn't mean she was pining.

Briar glanced between the two room-mates. Ethel, always so serious and working hard to reach her goals. Mim, always out for fun, yet not lazy in the least. Handing out more leaflets suddenly seemed exhausting.

"Quit fighting over me." Briar held up her hands. "I just want to have a night of fellowship. Getting in on that scissor game last night made me realize how much I've missed the fun." Her voice cracked and she looked away.

All she said was true. Ever since Nanny left them, she'd been winding herself up tighter and tighter with worry over the future. It was nice to play for once. And she was so confused about Wheeler. Was Mim right, and he had only gotten cold feet with her? Or was Ethel, who thought Briar should get on by herself, taking up the cause of suffrage to change her future instead? She let out a deep breath. Mrs. Tuttle, the lecturer who came to the house, was a married woman. Briar could marry and still stand for herself and women's rights.

"You've been shouldering so much," Mim said, sympathetically.

They have no idea. Wheeler, Fanny, the spindle, and the children. Briar's head would explode if she tried to think about it all at the same time.

Mim turned to Ethel. "She's only going to be sixteen for a few more days. Why push her to act twenty-five?" She went over to her dresser and pulled out several outfits. "Did you want to wear my dress with the leg-o'-mutton sleeves?" Mim had a satisfied look on her face, like she had won the argument.

"Yes, she's young, but she is flirting with trouble. There's a difference." Ethel moved to leave the room, her nose in the air in protest. "I've given all my advice to deaf ears," she said as she stalked out the door. "Heaven help you now."

Briar sighed. Her room-mates' intentions were good, but some things she needed to learn on her own.

"I don't know if I can wear something that fancy," Briar said, examining the dress Mim was pulling out. Everyone marveled at how many dresses Mim had managed to acquire. Besides being an excellent seamstress, she was quite verbal to her sweethearts about what she wanted them to bring her. "No flowers" was rule number one, but yards of material were always welcomed. "I wouldn't look like me anymore." *And it would look like I was trying too hard.*

"Nonsense," Mim said, holding up a buttercream gown to Briar's shoulder with one hand and placing her other hand on Briar's waist. "Do you have a better corset than that?"

"This is all I have."

Briar looked uncertainly at the cosmetics. Mim was laying out cheek powder, some kind of cream, two bottles of perfume, and a handful of other products Briar had no idea what they were. Would Mam have approved? It was only a certain kind of girl who painted her face with store-bought items.

Mim rolled her eyes. "Don't look like I'm about to teach you how to lose your virtue. When I'm done with you, you will still look like you, only better. Wheeler won't even be able to tell I've done anything to your face, but he'll notice you look especially attractive today. What you do with your virtue is your own business."

Briar gasped. She crossed her arms and legs uncomfortably and looked at the empty doorway. Ethel had a point. A boy ought to like you the way you were.

But Mim wasn't done with her lecturing. "Once you are all dolled up, you'll have his eye. Be sure not to waste it. Hang on his every word, even if he is boring."

"Oh, Wheeler's not boring."

"Sure he's not," Mim said.

"What's that supposed to mean?" asked Briar. Mim's tone was starting to sound like Ethel's.

Mim grabbed Briar's chin and tilted her face this way and that in the light. "I only mean that you seemed to have a better time with that Henry fellow than with Wheeler. I hate to admit that Ethel might have been more observant than me about this, but are you sure there isn't anything between you?"

"Henry isn't here," Briar said, fully aware she wasn't answering the question. She didn't know what she thought about Henry anymore. He was *Henry*. There was no one else like him.

"At least Henry let you talk. Wheeler just goes on and on about himself. You do have a lot of freckles, don't you?"

Briar pulled her chin back. Her freckles were a sore spot for her. Instead of an ivory-white complexion like a heroine in a novel, her skin was all blotchy. Leave it to Mim to zero in on it.

"Awk! Don't take offense. A lot of you Irish girls have freckles. I've got rice powder to tone it down. When I'm a wealthy woman I'll have pearl powder instead." She'd already opened a canister and dabbed a brush inside. She gently patted down Briar's face, stepping back to examine her work. "Hmmm, this blemish is a tricky one."

Briar held up her hand to cover the red mark that had appeared on her chin that morning.

"Put your hand down. I can cover it better than that. You don't see my blemishes, do you?"

Briar examined Mim's always-flawless skin and shook her head.

With a sigh, Mim leaned forward and pointed at a tiny spot on her forehead. "We all get them. Some of us are just better at hiding them."

Briar chose not to comment. Mim thinking her tiny dot was a big blemish was an overstatement.

Mim dabbed a bit more on Briar's face, then tapped the lid back on, and opened another jar.

"What's that?" asked Briar nervously.

"Settle down, it's only rouge."

"I don't need any cheek color."

"Will you trust me?" Mim stepped back. "Look at me, and tell me what cosmetics I have used on myself today."

"I don't know," Briar said. "You look like you always do during the day."

"Exactly. I look natural, but I'm wearing everything I'm

going to put on you."

"I don't know why you wear cosmetics to the mill," Briar said. It seemed a waste. The only single male-folk on the spinning floor were the doffers, and they were all young-uns except for Henry.

"You never know who you'll meet on the street coming home for dinner, now do you? A girl has to be prepared."

Briar nodded. Since she agreed to let Mim help, there was no point in complaining at every turn.

As Mim applied ointment and more powder, she began to hum, clearly enjoying making Briar up. But when Mim lit a candle and stuck a hairpin in the flame, Briar couldn't remain silent. She jumped out of her chair. "I don't want you burning my hair." She grabbed at her locks to protect them.

Mim laughed. "This here pin is not for your hair. 'Tis for your lashes, to make them darker."

"No! You're not coming at my eyes with that hot poker."

Mim calmly held the pin in the flame. "It won't be hot when I 'come at you,'" she said. "I only want the soot. Try not to rub your eyes or you'll look a mess. And no crying."

"Why would I cry?"

"Girls just do sometimes," said Mim. "Now hold still."

Briar stared at the spot where the wall met the ceiling, resisting the urge to blink while Mim attempted to *bring out her eyes*. She was surprised at the lengths she was willing to go to test Wheeler. Would she know at the end of the night what to do? Could it be that easy?

CHAPTER THIRTY

Feeling self-conscious, Briar slipped downstairs and into the parlor. She'd not put on Mim's fancy dress, thinking that was overdone. Instead, she wore her best dress, which only meant the one she didn't wear to the mill. The cosmetics made her feel out of place, as if she were wearing a fur coat in summer.

When she stepped into the room, the girls sitting around glanced up to see who was new, then went back to the games or activities they were working on. Briar was glad she'd not worn Mim's dress. The parlor was busy tonight and she didn't need to give anyone more fodder for gossip.

Nell was on the piano. Mary and Lizbeth were deep in conversation, and the others were around the coffee table, playing Tiddledy Winks already. The two chairs set off by themselves, most often used for courting couples, were empty, and Briar sat in one. These were the seats she and Wheeler used to occupy all last winter.

"I hear a doctor over in Rutland is calling it an epidemic. He's got more than fifty patients, and several have died already. Some only a few days after getting sick."

Briar leaned in to the conversation. An epidemic meant it wasn't the spindle. Some of the pressure weighing her down eased. She was already responsible for her siblings; she didn't want to be responsible for a whole floor of operatives.

At the first knock on the door, Briar shot up to answer it, but was beaten there by another eager girl. Everyone was ready for the fun to start.

They began where they ended the previous night, with the Crossed and Uncrossed scissors game. Wheeler came in late, but the circle opened up to allow him in. He smiled and waved as he moved in his chair across from Briar, and they started passing the scissors around.

Twenty minutes later when the boys still weren't figuring out the trick, the girls began exaggerating their motions to give hints. Finally, Nell crossed her legs and said "crossed" then uncrossed her legs and said "uncrossed." And if that wasn't enough, the next girl crossed her ankles, saying "crossed" then uncrossed her ankles and said "uncrossed."

George smacked his forehead. "It's the legs, not how you pass the scissors."

The laughter from George's comments set the tone for the rest of the night. Briar let go and allowed herself to be just a girl instead of a caretaker of her siblings, an operative at the mill, or the guardian of a dangerous spindle.

At the end of the night she walked Wheeler to the door, like she used to do.

"I had a good evening," Wheeler said.

"Me, too."

"It was like old times."

"Mm-hmm," she agreed, and yet it was and it wasn't like old times. She'd had fun, but so much had changed since they were together. Briar felt like she had grown, gained some perspective. Had he?

Wheeler walked out to the porch, almost the last guest to leave. He lingered. "You look nice tonight. I found myself wishing we'd land at the same table, but we never did. Maybe another time?"

To Briar's shock, when she tried to answer, she teared up. She blinked rapidly, afraid of smudging the soot Mim had so carefully placed on her eyelashes. But it was no good. He seemed like his old self, playing games and having fun, but not showing Briar much deference over anyone else, despite what he said. She got the impression any girl could sit by his side and he'd be content. It didn't have to be Briar. She fled back inside. "Good-night," she called over her shoulder as she ran down the hall.

If only Mim hadn't planted the idea of crying into her mind. She never cried. At least not in front of Wheeler. How ridiculous to cry when a boy says you look nice.

Ethel caught Briar at the base of the stairs. "What happened?" she asked.

Briar pulled out a handkerchief and began wiping Mim's hard work off her face. It felt wrong to dress up for Wheeler now, but how could she explain that? They weren't the same together, and she didn't think she wanted them to be. She had the chance to put everything back together for the children, just what she'd been working toward, and now she didn't know if she could sacrifice her happiness for it. Tears welled up and she blinked them away. If she had the opportunity to save the children, shouldn't she do it? What kind of sister would she be if she didn't?

"Well?" Mim joined them in the hallway. "I could hear the party down the street." She narrowed her eyes as if trying to examine Briar in the dim light. "Didn't I tell you not to cry?"

Briar's lower lip started to tremble.

Mim pulled her into the parlor where they could sit down. "What happened?" Mim's voice was soft, sympathetic.

Briar rested her head on Ethel's shoulder and took a deep breath. "The feeling was different. But how can I walk away from keeping the children together?"

"Listen, honey." Mim grasped her hand. "You've got three siblings counting on you and you almost had a home secured for them. That's why I'm so willing to help you find out if you two can work it out. Don't feel guilty about wanting to be happy, too. Wheeler isn't the only eligible bachelor out there."

Ethel stroked Briar's back. "If you both still care for each other, it'll take some time. You can't go back to where you were overnight." She stilled her hand. "But don't force something that's not there. You'll only regret it."

The other girls of the boardinghouse were restoring order to the parlor when the front door banged open. A grisly young man burst through and staggered into the house. "Lola? Lola! Show yourself."

All the mill girls looked at one another with wide eyes. There was no one named Lola living there.

Miss Olive came from nowhere and blocked his passage into the parlor. "Sir, you must leave now." When he took a step closer she wrinkled her nose. "You've been drinking. Out you go."

Ethel leaned back and hid behind Briar.

"Don't worry," Briar reassured her. "Miss Olive won't let him in." She'd never seen Ethel afraid before.

By now, Miss Olive had managed to maneuver the stranger back to the front door, but he wedged himself in the door frame so that she couldn't close it.

"I'm not leaving until I've seen her. Lola! I know you're here. I found you. You can't hide from me." The commotion he made was so loud it had to be echoing out onto the streets.

Ethel began to tremble and Mim looked at Briar with raised eyebrows. Wheeler and two other men returned to the house to assist Miss Olive.

Meanwhile, one of Ethel's temperance friends addressed the girls. "This is a prime example of what we are talking about. This man is obviously under the influence of the drink and can't be reasoned with. This poor Lola would be glad to be away from him in this state. Heaven help her if he finds her. For her sake we should double our efforts. If you haven't signed a pledge yet, come forward now and add your name to the cause." She waved the petition in the air.

There was a bang as the man pounded the wall. Several of the girls jumped to their feet as one and lined up to sign their names to pledge temperance.

Ethel continued to shrink from the noise. Her eyes were fixed on the parlor entrance.

"Wheeler's out there now. He'll get him away," Briar said.

Ethel nodded.

The disturbance moved out to the porch. Ethel darted from the room and ran up the staircase. Briar and Mim looked at each other in bewilderment before running after her. The man at the door saw Ethel and broke away from Wheeler to follow her, almost knocking Briar over.

"Lola! Pack your things. You're coming home with me," he yelled up the stairs.

Wheeler tackled him, smacking the man's face into the stairs with a *thwack*. Assured Wheeler had the man pinned down, Briar stepped over them and ran after Ethel.

"Is he still breathing?" Miss Olive asked.

"Yes," Wheeler said. "He'll wake up with a big headache, though. Help me get him to the porch and I'll get some of the other fellows to help me deal with him."

Briar found Ethel packing her carpetbag.

"You can't go with him," Briar said.

"No. Never again," Ethel said with fire in her voice. "I need to run farther away."

"Who is he?" Briar asked.

"My husband."

Mim stood in the doorway. "Your husband! You never said anything about being married." Mim sat down on her bed. "You must have thought I was so silly with my imaginings of what married life was like."

Briar turned back to Ethel. Leave it to Mim to focus on herself at a time like this. "You can't leave, not now anyway. He's still downstairs. Wheeler knocked him out cold on the stairs."

Ethel stopped packing and faced her room-mates. "I'm sorry I didn't say anything."

Briar reached for Ethel's trembling hands and pulled her to sit on the bed. "I can see why you didn't." They sat for a minute, Briar and Mim watching Ethel stare at the floor.

"Your name is Lola?" Briar asked.

"My husband is a mean drunk and if I try to divorce him he'll get custody of our baby. I have no rights to her."

"You have a baby?" Mim said.

Ethel took a shaky breath. "That's why I'm so interested in both temperance and getting the vote. If we can stop our men from spending everything we earn on drink, we'd have our husbands back. And if we can't do that, at least if we get the vote we'll have options. We'll be able to change the laws so women like me can legally leave with our children."

"Where is your baby?" Briar asked softly. She thought of her siblings and how hard it was to be away from them, and she saw them every weekend.

"With my mother-in-law. She's a good woman and promised to keep Addie until I was able to find a way to make a living for the two of us. I didn't tell anyone where I was going, and I changed my name. If he shows up at the mill he'll either cause trouble or take my wages. Either way, I can't stay here." She rose again and stuffed more clothes into her bag.

"How do you think he found you?" asked Mim.

"That payday when Briar and I went to the bank, remember, Briar? A man on the wagon called out to us. I knew him. I hoped he'd think he'd been mistaken if I pretended I didn't know him. He must have told my husband." She started breathing in great gasps, clutching her shirtwaist at the neck. "I don't know what I'm going to do." Her voice rose in pitch.

Mim sat on Ethel's old carpetbag. "For starters, you're not leaving us. You need to stay here so we can help you. It'll cost you time and money to move and set yourself up again. It'll be a step backward. Wait and see how this works itself out before you make any decisions. You're not going to get a better house than this one. Miss Olive will know what to do."

Ethel fell to the floor, rocking back and forth as the tears streamed, keening in a way Briar had never seen before.

Briar and Mim looked at each other in shock before falling to their knees with Ethel. Their strong, practical, logical room-mate was unraveling.

CHAPTER THIRTY-ONE

"I'm not going," mumbled Ethel, her face buried in her pillow.

"It's the WCTU. You need to go. You have the white ribbons." Briar turned to Mim. "See? She's really not going."

Ethel continued talking into her pillow. "You take them. You're better poised to change the world than me, Briar. I'm not strong enough."

"It's a crisis of faith," said Mim. "That's all. Your drunk husband came 'round and now you're back in his grasp. Snap out of it. You've been preaching this stuff to me since we met. Don't make me go alone."

Ethel lifted her face. It was puffy and wet with tears. "You? You'd go to the meeting?"

Mim crossed her arms and huffed. "If it'll make you go, yes. Otherwise you'll keep moping forever. You're hard enough to live with when you're happy."

Ethel looked at Briar. "And you?"

Briar nodded. "Of course I'll go." She pointed to her

shirtwaist where she had already pinned a white ribbon.

"'Do Everything,'" Ethel said, pushing herself up. "That's what Miss Willard says." She wiped her eyes. "I'm sorry."

"For what?" asked Briar.

"Not telling you. It was my deepest secret, and the one I wanted to talk about every day. At least, regarding my baby. Briar, you don't know how many times I was tempted to go take her and bring her to your cottage to be raised by Nanny so I'd have her close by me." She swung her feet over the side of the bed. "And you, Mim. With your ideals of marriage. I didn't know what advice to give you. My experience has not been ideal in the least."

"Well, didn't you know what he was like before you married?"

"A little, I suppose, if I'm being honest. But I didn't think he'd get worse, I thought he'd settle in once we married." She splashed water on her face. "Let's check on Sadie before we go. I feel like we ought to include her on this room-mate outing."

Miss Olive let them poke their heads in the door but enter no farther. Sadie was sitting up but had the look of misery about her.

"Glad to see you up," said Ethel, her voice attempting to be cheery but coming out strained.

"Ethel is dragging us to the WCTU meeting tonight. Be glad you're stuck in bed," said Mim.

"You're looking much better," added Briar.

Sadie gave them a slight smile in return, pointing to her right leg, bent slightly at the knee. "It's froze that way. Can't straighten it, but the doctor thinks I might be able to eventually." She cleared her throat and forced a brighter smile. "Looks like you'll have another new room-mate.

Sorry we didn't have time to know one another. You three always look like you get on well. I was looking forward to being part of your group." She paused before addressing Briar directly. "I hope everything works out for you."

She's talking about Wheeler.

The three room-mates exchanged wondering glances before giving a wave and backing out of the room.

"Do we really get on so well?" asked Mim.

Briar laughed. "Miss Olive said she put us together for a reason. She seems to think we need each other."

The community hall above the mayor's office was starting to fill up by the time they arrived. The room-mates split up with bundles of ribbons each to pass around. Once they were empty-handed, they met up again, and found seats to the right of the lectern.

"If this is such an important meeting, why can't Frances Willard herself show up?" whispered Mim.

"Shhh! Just listen. The woman can't be everywhere at once."

A woman in her thirties stepped out onto the stage. "Welcome, ladies. It's exciting to see such a good turnout tonight for our guest speaker." She went on to introduce Miss Nan Whitaker, a representative of the Woman's Christian Temperance Union. The topic of the night was to give a global perspective on the movement, including suffrage in other countries.

"Good evening, ladies!"

A resounding applause lit the room.

"I bring greetings from our president, Frances Willard,

who is at this time at Eastnor Castle in England, working tirelessly with our British sisters as they seek the vote. Temperance is at the heart of what we do. Prohibition, Women's Liberation, and Labor's Uplift are the three major avenues, all undergirded by temperance.

"Not everything is in temperance reform, but temperance reform should be in everything we do. We have unequal laws in marriage, in property rights, and add to that the risk of intemperance at home, which makes these inequalities unbearable. Money that is spent on drink is not available for other pursuits, and women and children get the worst end of it, drowning in poverty."

Briar stole a glance at Ethel. She was completely engrossed in the lecture. Her face upturned and her focus keen. Mim, sitting on Briar's other side, reached over and squeezed her hand. Briar nodded. They were going to help Ethel get through this.

When they left the lecture hall, the sun was down and the lamplighter was working his way along the street, turning on the gas lights. There were several men waiting outside, and as soon as the women exited, the men began hurling insults.

"Just walk on by, ladies," said Ethel, her strength and resolve clearly having been restored. She pulled back her shoulders and lifted her head high. "We've made them nervous tonight is all."

On the edge of the crowd, a familiar form stuck out from the rest.

"Wheeler?" said Briar. He was standing in the shadows of the mercantile, with his hat pulled low, but she could make out his tall, lanky form anywhere.

"You didn't come here to listen to that speech, did you?" He stepped forward, closer to the streetlight.

"I-I came for Ethel's sake," she said, self-consciously touching her white ribbon.

"You know you girls are only biding your time until you get husbands. You don't need the vote. Your husband will make the decisions on how the family votes, same as it's been done for years. Besides, I'll never sign a temperance pledge. None of the fellas I know will."

"It's about home protection," said Briar, reiterating what she had learned that night. "Women need the vote to help make laws suitable for women and children, not just the men."

"Home protection? You don't need that, Bri. I'll protect you."

He looked deep into her eyes, and the others on the street seemed to fade away. *Is he making a declaration? Now?* She let her hand fall from the ribbon.

Before she could properly react, he smiled like he knew the reaction he had caused, doffed his hat, and was off. He thought she was pleased. No. She wasn't. That was the problem. What was she going to do?

Chapter Thirty-Two

By Saturday morning, the excitement of the WCTU meeting had worn off and Ethel had resumed her murmurings about leaving town again. Fortunately, Mim was doing a good job of keeping her talked out of it.

Briar had even considered staying in town for the night in case Ethel decided to leave while she was gone. Perhaps it was best if the two older girls were given time to speak privately. Ethel's problems were so much more than Briar could imagine. Miss Olive would have her hands full this weekend between Sadie's physical needs and Ethel's emotional ones.

After work, Briar reluctantly pulled the bicycle out of the shed for her trip home. She'd never been so torn about leaving. She wanted to stay, but if she did the children would worry about her. Besides, she had to find out if Fanny had managed to devise a plan about the spindle.

Since Briar's frames were working so well, the overseer had given her two of Annie's old frames to run, and even they ran without mishap now. No one was running as many frames as she was. It seemed the curse might be too old to cause any problems, so if there was a way to safely keep the spindle, Briar would be all for it.

She swung her leg over the bar and got ready to push off when she heard her name.

"Briar!"

Wheeler grinned at her and made his way over to her side of the street. "Walk you to the cottage today?" he asked.

Her stomach knotted. Should she try one last time to see if they could connect again? So many pressures were weighing in on her that she questioned her judgment on everything.

In reply she hopped off the bicycle, and he fell comfortably in step with her. He took one of the handlebars.

"Thanks for helping Ethel the other night," she said.

"No problem. I meant what I said earlier. If you ever need me, I'm here for you." He gave her the look that used to make the butterflies in her stomach explode.

She smiled tentatively back. No butterflies. Just a general feeling of unease.

"What happened to that man after you boys took him away?" Briar had a hard time saying the word *husband* in relation to someone married to her room-mate.

"He left town. We saw to that. He had a friend here who he was staying with and that fellow said he'd make sure he was on the train today. If it was running. With these rail-worker strikes going on, you never can know."

"What if the train didn't run today?" If Ethel were to catch sight of him still in town, that would be it. She'd pack her bags and be gone before Mim could talk her into staying.

Wheeler shrugged. "I wouldn't worry about it. It's not your problem."

Of course it was her problem. How could she not worry about her friend?

"You know, the other day Mr. Smith came in to observe how I handled a conflict in the bailing room. He wanted to see if I was up for the challenge, and if two older men would listen to me."

"And?"

He stood tall, a big grin spread across his face.

"Well done," Briar said, knowing he was fishing for praise.

"You know," Wheeler said, dipping his mouth close to hers. "You're the prettiest girl at the factory again."

"Oh." *Oh.* Briar's face grew hot. That was a clumsy compliment. Her mam's saying came to mind: where the tongue slips it speaks the truth.

He produced a flower and handed it to her. When she didn't immediately reach for it, he plucked off the bloom and tucked it into her hair above her ear. His finger traced the line of her cheek and, for a moment, she thought he was going to kiss her. She turned her head away. He took a step back and crooked out his arm for her to hold.

Instead of taking his arm, she took over pushing the bicycle.

"How is your family?" he asked, letting his arm drop to his side.

"The boys are causing trouble as usual, and Pansy is ever the little mother over them, and Nanny has gone—"

"That's great! I forgot to add that Mr. Smith must have told Mr. Albans, because then he stopped by my area and congratulated me on the move to Burlington. I leave Monday after next. They've also been impressed with you lately. We could both be moving to Burlington and then, who knows?" Then he smiled the smile that used to make her weak in the knees. But not this time.

She tried to smile but suspected it came out like a

smirk. He was leaving on her birthday and he didn't even realize it. The date held such importance for Briar, since she was afraid she'd have to give up the children then, and here he was, so nonchalant. Did he even see her? Know who she was? Had he forgotten everything that was important to her?

They walked like this the whole way to the cottage, Wheeler trying to impress her with his accomplishments, and Briar trying to convince herself that she'd finally achieved what she wanted. Her plans were back on track. She should be pleased.

Presently, Wheeler picked up a stone so he could demonstrate the accuracy of his throwing arm. Apparently he'd been practicing throwing at targets. They stopped in front of the little lane next to her house and he said, "Look, I'll aim for that pot."

"No! That's my—" Too late. *Smash.* Pieces of the pot thumped to the dirt. The geranium landed upside down with snapped flower heads and crushed petals. She took in a deep breath.

Oblivious to Briar's distress, Wheeler hooted his victory.

"Thank you for walking me home," she said stiffly. "But...but you should go back to town. We can't pick up where you left me. I'm not there anymore. I've changed." *Even if it means working every job I can find and begging help from all my friends and acquaintances, I'll find another way to keep the children.*

He looked startled, then smiled. "Till Monday," he said with a wink before turning around and strutting back toward town.

"No, Wheeler," she called out. *Find your voice.* "I'm staying here. You're moving to Burlington on your own."

He turned, cocked his head. Then shrugged. "Okay. See you, Briar."

Briar slowly shook her head as she watched Wheeler walk away. She used to love watching him walk down her lane, knowing he wouldn't get back till dark but knowing he made the sacrifice for her, for them. She sighed. Well, that was it, then. It was over. She wanted it to be over.

"Who was that?" asked Fanny, joining her on the road and craning her neck to see Wheeler's lanky frame headed back into town.

"Someone I thought I needed."

Briar turned around and joined her family feeling lighter than she had in a long time. Despite everything else being the same, she wasn't. All the meetings Ethel had brought her to had given her hope that she didn't have to settle. What she thought was a "this or that" decision had opened up to a third path. And that was a powerful realization. It wasn't marry Wheeler or lose the children. She could use her God-given tools to find another way. It may not be as neat and tidy and it may involve charity from others, but she wasn't feeling trapped anymore.

While she was wrestling with these thoughts, Briar went through the motions of listening to the children's adventures with their ever-growing menagerie. They had added a squirrel that Pansy had been coaxing into the garden with hazelnuts. Her face shone as she talked about his quick little movements. Watching Pansy blossom and enjoy her childhood helped bolster Briar's determination. She had to keep working hard for these little ones.

After the children were tucked into bed, Fanny handed Briar a cup of tea and motioned for them to sit outside on the stoop. The fireflies had begun to flit around in the woods and Briar remembered how she used to pretend they were fairies playing a game of tag or hide-and-seek with one another. She stole a glance at Fanny. Now she knew how far off those fantasies of tiny, carefree fairies were.

She sipped her tea, determined to enjoy her personal victory before she had to work on her most pressing problems again. The children. The spindle. Both needed protecting and she didn't know how to do either, yet. If Wheeler was a weight lifted off her shoulders, these other concerns were weights tied to each leg, dragging behind her, getting heavier with each step.

She'd have to temporarily lay aside her promise to her mam to one day set her feet on Irish soil. That was too big a promise and had the potential to get in the way of decisions she was making now. It had made Wheeler seem so perfect for her and made her blind to other options.

"The boys have probably captured every single one of those beetles at some point this week," Fanny said, breaking the silence. "They capture them in a canning jar and set them by their bed for a night-light. By morning they've all escaped, and the boys are convinced the fireflies team up together to unscrew the cap on the jar when they're sleeping. Every night they try to stay awake to catch them at work." Fanny laughed, wiping tears of mirth from her eyes. "Oh, I'm going to miss them when I leave. I never knew little boys could be so much fun."

"They are dears, aren't they?" Briar mused. Fanny was so good with them. *She would make a lovely nanny.*

"Do you have to leave us? Is there some fairy business that you have to go back to or can you stay? The children love you, I can tell, and it would only need to be until I get settled myself."

Briar held her breath, hoping. Praying. She should have thought of it sooner. Nanny always seemed to be acting out of duty, and now Briar understood why. But Fanny? She was acting out of love. Briar was certain of it.

Fanny was quiet. Finally, she said, "I don't make the decisions. This was the first time I've been allowed to live with people since, well, since Aurora. I'm not very good about hiding who I am. They like me to stay tucked away."

"Would we have to convince Prudence? It would be perfect…unless you don't want to?"

"How were your spindles this week?" asked Fanny, changing the subject.

By now, Briar knew not to push Fanny, but at least a seed was planted. "Great! I'm running more frames than ever before. Maybe we won't have to take out the spindle."

Fanny shot her a look of warning. "Don't let your guard down. I'm still working on how to remove it. You can't keep it."

"All the operatives are staying at their own frames. You might be worried for nothing."

"But girls are still getting sick?"

"A few. But I think it must be the polio after all."

Fanny pursed her lips. "Describe their symptoms again."

"They complain of different things: headache, fever, double vision, aching and weak muscles in their legs."

"I don't know. It's suspicious that at your mill it's only the girls on the spinning floor."

"Yes, but they're not falling asleep."

"We watch and wait, then." Fanny went around the dying petals scattered at the threshold and began to rejuvenate them. "And as a precaution, let's send you back with some old remedies for your sick friends." She picked up one of the briar rose petals and rubbed it between her two fingers. "The tinctures won't hurt anyone, but if the spindle is the cause, they will help heal."

CHAPTER THIRTY-THREE

anny and Mrs. Prince teamed up to put together a basket of home remedies for Briar to bring to those who had fallen ill.

"This one is a special liniment made with Solomon's Seal to rub into their feet and legs," Fanny said, holding up a jar. "The root does wonders for lungs and bruises and sore limbs. And give them this rose hip tea to start working on their insides."

The mention of Solomon's Seal reminded Briar of Henry. No one had gotten word from him since that first round of letters. She hoped he was okay. There had been no reports of shipwreck, so if he was on that boat then he'd made it across. But that was no guarantee he'd made it all the way to Germany.

"Do you know George at the mill?" Mrs. Prince asked.

Briar nodded, thinking back to the night they played Crossed and Uncrossed in the parlor. "We've met."

"Send him back with a message if more girls fall ill and you need additional supplies. He's been filling in for Henry, running errands for us. He'll let us know and we'll bring more remedies. It's no trouble at all."

"Do you think more will get sick?" asked Briar. She'd never lived through an epidemic but had heard plenty of stories from the elders in the community. Mention the words *potato blight* and you'd hear all you ever wanted to about starvation and typhoid and death, and even a few other random illnesses thrown in for good measure.

The two women passed a look between them. "Just let us know," said Mrs. Prince.

After squeezing the children tight—the boys wiggling away too soon for her liking—Briar raced back to town on her bicycle, driven by the worried looks of the valley folk. They might not welcome her back if the illness was spreading for fear of catching it themselves.

When Briar made it back to the boardinghouse, she parked the bicycle in the shed and, taking the basket, found Miss Olive. She was in the kitchen, putting the final touches on the evening meal.

"Briar. Welcome home. You'll be glad to know Sadie is stabilized and will be able to travel home to her parents by the end of the week. Isn't that good news?" Miss Olive washed her hands then dried them on the towel she had slung over her shoulder.

"Yes, very much so." Briar set her basket on the counter.

"The company plans to replace her immediately and we need her bed. Two more girls came down with the illness while you were gone."

"Oh, no. Now who?"

"Two more from your floor. The operatives don't want to come in to work, and the agent is concerned."

"We all are, but what's to be done?"

"Tomorrow the spinning room is getting a good scrubbing."

Miss Olive noticed the basket. "What have you got there?"

Briar pointed out the jars. "Remedies from Mrs. Prince and Fanny. They said to—"

"Briar rose tea and liniment?" Miss Olive hurried to unpack the basket.

"Among other items, yes."

Miss Olive scratched her head. "I don't know why I didn't think of it myself. Must be getting too old for this." She picked out one of the jars. "I'll get started on that tea now. The girls should have a restful night with this in them. Thank you, Briar." She cleared her throat. "Did Fanny send a message for me?" Her tone was light, sing-songy almost.

"No."

"Nothing? No matter how odd-sounding? It might be important, er, to the preparation."

Briar raised her eyebrows. "No. She just said to give you these and you would know why."

"Typical," Miss Olive whispered. "I'd go visiting her and Mrs. Prince for more details if I weren't up to my elbows in problems here." She smacked her elbows for emphasis, sending up a puff of flour that always seemed to surround her. "All the girls who have fallen ill have been on your floor. Makes me curious about what's going on there. Are you worried you might be next?"

An image of everyone crowded around her frame to touch the spindle flittered through Briar's thoughts. She swallowed. "A little."

"I'm sorry. I don't mean to be so insensitive to you operatives who are healthy. I've been so busy keeping an eye on the ill that I've been blind to other things. I clearly missed what was going on with Ethel and I feel terrible about that."

"We all missed it," Briar said. "She hid it well."

"Yes, you girls can hide what you want to, can't you?" Miss Olive pulled out a tray and it clattered on the counter. She looked thoughtful. "One other thing. Have you noticed an older woman loitering around the mill?" Miss Olive held her hand above her own height to indicate that of a potential stranger. "Calling girls over to her?"

"You mean looking for someone? Not recently. But Ethel said she had a mother-in-law. What if she came looking to warn Ethel about her husband?"

"No, Ethel received a telegram from her yesterday to let her know her husband is back home and feeling remorseful over what he did."

"Is Ethel going back to him?"

Miss Olive shook her head. "No, dearie. But she is going to stay with us. She's become a much stronger woman in Sunrise Valley and I'm glad she'll let us help her a little longer. You and Mim have been good friends to her."

"So who is this mystery woman?" asked Briar.

"What woman?" said Miss Olive. She pinched the tea into an infuser and set it in a teapot.

"The one you were asking me about. If I'd seen someone loitering near the mill."

"Oh, I haven't seen anyone. I was asking if *you* had." She pointed to the stack of plates waiting to go out to the tables. "Would you mind getting the girls started setting the table?"

"Yes, ma'am." Briar hefted a stack of plates to the table, wondering if she was in the right boardinghouse. Miss Olive was starting to sound a bit off, like Fanny.

• • •

Monday morning the overseers had the girls scrub the spinning room from top to bottom. At first their work was solemn, thinking about all the operatives missing from their ranks, but as the day wore on, they started singing and visiting with one another, something they couldn't do when all the frames were running.

"Be sure to clean and grease each and every spindle," the overseer had said. He had looked straight at Briar before rubbing his hands and trotting off to put his feet up in his office. "I'll be checking."

The work was tedious, and it took them a long time to complete a frame. Briar had begun with frame number one. She did a good job of cleaning her frames every Saturday, so there wasn't much fluff to find. However, wiping off the grease and applying more was a messy job, and soon she looked and felt as dirty as a doffer.

Finally she'd worked her way to the frame with the fairy wood spindle. She'd already decided that she would not clean it. She'd work as far as the neighboring spindles, but not let her hands go near the wooden one, and hope the overseer didn't check each and every spindle like he said he would.

She slowed down when she got near the wooden spindle, afraid it might compel her to prick her finger. When she was doffing, it was a quick off with the full bobbin, on with the new, and move along. She'd never been tempted to touch the tip.

The other girls started singing "Daisy Bell," a light, fun song. Those who started work as doffers took off their boots and slid on the oily and soapy floor like they did when they were children. It had been a long time since the spinning room had been so joyful.

Briar sang along to relax her nerves. She was now

cleaning the spindles on either side of the fairy wood. Hook in. Pull out. Sing the words. Pass over the wooden spindle. Hook in. Pull out. Sing the words. Breathe.

> *Daisy, Daisy give me your answer do.*
> *I'm half crazy, all for the love of you.*
> *It won't be a stylish marriage.*
> *I can't afford a carriage.*
> *But you'll look sweet upon the seat.*
> *Of a bicycle built for two.*

Briar was past the wooden spindle and she hadn't touched it. Elated, she joined in the circle of girls nearest her as they spun in a circle, singing, "I'm half crazy, all for the love of you."

She thought about how crazy Wheeler had made her. Even though the future was uncertain, she had no lingering regrets. As she continued to dance with the girls on the spinning room floor, her thoughts naturally drifted to Henry, who made her crazy whether he was here fixing her frame with a wink and a smile, or walking her home, showing surprising sensitivity for her feelings. The song seemed made for him. It wouldn't be a stylish marriage, but a life with him would be fun and filled with love.

Briar stopped dancing as she realized the great distance her thoughts had just traveled. She stepped out of the circle watching the operatives play. Was she only feeling this way because he wasn't there? More importantly, would she still feel this way if he came home?

The overseer stepped out of his office to see the commotion. "Inspection!"

The operatives immediately stopped their dancing and scurried to their frames. He started with the frames on Briar's side of the room. He was inspecting every single spindle.

When he got to Briar's wooden spindle, he barely looked at it when he said, "This one is dirty. Do it again." He stood, waiting for Briar to clean it right then.

She took out her hook and rag and, with trembling fingers, pushed the hook in and around the base of the spindle, pulling out a tiny bit of cotton fluff. She wiped it on her rag, hoping that was all the overseer wanted.

"Wipe off the entire spindle. Especially near the tip. It looks like it's not been touched."

Briar swallowed.

"The tip?" she whispered.

A girl named Grace who worked the far side of the room stepped in. She took her rag and wiped the spindle and put on a fresh bobbin. "There you go. A clean spindle." She stood with her arms crossed between Briar and the overseer. "Maybe now you can go pick on someone else. Briar is your best worker, and I can't take it anymore how you single her out."

"Impertinence. This is the last day you'll work here or in any mill. You're fired." The overseer marched into his office, presumably to fill out the paper work.

Stunned, the operatives gathered around Grace.

"Thank you, but you shouldn't have," said Briar. "Now you're out of work."

Grace smiled. "Don't worry about me. Today was my last day anyway; I was quitting and moving to New York. Now I can say I did it with style." She twirled a little pirouette. "Stick together, ladies!" she said before following the overseer to pick up her final paycheck.

The spinning room was now cleaner than the day it had been built. The operatives were eager to return to the usual routine, and their spirits were high, convinced that they had gotten rid of whatever germs were lurking.

• • •

But they were wrong.
During the rest of the week, one by one, more girls in the spinning room started to complain of headaches. Then their faces turned flush. And then, finally, they collapsed in sickness and were carried home to their boardinghouses.

Grace was the first one to collapse that night at her going-away party.

CHAPTER THIRTY-FOUR

The knot that had been forming in Briar's stomach twisted tighter. How could the spindle be making the girls sick? They were all over seventeen and none had pricked a finger. It made no sense for these other girls if Briar was the targeted one, and she didn't have so much as a runny nose.

The doctor was convinced it was polio, but Briar didn't think so anymore. There were so many girls ill now that Miss Olive turned the whole first floor into an infirmary. The healthy ones sat around in the parlor, postulating about who would be next. The parlor game players had met during the beginning of the week, but as the number of sick girls climbed, the games weren't as much fun, and they spent more time talking about illness and worries than laughing over who was cheating at Tiddledy Winks.

Friday morning, Briar found George and sent him into the country with a message for Mrs. Prince: *We need help.*

When Briar arrived at the boardinghouse for dinner, she found Fanny and Miss Olive conspiring in the parlor,

Fanny looking guilty and Miss Olive frustrated.

"The children?"

Fanny stood, straw hat in hand. "They're fine, dearie. With the Princes. The Mrs. sent me with the remedies." She indicated the pile of baskets gathered on the floor of the parlor.

Miss Olive stood and took two baskets with her. "I'd better get started. Girls?" she called to the returning operatives. "Hurry up and eat."

"Are you staying the night in town?" Briar asked Fanny.

"Oh no, I'll stay long enough to help Miss Olive with the ministrations, but I'll be back to the children by nightfall. Don't want them to worry. Although, I'm sure they are having fun at the farm. I'm afraid they'll try to talk the Princes out of more animals if I leave them too long."

"How do you travel so quickly from place to place?" Briar asked.

"Oh, I have my ways." Fanny winked.

Briar's curiosity was piqued. How did a fairy travel? Via the wind, according to Briar's mam.

"Now, you wouldn't consider moving out to the cottage until this…this trial has passed, would you?" Fanny asked. "The children would love to have you home for longer than a speck, and you've only got two more working days until your birthday."

"I'd get fired for breaking my contract if I didn't show up for work."

"Take special care, then. I haven't been able to find Isodora, but she's bound to be close and watching. She'll be getting anxious that you haven't pricked your finger yet. Especially after all she's put into escaping my surveillance, finding the spindle, and then finding you. All too perfect for her to walk away from. You won't expect her tricks, so be extra careful. If you feel weak about touching the spindle, feign illness and go home. In fact…" Fanny felt Briar's forehead. "I think you've got a fever. Let's get you home now." She grabbed Briar's arm and started to tug.

"Maribelle. I can't leave her. Don't worry. I'll be careful, and in a few more days, I won't need to be so timid around the spindle. I'll be seventeen and can help you get it off the frame without fear of sudden death. Then you can take it back to wherever it came from."

Later that afternoon, Maribelle was doffing as usual when a movement caught Briar's eye. It was quick, but after years of intervening in the twins' mischievousness, Briar could sense when a little one was about to be foolish. Briar turned her full attention to the girl. She was pushing her cart of bobbins down the aisle when, quick as anything, she pulled the bobbin off the wooden spindle and then reached out with her other hand to run a finger along the spindle.

"Maribelle, don't!" Briar cried out, but she was too far away to be heard above the machines. Briar ran for the girl, but she wasn't in time to stop her from licking the sticky sweetness off her finger. Shaking the startled girl, Briar yelled, "What did you do?" She pulled her kerchief from her pocket, dropping the blue silk onto the oily floor. "Spit," she demanded, handing Maribelle the cotton handkerchief while Briar picked up the silk one.

Maribelle complied, keeping her head low. "Sorry, Briar. I know you didn't want me near the spindle, but it was a dare. I had to do it."

Briar bent down so she could look Maribelle straight

in the eye. "What do you mean?" She used the blue silk kerchief to wipe the tears from Maribelle's cheeks.

"The other girls dared me to do it. Said they all had, when we weren't looking. I didn't 'cause I didn't want you to be angry, but today, I couldn't help it. It's all I've been thinking about and I couldn't stop myself. I wanted to know what the syrup tasted like. They all said it was the best thing they'd ever tried."

Even though she knew the answer, Briar had to ask. "What other girls?"

"The spinner girls. It's a game they play when you're gone or not looking and the overseer's in his office."

Briar immediately shut down all her frames and dragged Maribelle to the drinking bucket. "Rinse out your mouth now. Keep rinsing till I tell you to stop."

That had to be the connection. Sadie, foolish girl, was the first to lick the sticky residue and the first to come down with symptoms of polio. But it wasn't polio at all. At least not for the girls in the spinning room. It probably was polio in the outside cases, like the farm boy, but for the girls who'd taken the dare to sneak past Briar to her spindle, well, those girls were reaping the curse from *Sleeping Beauty*. Her spindle was poisoning everyone. There was no doubt now. She had to get it out of the mill immediately.

"I'm sorry, Briar. Truly I am."

"Rinse. Don't you dare swallow."

The overseer saw them and marched down the row. "Why are your frames off?" he yelled. "We can't afford any shutdowns. There are enough still frames as it is with all you weak girls falling sick."

"They'll be back on in a minute, sir. Just taking care of the wee one here."

"Another one? Is she ill?" The overseer peered at them with interest.

"Not yet," Briar said. She hoped she'd gotten the poison out quickly enough.

Briar guided Maribelle back to the frames and threw the shipper handle. "I'll doff for you the rest of the day," she told the girl. "You go see Miss Olive—do you know which house is hers?"

Maribelle nodded.

"Tell her Briar sent you for some of her special tea. And you let her know if you start to feel feverish."

Briar stood, hands on hips, staring at the bobbin covering the wooden spindle. Threads whirred up and down, up and down, so smoothly it was mesmerizing to watch. After finally solving her frame's problem, she'd have to get it out. The spindle was too much of a menace. If the operatives had turned it into a game, it was only a matter of time before it turned deadly.

While Briar watched over her frames, she waited for the opportunity to remove the wooden spindle. Since it was firmly attached to the frame, she'd have to knock it out. And if she couldn't knock it out, she'd sneak back in somehow and light it on fire to burn it out.

There'd be no good way to explain her broken frame to the overseer, and with his temper, she'd likely be fired, and then labeled a troublemaker. She'd never find work in a mill again.

Even knowing she was doing the right thing, her heart weighed heavy. She'd worked so hard only to have her plans unravel on her. Perhaps she could get a job as a domestic servant, but that wouldn't make her enough money to support both her and the children. Pansy would have to get a job as a doffer to help. It was everything she didn't want to happen, but it was the way it had to be. She couldn't risk sacrificing the operatives' lives for her family's happiness.

When the overseer went to the farthest corner of the room, Briar found the discarded metal spindle and used it as a wedge against the other spindles. She might damage the machine, but she planned to pop the wooden spindle out, or break it, or… She pulled and grunted with all her might but it would. Not. Budge.

She adjusted her grip and tried pushing the metal wedge to snap it off. Not one splinter. Briar hit the spindle with all her might to no avail.

She wiggled it at the base, but it held fast. Even after all that pounding, it wasn't a bit loose. The bell rang and the girls shut down their frames. Briar dawdled until the room had cleared out. She bent down close to examine the spindle. *How am I going to remove it?* She pushed then pulled, trying to see if it had a weak spot.

"Hey, what are you doing there?" called the overseer.

Briar jumped, pricking her finger on the tip of the spindle.

She whirled around, automatically putting her finger in her mouth and sucking the pinprick of blood. She turned back around and replaced the bobbin. "I was just leaving." She scurried out of the room and ran down the stairs. *Oh no, oh no, oh no.*

As soon as she was outside, she spat and spat until there was no moisture left in her mouth. Her fingertip was red from her sucking and a dark red pinprick revealed the spot where she'd accidentally touched the tip of the spindle.

The others had ingested the poison, but she had sent it right into her bloodstream. She hadn't immediately fallen asleep, though, like Aurora in the fairy tale. Or dead. Fanny was right, the curse was weak. Maybe she wouldn't die. Maybe the tea and liniment would help her, too.

She ran for the boardinghouse, the pain in her head growing with each step.

A crowd had already gathered outside in the shade of the porch. Seemed it was still too hot to be inside.

"You look flushed, feeling okay?" asked Mim, taking a step back.

Miss Olive felt Briar's forehead. "You are a bit warm. Any other symptoms? Mim, go get Miss Fanny."

"She's still here? I've no other symptoms, but I suspect they will show up soon." Briar thought about the progression from headache, to fever, sore throat, to leg paralysis, then weeks of recovery... At least she hoped there would be a recovery.

Miss Olive pulled her into the shade. "What happened?"

Briar shook her head. She couldn't tell her boardinghouse keeper that she pricked her finger on a magical spindle. Instead of calling for the doctor, they'd be sending Briar to an asylum.

"I'm here. What's happened?" Fanny ran to Briar's side. She felt Briar's forehead. "Miss Olive, please find us a ride to the cottage. We need to leave as soon as possible. Mim, get me a cold cloth."

Her orders dispatched, Fanny focused her attention on Briar. "Was it the spindle?"

Briar nodded. "It was an accident. The overseer startled me." She rubbed her temples. The pressure was setting in, making it difficult for her to think. "They're getting sick from that sticky substance on the spindle. The girls are licking it."

"They what?" Fanny sounded shocked. "I thought maybe that one girl was addled in the brain. The rest followed suit?"

"It became a dare to the other girls to get by me and taste the syrup from the spindle."

"So that is how it's being spread."

"Maribelle," Briar whispered. She gripped Miss Fanny's arms. "She lives in the shanties on the edge of town with her family. She's only ten and she completed the dare today. Such a wee thing, it's bound to affect her quickly. I-I made her spit and rinse her mouth." Briar should have taken better care of the child. As much care as she would have given to Pansy.

"Miss Olive is taking care of Maribelle. Briar? *Briar.* Stay with me."

Fanny's voice was growing faint, her face dark, as if Briar was falling into a deep tunnel, falling further, falling faster, falling deeper. She couldn't move, only fall.

Fanny felt Briar's forehead again. "Oh dear. It's starting."

Chapter Thirty-Five

What happened next all came in a blur. There was Ethel, who bundled Briar up and sat beside her in the wagon. Briar had no idea whose wagon it was; the sun was too bright in her eyes, making them tear up in pain. There were voices, but it sounded like they were talking underwater. Distant and distorted. A wet cloth was pressed to her forehead, but soon the cloth was as hot as her skin and offered no relief.

She tried to keep her thoughts and prayers focused on little Maribelle, but her mind kept slipping into nothingness. When a bump jostled her, she woke, only to wish she hadn't. She tried to lift her head to see what was crushing her lower legs. They hurt and she wanted the weight off, but her mouth wouldn't say the words. A moan finally escaped and Ethel got busy wiping her brow again.

"It's hitting her faster than the others," Ethel said. "I'm worried."

Next thing Briar was aware of was being carried, feeling the gentle *thump, thump* of footsteps. It reminded her of when she was a child and her dad would carry her off to bed if she'd fallen asleep in the wagon. It was a comforting feeling, even if her body felt aflame. She was transferred to her bed, and refreshingly cool water was applied to her forehead.

"I'll take it from here," said Fanny. "Thank you, dears."

"I have to get back, but you should stay. For when she wakes up." The voice was Ethel's.

"No. No, I can't. I'm leaving, too."

A deep voice. A man's voice. Henry? Could Henry be home and back at the cottage? Oh Henry. It would be good to see him again. She missed him terribly. Missed the way he would tease her on their walks. How kind he was to the children. Henry, sweet Henry.

"I have to leave for Burlington." He brushed her hair away from her forehead. "I'm sorry you're hurting. Get better soon, okay?"

A flash of light as the door opened, then back to darkness. A jingle of reins and clomp of hooves. *Wheeler*. It was Wheeler who carried her in. But he wasn't staying.

Where was Henry? He was missing. He was the one who should be here. Why wasn't he here? He loved it here.

And where were the children? She couldn't hear them playing. It was too quiet in the little cottage, as if everyone were holding their breath.

She tried to tell them it would be okay, but her mouth wasn't working. So hot. So raw. She tried to fight the darkness but it was too strong. She let it overtake her.

• • •

When she came to next, there was a glow of candlelight and hushed voices of the children and scraping of plates. It was comforting to be home with family, even if she wasn't at the table with them. She turned her head, letting her eyes adjust to the light. Even the dim, smoky haze was too much for her sensitive eyes, and she closed them again, but not before Benny saw her.

"She's awake."

"Briar?" Pansy came over, her sweet voice thick with concern. "Are you alive?"

Briar forced herself to smile. At least she hoped it was a smile. Her body didn't seem to be responding to the commands she tried to give it.

"Fanny, look. She's okay."

"All right, child. Come away and finish your supper."

"Will we get polio, too?" asked Jack. Last winter both boys came down with the chicken pox and, once the worst was over, thought it great fun to be allowed to eat and play in bed. Until they grew so restless they were begging to be let outside.

"No, dearie. What Briar has can't be caught. You'll be fine."

While everyone was distracted, Briar tested out her limbs. Her legs hurt and she couldn't move them no matter how hard she tried. She couldn't tell if she was moving her toes at all. But her arms allowed her to slide herself up on her pillow. They ached a little and this worried her. What if the paralysis worked its way up even farther? To her lungs? Her heart?

Briar must have drifted off again, because the next thing she knew, Fanny was bustling around the room, putting up dishes and hustling the children to bed. Once gentle snores indicated the children had fallen asleep,

Fanny came over, a cup of tea in hand.

"A good, strong briar-rose tea. Not at its full strength this time of year, but it should slow the progression of the poison," she said. "Good thing I make it a habit to grow a variety of roses no matter where I am, don't you think?" Fanny helped Briar sit up with extra pillows, enough to drink without spilling. The extras would have come from the children's beds. Bless those wee ones for sharing.

While Briar sipped, Fanny lifted the blankets and applied liniment to Briar's lifeless legs.

It was a strange sensation. Briar couldn't feel the touch on her skin, but there was pressure and it hurt from the inside out. She winced.

"Sorry, dearie. It must be done."

Briar gritted her teeth. Fanny had the boniest fingers.

"I know your throat is sore; don't try to talk." She paused, and Briar nodded for her to continue. "Even after all you knew, you still pricked your finger on the spindle."

Nod. Briar held up her finger, showing the spot of blood.

"How does she do that?" Fanny whispered. She sighed and rubbed liniment on the spot. "Too late for this, but it won't hurt."

Briar held back her tears. All those years of avoiding any mill accidents only to be pricked by a spindle. And of the thousands of spindles, Briar had to go and prick herself on the one that could cause her the most harm.

"Well, you're not dead yet," Fanny stated matter-of-factly. "For that, we can be thankful. As long as there is life there is hope, yes? Let's go over everything again and see if we didn't miss something important."

Briar closed her eyes, trying to concentrate on Fanny's voice over the pain.

"As the youngest fairy, I always have to wait until the end to give my blessings to the babies. And tiny Aurora—she was a sweet little babe—had been given such wonderful ones already. My blessings had been taken: beauty, cleverness—that's my favorite—and singing. I was slow trying to come up with something unusual and the other fairies—there are several of us—were getting impatient. You should have seen Prudence! Was she ever giving me *the look*. I'm sure you've seen it."

Briar managed a smile. Yes, she did know the look.

"Is that the blue silk?" asked Fanny, reaching to pull it out of Briar's pocket. "I forgot all about the cloth. I'm cleverer than folks give me credit for. Have you been using this to protect yourself? It provides a small barrier to Isodora's magic."

"When I put the spindle on the machine, I had it wrapped in the cloth, to hide it." Briar paused to swallow. "I thought maybe it would look like I was cleaning my frame. I hadn't physically touched the spindle at all until today."

Fanny tucked the cloth back in Briar's pocket. "Is the light hurting your eyes?" she asked. She blew out a candle, dimming the room even more. White smoke rose in a swirl and looped around Fanny's head. Fanny watched the smoke, her eyes growing distant. She let out a deep breath. "Seems I lost track of the evil one, and that made the others nervous. And a bit angry with me." She held up her hands in a stop motion. "In my defense, I told them I wasn't the best fairy to put on the job, but the others didn't want to be tied down. And since I'm the youngest, it seems I have to do what they say.

"They're always giving me the worst jobs—not this one. Goodness, I don't want you thinking that watching you and the children is on the same level as tracking Isodora. No, no. This"—she looked around the room with a contented smile—"is a privilege." She sighed, and a hint of wistfulness escaped. "This I would like to keep doing, for your sakes and mine. I knew children were fun, but my, oh my." She giggled. "You wouldn't believe what the boys did to Mrs. Clover. She came by for tea and they tried to hide under the table to listen to the grownups talking. We let on like we didn't know they were there—who knew she was such a sport?—but with them knocking our knees and the whispering, it was like a barrel of squirrels had infiltrated the house."

Fanny appeared to get lost in her thoughts and Briar prompted her with a whimper.

"Sorry, dearie. How is that tea?" She looked into Briar's almost empty cup. "Drink it all. Now, where was I? Oh, yes. My history with Isodora. Well, while I was dreaming up my gift for Aurora, Isodora arrived in the great hall. Late and angry. Past angry. There was no reasoning with her. Personally, I think she was just looking for a reason to be mean. There was no need for her to curse the princess with death. Nor to have her parents live every day in fear of when it would happen.

"The whole family was at the party, pleased as anything a princess had been born. The family is prone to boys, you know, so she was special, even for a princess. There were platters of fruit and quail and currant cake. It was a party like the kingdom had never seen before. You know the story, yes? Isodora was left off the invitation to the christening—serves her right for staying away for so long. We'd all forgotten about her, though even if we remembered, we still wouldn't have wanted her. She's impulsive and spiteful and ruins everything. Her pride is so easily offended. Before I was able to give my blessing to the child, Isodora cursed her, then left in a huff.

"That's when I had my great idea. I couldn't change the curse, but I could soften it. Aurora didn't have to die; she would just sleep for as long a life as she would have had, and then wake up and lead a new life. Clever, wasn't it? Not everyone agreed with me. Some of the others thought if they had the chance they would have come up with something better, but I doubt it. You'll find that a lot of the fairies are too proud for their own good."

Fanny took the empty cup from Briar. "Good girl. It won't make you feel better, but you won't get worse for a while yet. I'm good at delaying things. Your Nanny is good at tracking things. I suppose that's what I started to tell you. When Isodora got away from me, I came straight to Prudence. Now you can understand why she had to leave so suddenly."

"What do you mean 'got away from you'?" The words sounded dry to Briar's ears.

"Well, when Aurora—the silly girl—even after we told her and told her, still pricked her finger, she fell asleep instead of dying. As you may already know, she slept for almost one hundred years. She awoke after a brave and handsome prince—through my prompting, by the way— found her and kissed her. Everything would have been fine after that except for one small problem." Fanny suddenly looked deeply interested in the china pattern on the cup.

"What?"

"I didn't realize that by stopping Isodora's curse, I was tying up her magic in the spindle. It took her a while to figure out why she could only do little bits of magic, but was so limited when it came to the big things. Poor thing couldn't kill anyone, what was she to do? But after she figured it out, oh was she livid. And, unfortunately for me, because it was my blessing that stopped her curse, well, we have an unusual connection. I always know where she is. At least, I did until she got away from me.

"She has always been very good at hiding. That's why we all forgot about her that one time. If a person doesn't want to be found, she shouldn't be so upset when she doesn't get invited to a party, don't you think?" Fanny shook her head, clearly irritated by Isodora's lack of manners.

"How do you keep track of her?"

"Until a few weeks ago she and I could sense each other. I could tell it irritated her, but one day—nothing. I came to Prudence."

"And how is Prudence to find her?"

"Our fairy magic has a scent. Isodora's is quite strong, especially since she likes the stronger magic. And there is a faint color given off. Again, more so when the magic is big. You probably haven't noticed mine as it matches the smell and color of the primrose. Isodora's magic usually leaves behind a nasty sour apple smell." Fanny wrinkled her nose.

"What if Isodora can change the scent the way she changes her look?"

Fanny frowned and snapped her fingers. "That would be just like her to figure out something like that. Prudence wouldn't know what to track if it was different."

Briar's head hurt with trying to think about it. The pulsing behind her ear was like the pounding of the looms located above the spinning room. Relentless.

"I don't know why Prudence was the one who ended up with you children," Fanny said. "I was surprised to find her here in a house filled with young ones. Not her usual activity, if you know what I mean. She's not a bit motherly.

It should have been someone else." She felt Briar's forehead.

"Poor dearie. These cloths are as fevered as you are. Let me cool them off with fresh water from the well. I'll be right back."

Fanny flittered out the door, leaving Briar fading in and out of consciousness. What was dream and what was reality? Fairies. Sleeping Beauty. Curses. Spindles. Tired, so tired. Rest. It was time to rest.

CHAPTER THIRTY-SIX

Briar began to stir back to consciousness again. A warm light. A new smell, one of fresh air and freshly cut wood. She blinked her eyes open and felt like she was still dreaming. There was a handsome stranger leaning over her. He had tanned skin and rich brown eyes framed in shaggy hair falling against his cheeks. She blinked again in time to see the boy grin.

A recognizable grin.

"Henry Prince, is that you?" Her mouth was dry and she didn't know if the words were formed correctly. At least her throat wasn't on fire today. She struggled to make her limbs obey and push herself up, but she hadn't the strength.

"Sorry, I knocked on the cottage door, but no one answered," he said. He stood tall, blocking the bright light streaming in from the front door. The curtains dividing the room had been held back and Briar could see the entire cottage from her bed.

"I let myself in to surprise you all, and here you are

surprising me. What are you doing sleeping in the middle of the day?"

Briar smiled, or at least tried to. She couldn't tell if her body was obeying her commands or not. Henry Prince was home. There was so much to tell him. He was obviously freshly returned and hadn't heard what had gone on in town.

"Well, get up and welcome your old chum." He held his arms out as if waiting for a hug. "I would have been here sooner, but with the railroad strike, it took some doing. Can you tell where I've been, lass?" He emphasized the word "lass" like it was a clue.

"She can't get out of bed," Pansy said, standing in the doorway. Her arms were loaded with a basket of fresh pickings from the garden. "She can't hardly move at all." Pansy set down her basket, and then poured a cup of tea.

A look of concern marred Henry's tan and rosy face. "What do you mean?"

"She's got the sleeping sickness." Pansy brought the tea to Briar and helped her sip.

The sweet liquid took away some of the dryness in Briar's throat. "Polio," Briar said, quick to explain. "A bunch of us mill girls came down with it. I'm the worst. They're all starting to recover, but I'm…not."

"Are you sure it's polio? How long have you been like this?"

Briar glanced at Pansy. "The doctor hasn't confirmed my case, but he's examined the others," Briar said. "Mine came on yesterday."

"What about Fanny? Does she think it's polio?"

"Fanny's not the doctor," Pansy said. "Do you have any sore places, Briar? I could heat up more warm cloths for you."

"I'm fine. You can go play with the boys. Henry can get you if I need anything."

"Don't tell them I'm back yet. I'd like to talk to Briar first," he said.

Pansy nodded then reluctantly went back outside.

"Pansy has been a wonderful nursemaid for me," Briar said. "I think she feels she can save me. She's scared I'll die like Mam and Da."

Henry pulled up a chair and held Briar's hand. "You're not going to die. Don't even think it."

"I feel it moving up my body," Briar said, and she couldn't hide the tremble in her voice. She'd not told the others because she didn't want them to worry, but she knew Henry could be strong for her. He always had been. "When it gets to my lungs I won't be able to breathe. There's nothing else to be done but wait." She swallowed. "It's so good to see you, Henry. I never thought I'd lay eyes on you again."

"Don't talk like that."

"What about the letter? Were you able to find my aunt?"

Henry shook his head. "I tried. I found someone who knew your family. An old farmer who thought they'd all left at the same time, but then his wife corrected him. Said your aunt and her husband left a few weeks after your mama did. They were going for work in the factories in England."

"That must be why they lost touch. Neither had a home, so their letters couldn't find each other."

She took another sip of tea. Her throat burned, but she needed to talk more. "I got your gifts. The acorn, the heart-shaped pebble, Solomon's Seal."

He grinned. "How did you know they were from me?"

"I don't know how you did it, but only you would have

given me those things. Tokens from the valley you love. Plus they were left in that spot you always tap on my frame when you're leaving."

He looked pleased that she noticed. "I didn't want you to forget about me, so I found an accomplice."

Briar started to cough, which hurt her lungs and made her wince.

Henry stood. "Are you all right?"

She held up a hand. "I'm okay now. Was Fanny your accomplice?"

"Yes. How did you know?"

"Something she said." *That's why she told me she was a fairy. She knew what I'd done with the spindle because she was there leaving me a gift from Henry and saw what I did.*

Henry began pacing between the bed and the door. "When did everyone start getting sick?"

"A few weeks ago, but never mind that. You're back. I want to hear all about the big adventurous world out there. Come sit and tell me." She looked around him to the pack he'd left by the door. It was much fuller than when he left. "What did you bring home?"

He looked back at the bag. "I have a gift for you." He took a step toward her. "But, I'll save it for later when you're feeling better."

"There might not be a later."

"Well, I'm not going to show you now. I believe you're stubborn enough to get better if only to look inside that bag."

Briar struggled for a breath. "Maybe."

Henry continued pacing. "I was all set to tell you of my adventures, but it doesn't seem appropriate now, with you so ill. How can I help? Where is Fanny?" He paced over to the door and scanned the valley.

"I'm sure Fanny will be along soon. Meanwhile, your tales of adventure are exactly how you can help."

He nodded. "All right." He poured himself a glass from the water jug and pulled up a chair from the table. "After I left you at the train station, I traveled to the east coast where I boarded a strong sailing vessel. You should see New York, Bri. I've never seen so many people meeting in one place before. The captain told me there were more than a million and a half people living there, and I believe him.

"The ship was sturdy, but I wasn't. I'm no sailor, that's for sure. I've never been so happy to see land in my life. When the ground is taken away from you, you sure miss it."

Briar closed her eyes. Henry didn't know how right he was.

"A huge storm picked up halfway through the trip and even the seasoned sailors were praying for deliverance. They made all passengers go below decks as wave after wave crashed over top. It was as if the sea were trying to spit up everything in it, and take us down at the same time."

"How terrible," Briar whispered.

"After we made it across the Atlantic and landed in Southampton, I stepped off that ship with a skip in my step and my burdens all gone. My parents had letters they wanted me to deliver to our family near the Black Forest in Germany, so I made my way there." He stroked her arm. "Are you sure you're up to this? Would you rather rest?"

"Keep going." She opened her eyes. She could hardly believe Henry was back. He was the same boy who left months ago, but not. He was taller, shoulders broader, his face thinner, more determined-looking than it used to be. This felt right, him sitting here with her. She never wanted him to leave again. He was home.

She worked to keep a look of peace about her as her mind fought her body for control. *Breathe. Breathe.* Her lungs rebelled, wanting instead to stiffen and not allow air through.

Henry continued to describe his trip through Europe, and Briar closed her eyes, focusing on his voice and her next breath. How had she lived when he was gone? She'd noticed the hole he'd left right away, but now that he was back, she was hit with how much better life was with him in it. Not only was he a part of the valley, he was a part of her. They may not share the same heritage but they shared so many other things—most importantly, the same heart.

When she felt herself drifting off to sleep, Henry grabbed her hand again and she squeezed it. *Thank you.*

There was a rustling at the door and in walked Fanny, her hair a bit ruffled. "Oh. You're back," Fanny said. She worried the apron in her hands.

Pansy ran in after, out of breath. "Where were you, Miss Fanny? I was looking everywhere for you."

Fanny glanced at the girl, then back at Henry, looking like she wanted to say more. "How was your trip?"

"Successful. I thought," Henry said hesitantly, returning eye contact with Briar.

"Run along outside, now, Pansy. I think it's time to feed the chicken." Fanny gave Pansy a little push.

Pansy frowned and looked to Briar with pleading in her eyes. She knew she was being sent out so they could talk about things they didn't want her to know.

Briar nodded. *Yes, sweet Pansy, you need to go.*

Reluctantly, Pansy walked out as slowly as she could.

Fanny followed behind and shut the door.

"What is Briar really sick with?" Henry asked. "Is it polio like the doctor thinks?"

Fanny shook her head. "No, dearie." Her voice was sad, almost defeated. So unlike the bubbly Fanny they had grown used to.

"How bad is it?"

Fanny held his gaze. "Quite."

Henry's face paled and he ran a hand through his hair. "No. It couldn't be." He stood. "I did just what you said. I filled the box with rocks and locked it."

He dug under the collar of his homespun shirt and pulled out a fancy scroll key on a chain. "I waited until we were crossing the deepest part of the ocean and threw it in. I watched it sink, and waited a full day, two days, three days. Nothing. I thought it worked. How could it end up back here? If anything, it should have found me. I was the closest. How does that blasted thing keep ending up here?" He gripped the back of his neck, staring up at the ceiling.

"What are you talking about?" Briar asked. He didn't mention any of this in his accounting to her, and what did it have to do with her illness?

"I hoped it would work this time, too," Fanny said.

"This is worse than not working out." Henry pounded the table. "Now she's being punished." He pointed at Briar. "She's innocent. It should be me lying there."

Fanny pushed her hands down in a calming motion. "You had a good plan. We were right about one thing, the curse is weak. Since my connection with Isodora has thinned I thought it was time to try, too. Don't be so hard on yourself. I think it was a trick. She found some way to get around our connection." She slapped his shoulder. "It's time we forge ahead," Fanny said. "I've come from the mill. The spindle is set firm into Briar's spinning frame and I can't get it out. Isodora gave it to her, so she's still here somewhere."

Realization forced its way through Briar's muddled brain. Henry knew. Henry Prince knew everything.

He let out a deep breath filled with anger and frustration. Then he turned to her, his eyes sad. Before Briar could register his motives, Henry leaned down and kissed her, full on the lips. The sensation was cold from the water he'd been drinking but soft with tenderness. He pulled away, his eyes searching hers.

"Well?" he asked. His hand still cupped the back of her head where he had grabbed her to lift her lips to his, and his face hovered inches from hers. "Do you feel anything?"

CHAPTER THIRTY-SEVEN

Briar lay stunned, staring back into Henry's deep gaze. The kiss happened so quickly she didn't know what to think or feel. She certainly didn't have time to feel any fluttering in her stomach or the warmth of a kiss inside, or even a quickening of her pulse.

"Wh-what kind of non-romantic question is that?" Briar said. If a boy was to kiss a girl for the first time, he should try harder to make it meaningful.

Looking disappointed, Henry gently pulled his hand away and tucked the patchwork quilt around her.

He shrugged at Fanny. "I've failed in every way. My kiss didn't even heal her."

Briar blinked. "You thought you could heal me with a kiss?" Okay, that was a *little* romantic, even if the setup was lacking. "Fairy tales are best left to children," she said. Hot tears flooded her eyes and she turned to face the wall. How humiliating to be so hopeless that Henry had to resort to kissing her in a final attempt to save her.

"Maybe she needs Wheeler," Henry whispered to Fanny,

but Briar could hear him. Now her face truly burned. She did *not* need Wheeler.

"No, dearie, it's an old curse, and therefore unpredictable. I can't say if the kiss would have worked even if you were grounded properly." She stamped her foot on the worn wood planks. "This floor feels all wrong. I can't believe it, but Miss Prudence forgot to set the foundation. She never forgets anything. Humph. Must be old age—but don't tell her I said so."

Briar stole a glance to see Fanny nudge Henry back to the bed. "Take her out into the woods and tell her your part of the story. It'll make you both feel a whole lot better and give me time to think."

"I can't walk," Briar reminded them. "I can't even stand. My legs are asleep."

Henry shook his head. "They only think they're asleep. We have to convince them otherwise. I can help."

Briar tried not to be annoyed. The last thing she wanted to do was attempt to walk in front of Henry. He really didn't understand what was happening to her. Or maybe he did. The kiss had distracted her. He knew about the spindle. Which meant her early suspicions that he knew Fanny were correct, too. He knew all about Fanny. And he hadn't told her any of it.

"That's kind of you, but no. Thank you. I'd rather stay here." She smoothed a wrinkle in the sheet with her fingers, pretending that even that much motion was no big deal.

"You can sit, can't you?" Fanny retorted. "May as well get some fresh air." She exited the door and then returned with a wheelchair. "From town," she said. "It's a bit dusty from the walk up the lane, but it'll do."

Briar eyed the set of wheels with distaste. To go from the freedom of a bicycle to the confinement of a wheelchair was too much.

Henry lifted her like a bale of cotton and transferred her to the chair. Her legs wouldn't cooperate, and Fanny had to bend them as best she could so they weren't sticking out too much. So stiff.

They positioned her like a porcelain doll and she couldn't fight them. She wanted to punch and kick and flail her arms in protest, but it took all her energy just to breathe.

"Off you go, then," Fanny said, tucking the patchwork quilt around her.

Briar tried to relax as Henry pushed her along the bumpy path, but it was hard to have so little control. The path was narrow and filled with rocks threatening to bump her right out of the chair. She had to completely trust him to steer clear of the branches and keep her from tumbling over. That he could take care of her in the forest, especially if something were to go wrong.

"Why did you kiss me?" she asked as soon as they were out of sight of the cottage.

"You mean a reason other than I've been wanting to kiss you for months?"

She could sense the grin in his voice. There it was. The old, incorrigible Henry. Never serious.

"Tell me. Life has gotten a bit strange since you left. Nothing can surprise me now." She wanted to hear him say it. To hear him explain how he was not the person she thought he was.

"I will." His voice sounded sad again. "But in the proper place."

After several minutes of silence, and Henry struggling to push the wheelchair over the forest path, he said, "We're nearly there."

"Thank you for the fresh air," Briar consented. "I feel better already." She didn't really, but it had broken the monotony to get out of bed.

They continued on until the path ended. Henry tried to forge his own path, but the wheels got stuck in the undergrowth, nearly toppling Briar out. Without a word, he reached down and scooped her up, bouncing her a few times until she was settled snug against his chest. With great effort she put her arm around his neck. "Where are you taking me?"

"You'll see," he said. His voice rumbled from deep within his chest and her stomach flip-flopped at the sound. She wasn't used to her body reacting this way to Henry. She was used to him being her chum. It didn't matter that he kissed her not twenty minutes ago, it was going to take some time to get used to thinking about him differently. Time she didn't have, but desperately wanted.

His jaw was set in a determined line as he proceeded through the forest. Then he stopped and said, "Here we are."

Briar pried her focus off his mouth to see where he had taken her. It was the place with the hollow tree fallen across a little brook. She drew in a deep breath. She hadn't been back to this place in years. Not since her mother died. If she closed her eyes she could picture Mam bent over the fallen log, arranging the moss for their fairy garden, teaching Briar and also Henry, who insisted on following one day.

"You remembered," Briar whispered, looking up into Henry's eyes. He was grinning like the twins did whenever Briar caught them being especially good. Her gaze dropped to his lips, which were close enough he could kiss her again if he wanted to. *Does he want to?*

Again, her pulse quickened. She wanted to stay snuggled in Henry's arms as long as he could hold her. Too soon, he carefully lowered her to a moss-covered spot on the edge of the glen, and then disappeared back through the woods. He returned with the quilt that had fallen off when he picked her up.

After spreading it on a flat area, he helped her onto the quilt, finally settling himself behind her. He lifted her up so she rested against his chest. "Comfortable?" he asked.

His deep voice rumbled through her back and into her chest.

"Yes," she squeaked.

"Did you know that this was where my family first built a home? When they came to America?"

"I never thought about your family coming to America. Guess I thought they always lived here." She looked around for a stone foundation but didn't see one. "It's so far away from everything."

"Exactly. They wanted to stay away from everyone. But the well they dug dried up in the summers and then they decided it would be better to move closer to the big creek, where the house is now."

"Where did they come from?"

"Now that is where the story gets interesting." He leaned back on his hands.

CHAPTER THIRTY-EIGHT

The woods were silent except the call of two warblers on opposite trees talking back and forth. To Briar it seemed like the one bird was trying to get the other bird to come over to his tree, but his friend was reluctant. Briar waited for Henry to continue. *Breathe in. Breathe out.* He was taking an awfully long time to collect his thoughts.

"I hoped that one day I'd be telling you this story, but I didn't expect it to be like this." He reached out with his hand to indicate her lifeless legs. He wrapped his arm around her waist, and she nestled back against him.

"My family roots go way back to the Black Forest in Germany." He held out his calloused hands. "Not that you can tell by looking at us now, but we come from kings and queens. Back then, my family used to throw the biggest parties. Everyone would come, decked out in their finest, wearing their most expensive jewels, so I've been told. The last party was one to celebrate the birth of a special princess. You see, my family tends to produce boys, boys, and more boys, so the arrival of little Aurora was special."

Briar lifted her head to see Henry's face. "Fanny told me about the story of Aurora. I didn't realize you were related to her. I thought maybe I was, my name being what it is and, well, with what is happening to me."

"Yes, Briar Rose. Your name caused quite a stir when you and your family moved into the valley. Miss Prudence put everyone on alert. Your name was too much of a coincidence for her liking. You know how she prefers life to march along in a particular, unchanging way."

"Is that why you started following me everywhere?"

"What? No. Yes. No." He laughed nervously. "I followed you around because I thought you were pretty. And then when I saw how kind you were to others, the way you are taking care of the children, your tenderness with them, your patience with the boys, I fell hard for you. You are unlike any other girl I know."

Briar's face warmed. She had no idea Henry noticed all those things about her.

"And if it weren't for me," he continued, "you'd be outside playing with the children right now same as always. I should have left well enough alone."

"What are you talking about? You didn't make me prick my finger."

"I'm getting to that. So, you know about Aurora from Fanny's telling. Did she tell you what happened after Aurora woke?"

"Only that Isodora figured out what had happened and was furious about it."

"Yes, but the fairies dealt with her. Aurora was the one left with the problem of the spindle."

"What do you mean?"

"The spindle was still poisoned. The handsome prince, as they like to call my long-ago grandfather, tried to hack it to pieces with an ax, but it wouldn't bust. Aurora tried to burn it in the hottest fire, but it barely singed."

Briar thought of the spindle and the burn mark she had noticed.

"They tried to bury it in the ground, but the earth would shift and spit it back up again. They could not be rid of the thing. It was terrible. They tried for years, and nothing they did would destroy it. They lived in fear of someone in their household pricking their finger. It tempts people to touch it."

"The girls at the mill said it smelled like apple pie."

"Apple pie? I suppose. I always thought it smelled a bit rotten."

Briar wrinkled her nose, thinking of the smell. "Me, too. I didn't know why the girls liked the smell so much. Anyway, I'll tell you about that later. Please continue." Briar put her hand to her throat. It was starting to hurt again.

"Aurora was convinced that the spindle would get its revenge on her daughter. She was scared to have children, but fortunately for her, all her children were boys. Mama thinks the fairies had something to do with that. Even though the family is prone to boys, there has not been a girl born into the Prince family since Aurora."

"That is unusual."

Henry took Briar's hand from her throat and held it, stroking his thumb in circles, taking her mind off the pain. Why did she have to find out now, when it was too late, how good it felt to be in Henry's arms?

He cleared his throat. "Fear grew and spread. The servants gossiped about what was going on at the castle and it began to affect the kingdom. Normally parents push their daughters at princes, hoping to make a match, but no one who knew the story was willing to part with a daughter, even if it meant she would become royalty. The family was shunned, blamed for the problem.

"Many generations later, and many attempts to rid themselves of the spindle, they finally decided to do something drastic. They sent a youngest son to take the spindle to the new land, America, to hide in a remote valley and guard the spindle to his dying days. The legacy of protection would pass to each generation. No one leaving the valley. No one calling attention to themselves. No one tipping off Isodora to the spindle's current location. They would live in poverty and seclusion, the opposite of royalty so as to keep the secret. He was the one who named the area Sunrise Valley in memory of Aurora. She had long passed, and they thought it would be a fitting tribute, since her name means sunrise."

"So your family has been guarding the spindle all this time? At least until Isodora found it." A shiver ran down Briar's body as she remembered speaking with the fairy who wanted her dead.

He shifted, pulling her in tighter. "Cold?" He wrapped his other arm protectively around her, and rested his chin on the top of her head.

Briar nestled in deeper.

"This is the part that's going to be hard to confess," he said. "Know how deeply sorry I am, Briar. I thought I was doing the right thing. My parents tried to talk me out of it, but finally relented after I was so persistent. Perhaps they were as hopeful as I was to rid ourselves of the responsibility. When I saw Fanny here in place of Prudence, I thought you were in danger. Something had changed. We had been protecting you, just in case, for so long, and I panicked. They told me they didn't know where Isodora was, so I wanted to get the spindle as far away from here as possible. As far away from you as possible." His hand squeezed tighter. "The irony is, if I had continued on with my regular life, going to the mill as if nothing was wrong, acting the way my family has for generations, you wouldn't be lying here in my arms now."

Briar lifted her head so Henry could see her face. See that she didn't blame him for anything. See how much she wanted to be lying in his arms.

"You couldn't have known what would happen."

Henry's intense gaze met hers. "But I did. The first time I met Fanny was when my parents told me who we really are. They waited until they thought I was old enough to keep their secret, yet young enough to have not made real plans of my own. Fanny helped explain the seriousness of what we do. They told me the consequences of losing the spindle. She feels responsible herself, since her blessing over Aurora and the spindle continues on in ways she didn't expect."

"Can't you walk away?" Briar asked the question she already knew the answer to. Henry was too dependable to walk away. That's what she loved about him. Everyone else in her life who left, left for good. But Henry came back. Always Henry.

"No. But if the town keeps growing the way it is, we are going to have to move. We're finding too many girls wandering onto our property even though we have fences and all those signs up. Remember that day I brought you home?"

Briar nodded. "I didn't think your mam liked me much."

"I'd never seen her so angry, and with good reason. I came back outside and you were walking in a daze toward the house. You should have seen your face. The spindle was pulling you in."

Briar remembered the jittery feelings she felt while near the house. She thought it was nerves because of the KEEP OUT signs. But it was the spindle. "I had no idea."

"The fairies would come every few years and supervise while we tried to destroy it. The only trial that even came close was when we submerged it in the river. It didn't seem to like the water. It came back to us, but aged. Fanny could feel that the curse had been touched somehow."

"Why does the spindle come back to your family?"

"Prudence thinks it's because of Aurora, her bloodline. The spindle seeks her out and we are the closest thing."

He took a deep breath, his chest rising and lifting her up with it, as if he were helping her breathe. "The day after Fanny arrived, I spoke with her in the woods, told her of my plan. She wants this to end as much as we do."

Briar nodded. That secret meeting was the conversation she overheard.

"I saw an opportunity. It was like a window in time had opened up. There was a change in destiny and I wanted to seize the moment and change my family's future. You helped me with that when you pointed out how strange it was that we never left the valley."

"I shouldn't have said that. I was only frustrated that *I* couldn't leave the valley."

"Doesn't matter anymore. You know already that I dropped the box in the middle of the ocean?"

"Yes. The spindle box."

"You want to know how Isodora could possibly get hold of the spindle from the bottom of the sea? I don't know. There was that storm." He nestled his head in the crook of her neck. "My family will never be rid of it."

"You might be soon," Briar said quietly. "If the curse is fulfilled...if I die...you will be free. Promise me you'll watch out for the children. They love you dearly and I know you'll do right by them, making sure they go to good homes."

"No. No!" Henry squeezed her tight against him, as if trying to keep her alive by sheer will. "We'll all think of something. You have life in you, Briarly Rose, and we're going to think of something."

She didn't want to hurt him, but she had to face reality. "My birthday is the day after tomorrow." What she didn't say was that she felt the poison pressing in on her lungs like fingers looking for a weak spot, and it was getting harder and harder to fight it. *No one can stop the curse now. It's too late.*

CHAPTER THIRTY-NINE

When Briar woke up in the darkness she could tell something was different. What felt like a wall keeping the sleeping sickness steady was gone. The pins and needles feeling was stronger now and once again traveling up her body. Her stomach. Her ribs. It was working its way through her bones and into her lungs, and then it would hit the target—her heart.

Afraid her panic would make the poison travel faster, Briar slowed her breathing and focused on the things that mattered. Pansy. The boys. Henry.

Henry had been so tender with her on the way back to the cottage, and the way he lowered her onto the bed. Even though Pansy was hovering, wanting to care for Briar herself, he plumped up Briar's pillow and tucked her in. Told Pansy she could take the night shift.

Like Briar did while she was spinning, she released what her body was doing and retreated into her mind. She imagined happier days. She looked over at the bundles in the beds near her. The boys. Jack soundly sleeping, but

Benny wrestling with monsters in his sleep. He'd gotten all twisted up in his sheet.

As the sunrise warmed the world and started to brighten the room, Briar drank in Pansy's sweet face. Her long eyelashes restful on her cheeks, her heart-shaped lips, parted open to breathe. She'd been such a help to Briar these last few days. As Pansy rubbed the liniment into Briar's sleeping legs there was a deep concentration etched on her dainty features, as if through force of will Pansy would save her sister.

Briar tested her limbs to see what would move. Not her toes. Not her knees. Not her thighs. She tried to bend at the waist, something she could do yesterday, but her body wouldn't respond today.

Alone, and not having to put up a front for anyone, Briar let herself fall apart. This was it, then. Today or tomorrow was all she had left.

What would you do if you only had one day left to live?

It was a question often asked at the boardinghouse in the middle of the night when room-mates couldn't sleep. Mim had gotten serious and said she'd hop on a train and go home. Ethel's answer made much more sense now. She'd said she'd hold a baby to remind herself that life goes on. Briar couldn't remember what she'd said. It was probably something grandiose like take the children to the ocean and pretend they could see Ireland off in the distance. But now that the reality was in front of her, she realized she just wanted to be. Be still. Be present.

She'd made her peace with God long ago and wasn't scared of what happened after she died. It was the dying part she was nervous about.

"Briar, do you want me to do your hair for church?" Pansy asked. She'd gotten out of bed and had started to pack up the bedroll.

Briar blinked away her tears and smiled wide at Pansy, putting all sad thoughts behind a facade. She shook her head. "I'll not be going today."

"But you always go," Jack said. He yawned as he climbed onto the bed.

"Who's going to keep us from getting in trouble?" Benny asked as he stretched himself awake. "We don't listen to Pansy."

Not pausing from her rolling, Pansy stuck out her tongue at the boys.

Briar touched Jack's hair, wincing as she raised her arm. "You are old enough to stop yourselves from getting into trouble," Briar said. "Behave, and look out for each other."

Briar blinked the sleep from her eyes. She took some experimental breaths. She had a few more hours, she guessed. Her lungs were tight, but the air still eked in. Her face was likely pale, and she hoped the children wouldn't be scared. Fanny should send them away for the night. Perhaps Mrs. Prince could take them in until Briar passed. It was selfish for Briar to want to keep everyone snuggled close to her.

The children were back and had gathered around her bed with big grins. Briar wondered if they'd found another stray animal to bring home. What time was it anyway? She smiled at them.

"They can't fit inside the house, so they made a ring around the yard. Everyone's holding hands and praying for you." Benny bounced on his toes as he spoke.

"Who?"

"The whole valley."

"And Miss Ethel and Miss Mim," said Jack, blushing. He had a little boy's crush on Mim ever since she slipped him those first sweets when they came to town to see where Briar lived.

Mr. and Mrs. Prince came into the cottage with apologetic, worried looks. "How are you, Briar?" Mrs. Prince said quietly.

They must feel as guilty as Henry. How to let them know how genuinely she was touched by their concern? "It wasn't your fault," she whispered. Now she knew why Mrs. Prince didn't want Briar at the farm. It wasn't because she didn't like spinner girls. She was merely trying to protect them.

Briar's attention was drawn to Henry hovering near the door, with Ethel and Mim. They might have news of Maribelle. If Briar were to go to her maker tonight, she'd like to go knowing Maribelle was on the mend.

The Princes expressed their well-wishes while Fanny organized all the food they'd brought: biscuits and eggs and onions and garlic. And what was that? A cake. Fanny met Briar's gaze. Someone had baked her a birthday cake for tomorrow.

Would she be alive to eat it? She looked at Henry with Jack and Benny climbing all over him. If Briar died from the spindle wound, Henry would be free. And she knew he would take care of the children. Not from guilt, but because he loved her family as much as she did.

The Princes excused themselves, opening up space for Ethel and Mim to move in. Ethel sat on Briar's bed. "Miss you back at the house. If you stay away too long I'll take on airs as a lady lounging about with a bed all to herself." She followed Briar's gaze. Grinning, she raised her eyebrows. "It's good to have Henry back, isn't it?"

Briar smiled. It was strange to feel so ill and so happy at the same time. "What have you decided? Are you staying?"

Ethel took a deep breath. "My mother-in-law sent me a letter that he's trying to get help. She thinks he's serious this time."

"You don't?" Briar asked, reading the skeptical expression on Ethel's face.

Ethel looked down at her hands. "His mom doesn't know how many times I've heard that. But for now I'll stay in town. He could have gone into work and claimed my wages, but he didn't. If he comes back I'll leave and go even farther away, but Mim said she'd move with me."

Mim chimed in. "Not that it will come to it. By the by, Miss Olive wanted us to let you know Maribelle will make a full recovery. She was barely sick, not like some of the other girls. We went to see her in the shanties. What a beautiful child she is. We brought her sweets and you'd have thought we brought her the moon."

While Mim caught Briar up on the house gossip, Jack was inching his way around the room, getting closer to them. He especially perked up when Mim said the word "sweets." Mim was pretending not to notice, but when Jack got within arm's distance she reached out and grabbed him, drawing him up onto her lap. "Gotcha, cutie pie." She tickled him until he squirmed away and chased Benny outside in happy embarrassment.

Ethel smiled at Mim. "You'll make a good mom."

Looking surprised, Mim nodded. "Thanks."

"Did you two become friends since I've been gone?" Briar asked. Her voice came out like a hoarse whisper. She hadn't the strength to be louder. While it was nice to have visitors, she needed rest. So much rest.

Mim put her hand on Ethel's arm. "You could say we've come to an understanding of each other. Nothing in life is a given and you really don't know what other people are going through, do you?"

Briar caught Henry's eye. "No, no you don't."

"All right, sweetie." Mim stood, then bent down to give Briar a hug. "I wish we could stay longer, but the sun is on its way down. You get better soon, all right? I don't know how long this truce with Ethel will last." Mim spun around and waltzed out of the room.

Ethel sighed, and started to tuck the quilt around Briar. "Oh, I almost forgot. I thought you'd want some things from the house." She disappeared outside and came back with the patchwork quilt from their bed and the novel Briar had left under her pillow. "The quilt will remind you of your second home and how we are missing you. The novel will remind you that you've left things undone. We've more lectures to attend, you and me." She patted the quilt. "I'll need this back before it turns cold again, so you must get on your feet soon, you hear?" She waved her hand in front of her face like a fan. "Not that it feels like this heat will ever end."

Briar shivered. While everyone else was fanning themselves, she was alternating between freezing and feeling like she was breathing in fire at the same time. She was grateful for the extra warmth Ethel had thoughtfully brought her.

With a final wave, Ethel followed Mim outside. Henry tapped the door edge. "I'll be right back," he said. "I'll just see the ladies off."

Briar nodded, trying to swallow the lump in her throat. Even if she could breathe well, she'd have a hard time watching her best friends leave, knowing it was the last time she was to see them. Amazing how close the three of them had gotten. Miss Olive said she put them together for a reason. She knew all along how much they needed each other.

"She's pale as death!" Mim said as soon as she was out the door, likely not realizing her voice carried. "Did you notice the blue tint to her lips? I didn't want to leave her."

"Henry? What do you think?" Ethel said.

"She's going to be fine. Don't worry. Tell Miss Olive things are as expected here." His voice faded as they walked away from the cottage.

The lump in her throat refused to go away. Briar tried to clear it, but breathing was still difficult. She tried a deep breath but could only manage several short pulls, forcing herself through the pain. Death was progressing. How much longer did she have? When Henry returned, she'd ask him to take the children home with him for the night. He could get them excited about sleeping away from home and then be there to help them grieve.

Pansy came over and collapsed into the chair near Briar's bed. "That was so nice of everyone, but I'm tired." She looked at the piles of food stacked up in the kitchen. "How are we going to eat all that?"

The two sisters looked at each other and started laughing at the rare abundance. Pansy's laugh grew and grew until she was sobbing into Briar's quilt brought from the boardinghouse. Briar stroked her hair in comfort, wishing she herself wasn't the source of this grief.

"I could eat a little now," Briar said, to give Pansy something to do. In reality, Briar had no interest in food. Her stomach wouldn't accept any, and certainly wouldn't process any of it. But Pansy, ever the help, jumped up to look through the goodies.

"Hope you didn't see your surprise for tomorrow," Pansy said, sliding the cake in behind a basket of potatoes. "Mrs. Clover made it, and you know what a good baker she is. She'll tell you so herself," Pansy added. She turned to share another laugh with Briar, but Briar couldn't join her.

The air wouldn't come.

Briar took her first strangled breath, and Pansy was immediately at her side. They looked at each other with wild eyes.

Pansy ran outside.

CHAPTER FORTY

Minutes later the door burst open and Henry was there, kneeling at her side. When Briar reached out, he took her hand in his. His breath came in gasps like he'd just run halfway from town. She was in full panic now. Her focus was gone. She could no longer retreat into her mind; the stress of breathing was all she had. Isodora had won. After all these years the curse would be broken.

"No, no, no," Henry coaxed, eyes fixed on Briar's. "Follow me. Breathe with me." He mimicked taking in deep breaths. "Come on, Briar, breathe with me."

A commotion was going on outside, noises with no meaning, getting louder and louder.

Briar shook her head. *No*. Keep Pansy away. Mim and Ethel okay. *Breathe. Breathe.* She gasped in air, but it burned like sparks and wasn't enough. The sounds died down to silence and Briar wondered if this was the end. She fought for each breath.

A woman in a rose-colored gown, plain bell skirt with layered lace bodice, strode into the room, Fanny at her heels. The woman's silver hair was tucked up into a matching rose-colored felt hat adorned with white flowers. She was aged but held herself proudly as if she refused to believe she was not in the prime of her life. To see her in the street, one would think she was an uptown society lady. But to see her in the country cottage was out of place.

"I tried to stop her." Fanny held out her hands, looking like a frustrated child. Her hair was askew is if she'd been in a fight and a scratch on her cheek was starting to bleed. Beyond the front door were oddly shaped trees, sprung up from nowhere, a dense forest with sharp branches.

Briar could only blink and continue to struggle to breathe. Who was this? Why was she in the cottage, crowding out the air with her smile?

Fanny threw some pebbles above the woman, and in midair there was a burst of pink, a smell of roses, and then the pebbles stretched and joined, transforming into a large silver birdcage with bars encircling the intruder. With a wave of her hand the woman walked through the bars and then sent them to encase an enraged Fanny.

"Let her go, Prince," the woman said. "It's too late now. She'll die, and I'll be released. I can already feel myself getting stronger with each breath she loses. And you'll have to live with the guilt that it was all your fault for losing the spindle."

Isodora. Her turquoise eyes were the same as the peddler's.

"Oh, look. She recognizes me." Isodora tilted her head, examining Briar. "The eyes, isn't it? Eyes are hard to change. Not that I needed a disguise to fool you, but it amuses me to play a role. A peddler is oft more trusted than a gypsy woman, and an overseer can push a spinner girl to her limits."

Briar blinked. Isodora was also her overseer? She imagined dark glasses over the face. Fanny was right, Isodora had been close by all along.

Henry stood protectively between Briar and Isodora. "Undo it. You have no reason to hurt this girl. She isn't a part of this."

"She is now. I've come too far to turn the other cheek, if that's what you want me to do. Silly notion. Your family line hasn't produced a girl since that ugly baby Aurora. It has to be an innocent. Don't blame me, blame them." She pointed at Fanny who was busy trying to break out of her own cage.

"Please," Briar gasped. "The children."

Henry looked pleadingly at Fanny. "Is there really nothing we can do?"

"Stay where you are, Henry," Fanny said. She rattled the cage door. "Love is the only thing that will protect Briar now. Isodora's magic can't get past it. Don't let her intimidate you."

"Where's Prudence? I thought she was coming?" he asked.

Isodora laughed. "Are you talking about that old tracker the fairies sent after me? She's not as good as she used to be. I lost her long ago. Doesn't matter. The Prince family doomed a girl the moment the young one here set foot on a ship. It was only a matter of time before a Prince became reckless. Or forgetful. People's memories are so short. They claim to learn from the past, but they don't. They think they can change destiny, but they can't."

The edges of Briar's vision began to blur. Isodora was smiling. She was happy Briar was dying. She was happy Briar's lungs were on fire and each breath brought sharp daggers edging their way into her heart, leaving tiny cuts behind. But Briar wouldn't stop trying to take a breath. Trying to live.

"There is a world beyond which human eyes cannot see. The elder Princes could tell you that my spindle calls to me. It had been dark for so many years. I'm not sure how you managed that." She looked at Fanny. "Your doing?"

Fanny scowled at her.

"But then one day it called out to me. It was on the move, looking to be free. And the best part?" She laughed. "I didn't know the girl would be this one." She jerked her chin in Briar's direction. "How fitting to find a girl named Briar Rose to exact my revenge." She looked at Fanny as if for agreement. "I couldn't have planned it better."

Fanny deepened her scowl.

"Fanny, please," Henry said. He bent close to Briar. "She can't breathe. What can we do? There must be something."

"Dearies, I'm so sorry. I-I've done all I know to do."

Isodora crossed her arms. "I won. Power lies in one's foundations. The fairies know this. If you could stand on the land of the Old Country you might be able to save her, but this land doesn't know me. It can't touch my curse."

"What do you mean?" For the first time Henry turned his full attention to Isodora.

Briar made a noise, trying to talk. *Get her out.* In her final moments she didn't want this awful stranger standing over her and gloating. She wanted Henry to sing the farewell reel. To release her. Da sang it for her mam, Briar sang it for her da, now it was her turn to let the notes carry her away.

He put a steadying hand on her arm as if to reassure her.

"Is that what you meant when you said I needed to be grounded?" Henry asked Fanny. "Is that the only reason the kiss didn't work?"

Fanny nodded. "She loves you, even if she doesn't realize it herself yet."

Briar's eyes were wide. She did realize it. Ever since Henry came home. Too late, though. And now she couldn't speak the words. Couldn't even breathe them.

But Henry turned back to her with his big grin. He squeezed her hand. "I have something for you."

He leaped up and began searching the room. Pansy was peeking in the doorway, watching it all. "Pansy," Henry said, "where is my bag? I left it here."

"Under the bed. I cleaned up." She stepped into the cottage and inched along the wall, like Jack had done earlier.

Quickly, Henry reached under the bed and pulled out his pack. "I never did give you my gift. Now's as good a time as any."

"Oh isn't this a sweet picture?" mocked Isodora. "A final romantic gesture."

Henry whispered in Pansy's ear. Her eyes opened wide, and she nodded. Then Henry pulled back the sheet covering Briar and reached under to scoop her up.

"Really, Henry," chastised Fanny. "She can see your gift fine lying down. Let the girl be."

But Henry ignored her, first lifting Briar up, and then positioning her so she leaned against his shoulder as he gripped her waist. Her useless legs dragged on the floor like marionette limbs.

"Now, Pansy," Henry said. His voice was urgent.

Pansy reached into the pack and fiddled with something inside. Then quick as a hummingbird she pulled out a small sack and dumped its contents over the floor. Dirt.

Before anyone else moved, Henry stood on the dirt

and kissed Briar with all the strength and passion that the first desperate kiss had lacked.

"No!" Isodora darted forward and shoved the two off the floor and onto the bed.

Briar gasped as she fell, and pulled in enough air to feed her blood. She felt the oxygen push past the poison and enter her lungs. As she breathed out, her mind began to clear.

"You brought me dirt?" she whispered. Henry was still a strange boy who said and did strange things.

He nodded, holding her protectively in his arms. "From Ireland. So you could stand on soil from the Old Country, like your mam wanted for you." His face reddened. "And I mixed it with soil from my family's Old Country. So we could join our histories and have a new beginning based on the old foundations."

Tears welled up in Briar's eyes. Sweet, sentimental Henry was helping her fulfill her mother's dying wish. His gesture was better than singing the reel. It was as unique as he was and came from his heart.

But would it heal her? She tentatively took another breath. The embers burning in her lungs weren't as sharp as before. She carefully breathed out, bracing for the pain.

"No!" screeched Isodora again. She kicked at the dirt, spreading it around Pansy's recently swept floor. "It's too late. She's too far gone."

Henry wouldn't look away from Briar. "*Is* it too late?" he asked quietly. "Breathe with me."

CHAPTER FORTY-ONE

Briar locked eyes with Henry and breathed. He held her close in his arms, and everyone else in the room was blocked from her vision. It was just her and sweet, sweet Henry. Eyes locked with hers. With each breath she took, his smile grew wider and wider until he was grinning so wide there was no more room for his smile to grow. It took Briar several tentative breaths to not be afraid of the possible pain.

"It worked." Henry threw his head back and laughed.

Pansy jumped up and down, clapping joyously.

"I don't know," Briar said. "I'm breathing, but I still can't move my legs."

Henry shifted. "It probably doesn't help that I'm lying on top of you. How about now?"

"No. Still can't." But her heart was racing, pushing healthy, healing oxygen to her limbs. However, she was pretty sure her heart crashing against her ribs had nothing to do with breaking the curse, and everything to do with being in Henry's arms.

Fanny finally pushed through the door of her cage, the bars shrinking and changing back into pebbles. "You're getting better, I can tell. Her power is weakening." Fanny made a move like she was going to transform something else, but Isodora backed outside before Fanny could settle on something.

"I'll find a way to fully unblock my magic," said Isodora. "And when I do I'm coming for you, Fanny. You've stood in my way long enough."

Fanny chased her out the door, but came back a few moments later. As she walked in, the spiky trees outside the door shrank down and returned to dried rose petals. "So much for the primroses," she said. "They didn't work when I needed them most. I lost her. But now that she's revealed herself, Prudence will be able to track her quickly and take care of her."

"The boys," Briar said reaching an arm to the door.

"Are with the Princes. No need to worry. Here, dearie, let's get you settled back in bed and continue the treatments. You're going to be fine. Just fine."

"But what about Isodora? Henry can stay here with us while you do what you need to do."

"My priority is you kids here. Prudence told me in no uncertain terms that I was to stay with you all no matter what. Besides, making you stronger will make her weaker. Let me do my job, yes?"

Briar shared a look with Henry. She wouldn't relax until the spindle was safely removed from her frame and locked back up wherever they usually kept it.

Fanny plumped up the pillow then guided Briar back to a prone position. "The curse was old and slow-moving. Perhaps the cure is as well," Fanny said. She beamed at Henry. "I'll get the tea and see if we can help speed things along. Pansy? Your help?"

Alone in their corner of the cottage, Henry kissed Briar. "In case another kiss would 'speed things along,'" he said, quoting Fanny. "Is it working? Because I can keep going." He kissed her again.

Briar laughed, very much enjoying Henry's doctoring. "It is." Her voice came out stronger.

Henry smiled. "How are you feeling now?"

"Are you going to ask every minute?"

"Purely scientific inquiry. I'm curious about how potent my kisses are."

Briar tried wiggling her toes. Nothing. Too soon. Her knees? No. But the pins and needles feeling was working its way back down her body. It had cleared her lungs and was now in her middle. The tea might do her some good at flushing out the rest of it.

Fanny and Pansy had finished their preparations in the kitchen, arranging a high tea service on the kitchen table with selections of all the recent gifts. "Can you sit up, dearie? We'd love to have you join us at table."

"May I?" Henry held out his hands to indicate he'd help her.

Briar put her arms around his neck and he swung her up, carried her over to the table, and settled her into her usual chair. She hadn't sat with the family for days. She was going to live! To think, Henry Prince—the boy who never took anything seriously—had saved her life. At the rate the prickles were traveling, she might have use of her legs by bedtime. Certainly by morning.

Fanny bustled about, pouring everyone their tea, and was in the midst of pouring her own when the door banged open again. They all jumped and turned at the sound, expecting an angry Isodora, but standing in the doorway was an angry Prudence.

Nanny had finally returned.

Her black bonnet was thrown back on her head as if she had traveled a long way in a great hurry. Her diminutive form seemed to fill the doorway.

Pansy rose in excitement, but noticing Fanny's shocked expression, slowly sat back down.

Prudence stared unwaveringly at Fanny. "Just what is going on around here? Sitting down to tea and cookies as if you have no other responsibilities in the world?"

Fanny's teacup began to overflow and Pansy intervened, pulling the teapot out of Fanny's hands. She mopped up the spill with a rag.

"I— We— She—" Fanny sputtered. She pressed her hands on the table and leaned forward. "I'm sorry. What should I be doing aside from celebrating? We won. Isodora lost again."

Prudence came forward and patted Briar's shoulder. "I'm pleased to see you up and about, but Fanny and I have business to attend to." She jutted her chin in Fanny's direction. "Well, where is it now? Is it secured?" Prudence crossed her arms, looking between Briar and Fanny.

"It's attached to one of my frames at the mill," Briar said. "It won't come off, I tried."

Prudence raised her eyebrows at Fanny for confirmation.

"Yes, 'tis true. I tried myself to remove it, but it won't budge."

Prudence gaped. "You mean to tell me you've left it there? Unguarded? Did you at least think to put up some sort of protection?"

Fanny looked away. "Of course I did. I used the same protection we put on the blue cloth we wrapped the spindle in before. I was reminded of it when I saw it in Briar's pocket. That's where I was when Henry here came home. This time it's the frame itself that'll keep the girls safe. Curious things those mill girls. Perhaps after their recent illnesses some won't be so nosy."

"Briar, will you be all right here?" asked Prudence. "Henry, maybe you should take Briar and the children to your house for the night while Fanny and I reclaim the spindle."

"How are the legs?" Henry asked. "I could carry you the whole way if you want."

Still seated, Briar tentatively wiggled her toes. She grinned. Toes, those largely ignored appendages, had never felt so good. Next the legs, swinging at the knee. "I can move them!" Not even a single shard of pain. She was healing, truly healing. The nightmare was over. "Let's see if they'll bear weight." With a deep breath, she pushed up from the chair, leaning against the table. Her legs wobbled but held. "If I don't have to run, I can make it."

"Excellent." Fanny clapped in excitement. "Let me get my shawl and we'll be off," she said to Prudence as if they were planning a leisurely walk in the woods.

"And where are the boys?" Prudence asked.

"With the Princes. I have everything under control," Fanny said, irritated. "You aren't the only one who can look after children."

"They are not with the Princes. I've just come from there."

CHAPTER FORTY-TWO

Briar's legs gave out beneath her and she collapsed back into her chair. "She has them." It was like a punch in the gut. All this time Briar had been focused on protecting the girls around her, and she'd not paid enough attention to the boys.

If anything happened to them she'd never forgive herself.

"Let's not jump to conclusions," Fanny said. "I'll go look for them."

"And I'll go look for Isodora," Prudence said. "She'll be easy to track now." With one last withering look at Fanny, she disappeared out the door.

"Always thinks she knows best. Always thinks she can do everything herself," muttered Fanny. "Pansy, come help me find your brothers."

Briar tried to stand again, but her legs wouldn't support her.

"Stay put. Pansy and I will visit all their favorite spots in case the boys got lost in the dark." She lit the lantern.

Henry started for the door. "I'll go home and get my parents to spread the word. We'll have everyone in the valley looking for them. I'll come back with the wagon for Briar." With an encouraging squeeze to Briar's shoulder, he sprinted into the night.

Briar stood up and took tiny, shaking steps forward to follow Fanny and Pansy outside, but Fanny stopped her. "You need to stay here in case the boys come home."

"I can't. I have to help. Pansy can stay and wait."

Fanny took Pansy's hand and walked her to the door. "No, dearie. I need her to show me all their hiding places in case they simply fell asleep after such a busy day. You stay here. Your legs aren't strong enough yet."

"But—"

Fanny paused at the threshold. "If the boys come home, bang on a pot so we know we can stop the search."

And with that, they were gone.

Briar couldn't just sit there and do nothing! She set to work lighting candles and putting them in the windows as beacons for the boys. Her legs refused to respond to her commands to move faster. Instead, she walked as if through mud, fighting for every inch.

Finally, Briar set the last candle in a window, grateful that her legs had grown stronger with each step, though not strong enough to pace like she wanted to. She moved a chair into the doorway to keep watch. It was a dark night. Even the fireflies weren't playing in the trees. She strained her eyes, looking for any sign of movement. Listening for the faintest of cries. Willing the boys to call for her.

While Briar sat waiting, a touch of fog descended into the valley. She shivered as the breeze blew the mist into the yard and pulled at her feet. Adrenaline punched her heart. She'd seen this fog before. *Isodora.*

Briar stood. *She wants me to go to her. It's not the boys she wants; it's me.* With hours to go until Briar turned seventeen, Isodora could still use her to break the curse. Briar started walking to the road to meet Henry and the wagon. Now she understood why Aurora was powerless to stay away from the spindle. Isodora could be very persuasive.

Soon, the glow of a swinging lantern cut eerily through the fog. The disembodied form turned into legs, then the thick body of a horse, and then the welcome sight of Henry at the reins on his da's wagon. Behind him, more points of light bobbed through the dark as more of the valley folk arrived to help. As they walked closer, Briar realized they formed a line and were slowly, methodically making their way through the tall grasses and undergrowth.

Henry stopped in front of Briar. "What are you doing on the road?" He hopped down from the wagon.

She swallowed hard. "I know where the boys are. I know where she wants me to go."

CHAPTER FORTY-THREE

Briar rubbed her temples, trying to halt her growing headache and dread. She thought she'd spared her family another heartache, but it was not to be. This terrible ordeal was not over, but it would be tonight.

"Isodora took them to the mill." Briar heard her voice rise in panic. "She brought the boys to the spindle so I would go to her."

Henry blocked Briar's path. "No, let's think about this first. You can't meet her on your own. We should wait until the others come back." The flickering glow from the lantern warmed Henry's face and danced in his eyes, but his set jaw told Briar he didn't want her to run off alone to save the boys.

Briar shook her head. "No, they'll try to talk me out of it."

"And they'd be right. Briar, they can do things we can't." Henry looked angry. "Isodora wants you *dead*."

"I'm not afraid. I thought I was going to die before. I was ready to die. But I'm alive for a reason. It's not fair for the boys to be caught up in Isodora's schemes."

He took a deep breath, stared out into the forest. "It isn't fair for you to be caught up in this, either. I should go and get the boys out."

"Can we talk about this in the wagon? Fanny and Prudence can find us later and try to talk me out of it, but we need to move now."

He rubbed the tension in the back of his neck. "Let's go."

For being such a warm day, the weather had taken a quick turn to cold. Briar climbed up into the wagon with a boost from Henry. The breeze blew harder, as if trying to snatch away the breath she had finally regained. It was refreshing to take in a crisp breath after feeling like she was on fire and breathing in embers earlier. But her arms complained, rising up in gooseflesh.

Henry settled beside her, his leg touching hers and his body blocking some of the wind.

"Ready?" He reached for her hand.

Briar welcomed his touch. She was still a bit shaky and could use some of his steadiness. What would they face when they got to the mill? Had Isodora hurt the boys? Briar squeezed Henry's hand before he let go to hold the reins.

The horses *clip-clopped* their way down the road, their hoof beats muffled by the fog, adding to the dreamlike atmosphere. If people were calling out for the boys, the fog was pocketing their voices before they reached her ears.

"It's good the horses know this route so well," Henry

said. "I can't even tell where we are. If I had to lead them we'd be stuck in the brambles by now." Henry continued talking, trying to keep Briar's mind off the trouble they were about to face.

"I'm sorry, Briar," Henry said again.

"Stop apologizing. It's Isodora. You were trying to end this for your family and for anyone else she would target. You saw something evil and you tried to destroy it. You didn't create the spindle. Isodora did."

He squeezed her hand. "We will end this." He clicked his tongue, urging the horses to trot faster.

Soon they were on the outskirts of town. The buildings materialized out of the fog as if from nowhere. Few lights were shining in the windows at this time of night, so the town was mostly dark shadows as the carriage light passed by, lighting up the fog. The street lamps were mere points of light, but the closer they rode to the mill the dimmer the lights and the more shadowy the buildings.

"I'll go in and get the boys out to you," Henry said, his voice like steel. "Once you put them in the carriage, head straight for home. Give the horses their head and they'll take you home to my folks. Don't wait for me, I'll be fine. It's not me she wants."

"Henry, I think that's the point. She won't let you have the boys. If I don't go in, she could hurt them." Henry couldn't be the sacrifice. Isodora didn't want Henry. She wanted Briar. They both knew it.

"Whoa," Henry said, stopping the horses. He looped the reins on the wagon. "Briar, do you see that?"

Her mouth went dry. "Yes."

They were parked in front of the gates to the mill yard, but you wouldn't know it from what blocked their way. Thick, thorny vines had sprung up out of the sandy ground and had wound their way around the iron, barring anyone from getting near the gate, let alone the lock. The vines creaked and groaned as they continued to grow thicker and Briar watched in fascinated horror. What were they going to do?

Henry hopped down and came around the other side to help Briar down. "You okay? Legs still fine?"

Briar bounced a little to prove to him she could do whatever was called for tonight.

"Does Miss Olive keep an ax?" Henry asked.

She nodded and they rushed down the street to the boardinghouse. Briar knocked gently, not wanting to wake up the whole house. Miss Olive opened the door like she'd been waiting.

"What do you need?" she whispered.

"An ax," Henry said.

"Stay right here." Miss Olive shut the door. She was back moments later with her overcoat and an ax. "Nice to see you well, Briar," she said. "The girls were worried."

"Thanks. No need to come with us," said Briar. "We'll bring the ax back in the morning."

Miss Olive responded by leading the march to the mill, carrying the ax herself. "I've been expecting something to happen ever since this fog rolled in. You two care to share with me what you are doing in town in the middle of the night?"

"I need to get inside the mill," Briar said.

"And the ax is to break the lock?"

Briar shook her head and pointed.

Miss Olive stopped and silently took in the briars, which had grown twice over in the short time they'd been gone. They were taller and thicker and the thorns sharper.

"Oh my," she said. "I didn't expect that." She handed

Henry the ax and then marched up to examine the briars. They seemed to shy away from her, pulling back where she drew close but not letting her pass.

Some of Briar's bravado faltered at seeing Isodora's magic at work. Alive and responsive, the briars were terrifying. *This is not going to be easy.*

Thwack. Thwack. Henry began chopping at the vine.

The sounds were muffled thumps in the thick fog. With every chink he made in one part of the vine, two others would spring up in its place, making the area he was trying to cut through thicker than when he started.

"It's enchanted. We're only making it worse," Henry said. He dropped his ax and looked at Briar with sorrowful eyes. "I don't know what else to do. When my elder grandfather broke through to the castle, the briars almost let him through, like they were allowing him to pass."

"That's because I put those briars there," Miss Olive said. "To protect Aurora until her prince came. But I didn't make these. These are meant to keep you out."

Briar did a double take. "You, too?" she asked. She had been surrounded by fairies and didn't know it. "Is there anyone else I need to know about?"

"No, dearie, just us three. Prudence is back now, is she?"

Briar nodded, searching her memory for anything in Miss Olive's behavior that could have tipped her off. After all Briar's mother had told her of fairies, had she known they were real?

The trio paced in front of the impenetrable wall. Henry hacked all along the gate, but found no weakness. "There's no way in," Henry concluded, wiping the sweat off his brow.

"But they might let *someone* in," said Briar. "The person who Isodora wants to come in." Briar tentatively pulled a vine, being careful to avoid the thorns. As soon as she touched it, the plant parted, leaving a small gap. "Me."

"That's it, Briar," exclaimed Miss Olive. "Keep going."

"I'm going with you," Henry said.

Briar nodded and reached out her hand. Together. They would go together.

"I'll be right behind you," said Miss Olive.

Briar reached out again and touched the thorny vine. It trembled under her fingertips, as if it knew it was supposed to do something for her. She tugged. She pulled. But the vine remained fast. She let go of Henry's hand to get a better grip, and when she did, she found she could easily move the branches. "It's working," she called out in excitement as she pushed her way into the thick of the hedge. "Stay with me, Henry."

"Briar!" came his frantic call. He sounded so far away. "Briar, stop!"

She looked back, but all she saw was thorns and dark, twisted vines. She began to panic. "Henry? Where are you? I don't see you."

"The briars won't let me in," he said. "They only want you."

Her breath came in little gasps. Briars. *They know my name.*

They only want me.

CHAPTER FORTY-FOUR

It was so dark. Darker than the night sky. Briar took a deep breath and tried to push away the claustrophobic feeling of the briars and thorns pressing in on her. Since she couldn't see anything, anyway, she closed her eyes tight to protect her sight. With arms out in front, she felt her way through the thorns and prickles.

Ouch. They jabbed at her, drawing blood. Their attack felt personal, vindictive. Her heart raced as she battled the thorns. They were letting her in, but reluctantly. Like stinging scorpions, they'd jab then back away and let her move forward one more step. After surviving the spindle, she knew she could tolerate a new level of pain so she steeled herself and slowly pressed on.

Henry's voice had long ago dimmed, and she was truly on her own now. She pictured him fighting the hedge with his ax, frustrated and getting nowhere. His family was the protector of the spindle, but now the spindle was back in Isodora's control. She would not be satisfied until she got her revenge and she'd come closer with Briar than at any other time. Her will was strong. Briar would have to be stronger if she were to find a way out of this alive.

The branches creaked and groaned in an eerie rhythm as they grew. The hedge towered over her head, and the way in front of her seemed endless. *How thick and tall would the briars get?* She fought against rising panic. Her head throbbed, and her competing instincts to flee and to save the boys pulled her in two directions. The boys. She needed to keep her mind focused on the boys. Those poor, scared boys. They were what mattered right now.

The narrow passage was like a tiny hallway that continuously closed in on her from behind, directing her forward. The thorns scratched at her arms as if disappointed they couldn't hold on to her. But as she moved away from Henry and Miss Olive and inched closer to the mill and Isodora, the branches parted more easily.

"Briar." A voice called above the rising howl of wind.

She peered through the darkness trying to see the dark form caught in the briars. "Nanny? Are you hurt?" Briar asked.

"No, but I can't move. Isodora is stronger than we think. Don't be fooled. I've never seen her so determined."

Briar swallowed nervously. "I'll do my best." She redoubled her efforts to get through the briars.

Finally, they let her go completely and she found herself alone in the darkened mill yard. The air here was still, despite the wind roaring around the briar hedge.

A flickering light shone in the window of the third-floor spinning room. The light drew Briar to it, the way the lightning bugs called the boys. Up the stairs she went. Trade her life for the boys'.

Thinking about it now, she wished she would have had a chance to say good-bye to Henry. He was going to carry the weight of guilt unnecessarily. Briar was making the choice, fully aware of the consequences.

She was just glad Isodora hadn't taken Pansy. The other mill girls didn't die because they were too old, and Maribelle had the protection of the cloth helping her. Briar patted her pocket and was relieved to feel the cloth. Could it do anything else to help her? The curse was for a girl before her seventeenth birthday. Pansy would have fit that description, too. But Isodora wanted Briar Rose.

At the door, Briar pressed her ear to the wood, straining to hear if the boys were unharmed. There was a noise, but she couldn't make out what it was. She turned the handle and opened the door a crack. The hinges were blessedly silent.

Candlelight shone from the back of the room. Briar couldn't see her frames from this angle but knew the light was coming from her area. She scanned the shadowed frames closest to her, looking for two messy-mop-haired boys, but all she saw was thread-laden spindles stacked like tiny soldiers in their frames, waiting to begin the day.

She slipped in, then quietly closed the door behind her, thankful that the wind was making enough noise to cover any rustling of her skirts. Taking a lesson from the children, she clung to the wall to quietly work her way around the room instead of taking the straight path to her frame. The shadowed plants along the windowsills made it feel like she was in a jungle, hunting down a tigress. A tigress who hadn't heard Briar come in. Or one who was so secure in her trap that she needn't lie in wait.

There. Isodora's silhouette bobbed around the frame. *What is she doing?*

Briar searched her memories for anything her mother might have told her about fairies, even if the stories were mere legend and tale. But her thoughts came up empty. All she could remember was her mother's singleness of purpose, to protect her family as best she could. To keep Briar out of the mills as long as she could. To be grateful for all they had, the sun, the rain, the forest. She gave Briar a childhood.

Next Briar thought of Ethel. Her desperate attempts to create a new life, no matter how hard she had to work. She was brave in the same way Mam was. Briar drew courage from the women who set the example in her life. Protecting the home. Not exactly what Frances Willard taught, but that's what Briar was doing.

She might see Mam and Da soon, if Isodora had her way. Briar would be able to tell them all about Pansy and the boys. Oh, how pleased Mam would be to know her children were growing so well. How responsible Pansy was becoming. How much fun the boys were to have around.

A loud snore broke the silence. Briar froze. The boys were sleeping. Was it a natural sleep or did Isodora do something to them? With renewed purpose, she ducked down onto her knees and crept forward to the row before her frame. A little foot stuck out into the aisle. If she could just grab it. And pull. As long as he didn't cry out. There. She had Jack.

Isodora was still preoccupied with the frame. Maybe she couldn't get the spindle off, either.

Jack stirred, and Briar held her breath. He blinked, then opened his mouth, but Briar quickly placed her finger to her lips to indicate silence. He nodded then mouthed: *Benny.*

Briar indicated Jack should sneak out the door, but he shook his head. "Benny." This time he whispered it. Briar knew not to push him, or he would speak it out loud and

Isodora would hear. Instead, she nodded, and peeked around the corner.

She couldn't see Benny. He must be farther up the row. There was no way for her to crawl over to him without risking being seen. She scooted back to regroup. Jack pointed and waved his arms like he was trying to communicate. Benny might have understood, but she certainly didn't. Oh, wait. He was telling her to go around the opposite way. Sure. It might work. She could hide behind Annie's frame and pull Benny to her that way. But she had to be quick, before Isodora noticed Jack was missing.

She mouthed, *Wait by the door.*

He agreed to that, and the two backtracked silently to the door where Briar left Jack to go get Benny. She prayed Jack would stay put. If there was trouble he could open the door and run. Hide somewhere on the mill grounds until it was all over. The boys were so good at tucking themselves into tight spaces.

Briar crept around the row of frames from the other direction. A mass of thread and roving had been spilled into the aisle. Obviously, the boys had been playing around frame number four. Briar would have laughed if the situation wasn't so serious. She imagined Isodora trying to make the boys sit still while they waited, but the boys having none of that. They'd pulled off all the bobbins and Isodora had let them unwind the cops. Thread lay like a cobweb pinned from frame to frame, around the spindles, and the fairy was poised like a deadly spider waiting for Briar.

With no time to think, Briar began crawling her way to Benny. He was curled up in a ball, sound asleep in the dim candlelight, and had rolled halfway under one of the frames. Her heart beat so loudly she was surprised Isodora couldn't hear it. If only Briar could get to Benny, wake him up, and make him run, he and Jack would be safe. He was too close to Isodora for Briar to hope she could crawl all that distance and not be caught. As long as she got him moving before Isodora captured her, the boys had a chance.

Briar knew the moment she crawled into Isodora's line of sight. There was the *clang-clang-clang* of a tool falling through the metal frame and a flurry of activity. Briar lunged for Benny.

CHAPTER FORTY-FIVE

"Benny! Wake up!" Briar yelled as she ran.

Too late. Isodora got to him first and locked him in her arms. A deep sleeper, he lolled against her unaware.

"Thank you for coming so promptly, Briar. You were so slow at deciding about the spindle the first time we met, I hoped these creatures would provide some added incentive."

Benny stirred, trying to turn and cuddle up against Isodora. She stiffened, pushing him away from her. He blinked his eyes open, and yawned as he woke up, groggy, but compliant. She made him stand, keeping her arm around his waist.

"Let him go, I'm here. You don't need the boys."

Benny looked up when Briar spoke. He started to smile, but another yawn broke in.

"Oh, but I do." She patted Benny's head, and looked around. "Where did the other one go?" Isodora muttered under her breath as she scanned the darkened spinning room. She took some of the thicker roving strands and tied Benny to the spinning frame.

Briar edged forward, closer to Benny. "Why do you need the boys?" She kept her movements slow and steady, hoping to distract Isodora with talk.

Isodora stepped back. "You want me to believe you'll kindly prick your finger again if I let the boy go first? I don't believe you. But if you are willing to touch the end of the spindle, by all means." She waved an arm at frame number four. "It's getting late and your birthday is fast approaching." She pinched Benny's ear, causing him to cry out in pain.

"No!" screamed Jack from across the room. He started running to save Benny. But instead of running for his brother, he ran for Briar. "That's like Sleepin' Beauty, Bri!" He stopped between Briar and Isodora, blocking the spindle, his hands out. "Don't do it."

"Stay back," Briar yelled.

But Jack was determined to help. "Miss Fanny told us all about Sleepin' Beauty. Pansy cried herself to sleep worried that you would touch one of these spindles and die, until Miss Fanny told her it wasn't the same kind of spindles in your machines." He paused to take a breath. "But that spindle there looks different. She's been working on it since we got here." Jack pointed to the wooden spindle. "Don't touch it."

The frame had been pulled apart so that the row of spindles was tilted out. Briar didn't know the frame could bend like that.

While Briar glanced away to the frame, Isodora grabbed Jack. He put up a fuss, kicking and squirming. "Let me go. Let me go!"

"I'll do it," Briar said, her voice sounding calm despite

her racing heart. "Just release the boys. As soon as they are out of the building, I'll prick my finger. I don't want them to see."

"No. You'll do it now." Isodora dragged the kicking Jack over to the spindle and held his finger over the point.

Briar ran forward. "He can't break the curse, don't hurt him."

Isodora shot her an annoyed look. "I know how my curse works."

"But she doesn't know how mine works," said a voice near the door. Fanny, hair out of sorts and filled with pieces of broken vine, her face and arms scratched and bleeding, stepped out of the shadows and into the flickering candlelight. Her connection to Isodora must have let her break through the briars.

"That is, I call it a blessing, not a curse. It's a protection I put over the frame to keep these silly girls from accidentally hurting themselves again."

"You." Isodora narrowed her eyes. "I can't get rid of you. What did you do to this contraption?"

"Miss Fanny," called Benny. He was now fully awake, his mouth trembling as he tried to squirm out of his bindings.

Fanny put her hands on her hips. "Tying up children? Really, Isodora?" She made a move to rescue Benny.

Isodora called out in a loud voice, "You are forbidden to let that child go!" The spinning frame began to tremble and Benny reached out for his brother.

Jack, who enjoyed exciting adventures, looked to Briar for help, his eyes wide and pupils dilated. Obviously scared, he was being so brave.

Briar's instincts took over and she lunged for Jack. Briar pulled on the boy, trying to get him out of Isodora's grip, but then saw that was only hurting him. She tugged at Isodora's bony fingers one by one, and Jack assisted with a bite to the fairy's forearm.

Isodora screamed while loosening her grip on Jack. He went limp, slid out from her grasp, and then wiggled away on the floor. He ran to help Fanny loose Benny.

Isodora clawed for Briar.

"No, you can't have them." Briar pushed her away with all her strength and ran for the twins.

As she fell backward, Isodora tripped on the tangle of thread left over from the boys' play and fell against the frame. The ends of the exposed spindles piercing Isodora's flesh, she cried out in pain and rage. She tried to lift her body forward, but stuck fast.

Briar covered the boys' eyes, watching in horror as Isodora writhed on the spikes. "Fanny, what do we do?"

Fanny twisted her hands. "I-I don't know. Try to get her off, I suppose."

Briar held her hand out to stop Fanny. "First, undo the curse," Briar said to Isodora. Her voice came out strong, even though she was trembling inside.

Isodora panted through the pain. "I can't, you fool. It must be carried out."

Fanny nodded. "That is the problem that got us here in the first place."

Briar didn't want to be cruel, but she couldn't let Isodora go free only to hurt someone else. "You must be able to do something. Release the Prince family. Seal up the spindle where no one can get to it."

"But then I'll forever be like this," Isodora seethed, glaring at Fanny.

"You'll be alive," Briar said.

Isodora made another move to save herself, and

gasped as the spindle pierced deeper. Her eyes took on a wild look and she began to wave her arms. In her struggle, she slapped her arm against the candle, which had been balanced on the frame. It fell, quickly setting fire to some cotton fluff along the way that then fell to the floor. It burned bright, fueled by grease that had dripped from the frame.

"No!" screamed Isodora in anguish as a sickly green cloud rose up from the poisoned spindle and surrounded her. Her own magic was working against her. The spindle must have gone deep enough to pierce her heart. The green cloud grew large and dense as it swirled around Isodora, until they could no longer see her. When her screams faded away, so did the cloud.

The fairy was gone.

But now the fire was spreading along the oil-soaked wooden floor.

"Run!" yelled Briar.

"Benny!" called Jack. His twin was still tied to the second frame.

"Go with Miss Fanny. I'll get Benny," Briar said. Before Jack could argue, Fanny had his little hand firmly in her grip and they were racing to the single door.

The smoke filled the room ahead of the flame. "Hold your breath," she said to Benny. "You're almost loose. When I say go, duck down to take a breath, then run with me." Her fingers worked quickly to break the rushing, thankful Isodora had used the loose cotton, which was easier to break apart. The smoke burned her eyes and throat, but she broke the bonds. "Go!"

The two ducked below the thick smoke for a quick breath, and they ran. Briar led the way, knowing the shortest path through the spinning frames. Fanny was waiting with the door open. Jack was already at the bottom of the stairs, immobile, watching for the rest of his family to emerge.

In the distance, the briar hedge was shrinking and snapping and disappearing with loud, angry cracks and pops. Miss Olive stood at an opening near the gate, holding Pansy's hand and waiting. Henry was trapped in one corner where the briars were still the thickest. Only his head and arm were visible. Prudence was to the right of Henry, and as the branches surrounding her collapsed to her feet she stood still, waiting. Observing. *Observing what?*

CHAPTER FORTY-SIX

Briar looked behind and saw the flames leaping out of the spinning room, but that wasn't where Prudence's gaze was focused. She was fixed on Fanny, who by now was carrying Jack. Briar hefted Benny to a better position on her hip. *Why is Prudence so intent on Fanny?* If Fanny were to get in trouble for any of what had taken place, Briar would be the first one to defend her. If it weren't for Fanny, who knew what would have become of the children when Prudence left so suddenly?

As the last of the sharp briar branches fell to the ground, Henry and Miss Olive were released. Henry, scratched and bleeding from the briars, rushed to take Benny. "Hey there, buddy. You okay?"

Benny coughed, but nodded that he was okay. "Fire." He wrapped his arms around Henry and squeezed hard.

"And you?" Henry asked Briar. He pulled Benny's arm to loosen the boy's grip around his neck, then reached for Briar. He tipped her chin, his gaze searching hers. "Are you all right? When I lost my grip on your hand I was afraid I'd lost you, too."

She smiled at him with nothing but love and hope in her heart. "It's over. I don't think you'll find a spindle in those ashes. Isodora intended for me to prick my finger again, but she fell onto her own spindle and it pierced through to her heart."

"It's not over at all." Henry looked very serious.

Confused, Briar glanced back at the mill, angry flames bursting out of broken windows.

Henry shifted Benny to his hip, and put his arm around her. Dipping his head close to hers, he said, "I want you to know that we are just beginning. We're not even close to being over, ever." He kissed her forehead, then transferred Benny into her arms.

Briar's heart fluttered. *Henry Prince.* Who would have thought? Her cheeks warmed, but not from the fire as she watched him run to the mill fire station to sound the alarm.

"Let's go quickly," Prudence said, waving everyone over to her. "The fog is lifting and Henry is calling in help. We shouldn't be here when they arrive."

"Can't you stop the fire?" asked Briar.

"Fire is not under our control. The townspeople will need to take care of this."

They hurried down the quiet street when the clanging of bells sounded out in the stillness. *Ting, ting, ting, ting,* trying to wake the whole town. Fires were serious business and a mill fire was dangerous.

Once inside, Miss Olive turned on one of the parlor lights, and at first, they all stood in a circle looking at one another.

"Sit down," directed Miss Olive. "I already had some tea brewing. Be right back."

The two other fairies gathered in whispered conversation near the piano. Briar chose the long sofa and the children all piled up around her. Pansy sat so close to Briar she might as well have sat in her lap. "I flew," she whispered. "In the wind, with Miss Fanny." Her face shone with excitement.

"What was it like?" Briar whispered back.

"It was like being on a cloud." Pansy thought for a moment. "Do you think she'll take me flying again?"

Briar examined the straight back, narrowed eyebrows, and pinched lips of Prudence as she listened to Fanny's enthusiastic telling of what went on in the spinning room.

"No, darling. I think that was it. Store up the memory in your heart so you can tell your own daughter one day." *Like Mam told us.* Briar shook her head. Oh, the questions she had for her mam.

Miss Olive came in with a cup of tea and handed it to her. The cup rattled in the saucer as Briar took it. Now that she was safe, the shock of it all was overwhelming. In the moment, one does what needs to be done, but anything could have happened in that room. To the boys, to her.

"They told us how flammable the room was, but I had no idea it could catch fire so fast."

Miss Olive nodded. "And you got everyone out. Your mam would have been quite proud of the woman you are becoming."

Briar gasped, her heart warming at the thought of her mother's approval. "You knew her?"

"We spoke once. When she first started at the mill and shared with me her concern that you'd have to join her. And you did. And now you have fulfilled her wishes for you."

But she hadn't. She had no home for the children, and no way to keep them together. Prudence didn't need to protect any girl in Sunrise Valley anymore, so they were on their own. Maybe the Princes could take the children now that the spindle was gone. She'd ask them next time she saw them.

Jack interrupted by patting Briar's arm. "I wanna watch them put out the fire an' see the fire wagon come. May I go back?"

"No, you curious thing," she said with a smile, happy that she'd thought of another way to keep the children together. "You'll want to join right in and carry a bucket."

"Can I?" Jack's face lit up at the idea. "Please, Bri? I want to make sure Henry is okay."

"Let's watch on the porch." Briar was worried about Henry, too. He would want to go to the exact location where the fire started to make sure the spindle was gone. He'd need to know he and his family really were free.

By the time Briar and the children had gotten to the door, a flood of boardinghouse girls in their nightclothes came streaming down the stairs, all blurry-eyed and wanting to know what was going on.

"Was that the fire bell?"

"What's happening?"

Miss Olive came in to restore order. "Listen. Listen, girls. Our mill has caught fire. But don't you worry. You are all safe here. I'm sure they'll have it out in no time."

"Fire!" The flood of girls continued out the door, pushing Briar and the children outside with them.

The dancing orange glow stood out against the dark sky. There were distant shouts and clangs from the horse-drawn fire wagons. All the boardinghouses up the road had their doors open and the mill operatives spilling out of them to see what was going on.

Miss Olive wouldn't let her girls get closer. She stood on the street with her arms open and waving her charges back into the yard. "Stay put. You can see just fine from here."

"Briar! You're back," someone called out, noticing her standing with the children. Quickly, the mill girls gathered around her. "Are you feeling better?"

"Completely healed," she said, glancing at Miss Olive.

"Look at that," said Lizbeth as there was a distant crash and a flare of orange. "There go our jobs."

"We can move to the new mill," said someone. "They'll take us since we don't need training."

Ethel shrugged. "We can check with the other factories in town first. Shame to leave all our friends." She smiled at Briar and Mim.

Briar smiled back, watching the fire reflected in her friends' faces. They'd grown so close these last few weeks together. She couldn't even imagine the hole they would leave behind if they moved to Burlington. She squeezed in between them and tucked her arms in theirs.

Briar no longer wanted to leave Sunrise Valley. She wanted to be near her family and the three fairies. And Henry. She rested her head on Ethel's shoulder. But with the spindle gone, there wasn't reason for any of the fairies to stay in the valley. What would they do next? The Prince family? Would they all leave? Briar still didn't know what was going to happen to the children.

"You okay?" Ethel asked.

"I will be," Briar answered. Her whole life could change now that she'd decided she didn't want it to.

By the time the sun rose, the fire was under control. The main building was a loss, but the surrounding outbuildings had been saved.

The boys had done their best to stay awake, but after Miss Olive brought them blankets, they each found a cozy spot in the parlor and fell asleep, much to the amusement of the mill girls.

With no work that day, the operatives set out to find word on employment in Burlington or to enjoy a rare day of relaxation. Several took turns using the bicycle to wheel to the mill and back with reports on the progress of the firefighters.

Briar was exhausted but fought to stay awake until she heard from Henry. The latest news was that the fire was out, but still he didn't come. She watched scores of men walk by, their faces blackened by smoke and ashes, but still no Henry.

The boys woke and wanted to play games in the parlor, so Briar propped open the front door to keep an ear out while she kept watch out on the porch. By the laughter she knew the boys were having a grand time playing Tiddledy Winks, and the mill girls were won over by their adorableness.

Jack came outside, bouncing. "Briar, they told me I should be a candy boy and they would buy all their sweets from me." He grinned wide. "But then Benny said I would eat it all myself, and I think he might be right. It would be hard for a fella to watch someone else eat all that candy and not take one or two for hisself."

"You would make a fine candy boy."

"I'll tell Benny you said that." And off he went, back into the parlor.

Finally, Henry came ambling down the road, soot-covered and looking more like a coal miner than a mill worker. Briar relaxed her clenched hands, relieved he was okay and she could see it for herself.

He had something wrapped up in his hand, and he wasn't smiling.

No. The spindle couldn't have survived. As much as Briar wanted things to stay the same, she didn't want *that.* She stood and braced herself for the worst.

CHAPTER FORTY-SEVEN

Briar craned her neck to see what shape the wrapped bundle was, but when Henry got closer, he hid it behind his back.

Her heart sank. Their family wasn't free after all. She rose and went to meet him. The Prince family was able to guard the spindle for hundreds of years. They would continue to do so. And now that she knew the secret, she could help.

Henry stopped to talk with Fanny, who, after checking up on the boys, had gone down the steps ahead of Briar to join Miss Olive and Prudence who were talking across the road.

When Henry saw Briar, he smiled.

"What happened in there?" she asked, being obvious about trying to see behind his back; he being just as obvious about blocking her view.

"We managed to save all but the one building. It could have been a lot worse." He sounded tired and not at all victorious as she'd expected.

"What's behind your back?"

Before he could answer, Miss Olive interrupted. "You are all invited out to the country, courtesy of Miss Fanny. She says she needs the help eating all the goodies the neighbors brought to her house." She turned to Henry, "Would you get the wagon for us, please?"

"I'll show you later," he whispered to Briar, mustering up a smile before jogging back down the road.

With several whoops, the girls ran inside to grab their bonnets.

"I'll go get Ethel," Mim said. "It'd do her some good." She followed the others inside.

"And I'll gather the children," Briar said, curious about when "later" would be.

By the time everyone filed back out to the street, Henry was there with his wagon, and he'd recruited George with another wagon to fit more girls.

George offered a hand to each girl as she climbed up in the back, but when Mim walked out with Ethel, he abandoned his post and jogged up to her with a silly grin.

"This way, ladies," he said with a wide, sweeping gesture to his wagon. In return, Mim flashed him her best smile and looped her arm through his.

Ethel and Briar exchanged a look.

"You go with Henry," Ethel said. "I'll take this wagon and keep an eye on them."

Briar hopped up on the wagon beside Henry. "What about the three ladies over there?" Fanny, Miss Olive, and Prudence were having a strong discussion across the street and out of earshot of the boardinghouse.

Henry shrugged. "I think they can get back to the cottage on their own."

Fanny looked over and met Briar's gaze. She smiled and nodded once as if she'd heard.

Briar turned back to Henry. "You'll have to tell me all you know about them."

"I don't know much, but I can guess what they are talking about now."

"The future?"

Henry nodded. "But I have no idea what they will decide."

"What about the mill? All these girls are out of work."

He smiled. "I heard there was an anonymous pledge to cover the cost of rebuilding. Some wealthy German investors, I believe. It shouldn't take too long to be up and running again. Those who can't wait can move on if they wish. It's not so terrible to leave the valley. It's a beautiful world out there, too."

The mill girls sang songs all the way, giving the ride a festive air. Briar wanted to ask Henry about the spindle, but she couldn't press him because then the girls would wonder.

She didn't want any more secrets between them and she didn't think he did, either. She watched his profile as he stared out over the valley, giving it that Henry look.

He turned and caught her staring. He wiggled his eyebrows, and she laughed. *Henry Prince.*

These feelings she could trust. Henry was true.

At the cottage, the girls spread out, playing with the animals and hiking in the woods. After Henry washed up, Briar tried to corner him about the bundle he was hiding.

"Later," was all he said, jerking his chin at all the people gathered around.

When it was nearing time to eat, Briar tried to go inside to help serve, but Pansy took her hand and led her out back to check on the bunny.

"We were gone all night and the animals missed us. They need to see you, too. They want to know you are healed."

It sounded like an excuse one of the boys would make to get Briar's undivided attention, so she played along. Maybe Pansy was overwhelmed with all that had happened, and now all the people invading their home. Briar could give her a quick bit of quiet and attention. "I feel great, Pansy. Almost like I was never sick. Don't you worry."

Pansy had knelt down and was petting the bunny, but kept looking over her shoulder like she wanted to join the gathering in the cottage.

"We can go back, if you think you're missing out on something," Briar said, confused by Pansy's mixed messages.

"No, a few minutes more," Pansy insisted.

Briar found a Solomon's Seal plant growing near Fanny's garden patch. She plucked it and tucked it into her Newport knot.

Henry sidled up next to her and bowed. "Your presence is requested in the cottage." He gallantly held out his arm and winked at Pansy.

Pansy raced ahead and disappeared around the corner.

"Alone as last," Briar said, looping her arm through his. "Now will you tell me what happened with the spindle?"

"It's gone," he said. "No trace of it or Isodora."

Briar was confused. "But I saw you bring something from the mill. If not the spindle, what was it?"

"Be patient. I'll show you soon." He dropped his arm and guided her ahead of himself into the cottage.

"Surprise!" yelled everyone. "Happy Birthday." Miss

Fanny stepped forward with the cake Mrs. Clover had made for her.

Briar held her hands up to her mouth. She was seventeen. She was alive.

"Now we can finally eat this cake," Jack said.

While everyone was busy eating, Prudence took Briar aside. "The ladies and I have come to a decision. Fanny is to be your new caretaker until the children no longer need one."

Briar looked up to see Fanny watching. Fanny grinned and waved.

"Is this acceptable to you?" Prudence noticed Fanny's enthusiasm and frowned.

Briar stifled a laugh. "She has done well with the children. It is acceptable. Where will you go?"

Prudence raised an eyebrow in answer.

Reminded that fairy business was not her business, Briar lowered her eyes and smiled. Prudence had cared for them, more than she herself realized, and that was something to treasure. "Thank you. For taking us in when you did."

"You are welcome, Briar Rose."

The mill girls were made as comfortable as possible for a sleep out under the stars. Briar walked Henry to the road so he could go home. His rough hand in hers a reminder of the changes in her life.

"What a day, Miss Briarly Rose Jenny. Do you realize your courage has redeemed my family's future?"

"Wasn't my courage, it was instinct to protect the boys."

"Call it instinctual courage, then, but it's one of the things I love about you."

She grinned, feeling the praise down to her toes. Her heart, once so torn apart, was whole again. All the people she cared about were here. They were safe. She pulled out the spindle's silk cloth from her pocket and wiped a mark of soot on Henry's cheek. "You missed a spot."

He reached up and stilled her hand. "I didn't know you had the cloth. Do you know what it is?"

"It came with the spindle. Fanny told me it would help protect me."

"More than that, it's a piece cut from Aurora's baby blanket. Dad told me to always keep the spindle wrapped up inside. I suspect one of the fairies did something to it."

"I'm starting to suspect those ladies of a lot of things."

Briar folded the cloth and put it back in her pocket, impatiently waiting for Henry to show her what he brought back from the mill. Did he have bad news or good news for her?

The fireflies blinked their lights against the dark, while the chatter of the mill girls floated over from near the garden, the children's laughter floating louder and higher. And right in front of her was Henry Prince. *Incorrigible, dependable, noble Henry Prince.* So many people to love in this valley. She never wanted to leave.

"About the spindle," he said.

She stopped walking. "Yes?"

"Technically, part of it survived the fire."

Briar's heart sank. "No. So it's not over?"

"It's over. Isodora is gone. Her spindle is gone. No more curses. But this remains." He held out the wrapped bundle she'd been waiting to see. "It won't hurt you. It's actually a family heirloom. Made by Aurora's father for her mother at Aurora's birth. I'm glad it survived. It's a symbol of love, of hope for the future."

Briar opened the bundle under the moonlight. It was the beautiful whorl, the disk that made the spindle spin. She ran her finger over the carved roses. There were now two darkened scorch marks that marred the wood.

"This was in my apron pocket. How did it end up in the mill?"

Henry frowned. "It's hard to explain anything with this spindle. Maybe Isodora found it in the cottage when we weren't looking. Maybe one of the boys had it?"

Briar handed it back, but Henry refused to take it. "It belongs in your family," Briar said. "You should keep it."

He shook his head. "That one hasn't been our favorite heirloom."

She held on to it with both hands. "Thank you." She would keep it as a reminder of what she could have lost if she hadn't been so blind to what was right in front of her.

Author's Note

Part of the fun of writing a historically based novel is trying to wrap a fantastical story around reality. What parts are real in *Spindle*?

Conditions in the cotton mills, the boardinghouses, the games they played in the 1890s, the lectures the operatives attended, the introduction of the safety bicycle...all real. (Hope you liked the quote from Susan B. Anthony about women, freedom, and the bicycle!)

Cotton mills were one of the first places where women joined together and realized the power they had to help each other when they acted together. Early mills, while not ideal places to work by today's standards, offered young women a chance to earn their own money, a novelty for many of the hardworking farm girls who flocked to the cities. But, as time went on, good intentions gave way to deteriorating conditions, and operatives went on strike to try to change their increasingly difficult lot.

In writing this novel, I wanted to get past the photos of sad and tired mill workers (mostly taken in the early 1900s by photographer Lewis Hine, whose powerful images were instrumental in shedding light on child labor) and remind us that these were real people who lived and loved, worked and played.

At the time this novel is set, the women's suffrage movement was well under way. However, Mrs. Tuttle and Miss Nan Whitaker are invented characters, as I couldn't find any suffrage or WCTU speakers who were in the area during my time frame. I patterned them after several other speakers, and in Mrs. Tuttle's case, had her quote Elizabeth Cady Stanton's famous "Solitude of Self" speech from 1892, just two years before this story takes place. Mrs. Stanton quite coincidentally mentions an example of a girl of sixteen, which was so fitting to Briar's circumstances I had to include it.

Sunrise Valley is my invention, but located near Rutland, Vermont, a real place and the location of the first polio epidemic in the USA during the summer of 1894. Also true to Vermont history, the Queen City Cotton Company built a new cotton factory in Burlington with 26,000 spindles in 1894.

The first of the strikes in the great railroad strike of 1894 started May 10. The issue was primarily a disagreement between workers making and repairing Pullman sleeper cars and Mr. Pullman. The conflict affected passengers, mail, and freight, and lasted until mid-late July of that year.

Lastly, did you catch the Easter eggs in the story? Briar's last name, Jenny, comes from the spinning jenny, an invention from the 1700s that utilized a row of spindles instead of a singular one as in a spinning wheel—get it? She's a spinner girl, a spinning Jenny. Ah, history is fun! Also, when the safety bicycle was being introduced, I mentioned Annie Londonderry, who set out on a bicycle trip around the world after the fashion of Nellie Bly's trip around the world in eighty days. Well, that Easter egg was a nod at my novel *Liz and Nellie*, which was a little side project I worked on between my fairy tale stories for Entangled TEEN.

The following resources were immensely helpful in helping me ground my characters in both the late 1800s time period, and in the life of a cotton mill operative: *Out of Ireland: The Story of Irish Immigration to America*, DVD narrated by Kelly McGillis and written by Paul Wagner; *The Lowell Offering: Writings by New England Mill Women (1840-1845)* by Benita Eisler; *The Belles of New England: The Women of the Textile Mills and the Families Whose Wealth They Wove* by William Moran; *Limping Through Life: A Farm Boy's Polio Memoir* by Jerry Apps; also, the novels *Lyddie* by Katherine Paterson and *Counting on Grace* by Elizabeth Winthrop.

ACKNOWLEDGMENTS

The acknowledgments section always seems to sneak up on me when my brain is exhausted from all the work my editors put me through... But what amazing editors I have! Stacy Abrams and Lydia Sharp challenge me to become a better writer with each edit pass. I am so grateful for their dedication. Layer by layer they pull the details of the story out of me, and when I'm stuck, they've got great ideas to get me going again. Thank you, ladies, for caring so much! Along with their tireless work is a whole team working away at Entangled: Christine Chhun, Melissa Montovani, Melanie Smith, Heather Riccio, Meredith Johnson, Lisa Knapp, Louisa Maggio, and Toni Kerr.

A quick shout-out to the booksellers, librarians, and English teachers who were so welcoming to me and my debut Cinderella duology and are kindly anticipating this book's release. You all rock the stacks: Brandi Stewart, Faith Hochhalter, Kirsten Flint, Dallas Parke (and family!), Allyson Bullock, Jared Duran, Jessica Wells, Traci Avalos, and James Blasingame.

What is a book without good beta readers to find plot holes, lapses in logic, and the joy in the story? Thank you Kristi Doyle, Sarah Chanis, Andrea Huelsenbeck, and Rebekah Slayton.

And, as always, I have to acknowledge the support of my family. The writing life can be an odd and unpredictable one, so everyone has to stay flexible. God knew what He was doing when He put us together. I need you guys, and I'm so glad that you need me too. (Because you do, teenagers of mine! You do.)

Now, you readers: I hope you enjoyed this story as much as I enjoyed writing it for you. If you want to stay in touch, the best way is through my newsletter. I send out exclusive content just for you and read all my own email. Sign up on my website: ShonnaSlayton.com.

Don't miss these other fantastic reads from Shonna Slayton

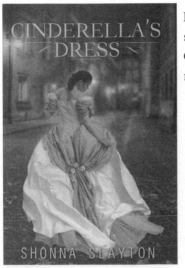

During WWII, Kate discovers she is the descendant of the real Cinderella...and the keeper of her mythical dresses.

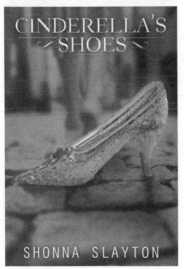

Kate's adventure continues as she searches for Cinderella's shoes... and tries to keep them out of the hands of the evil stepsisters.

Available now!

GRAB THE ENTANGLED TEEN RELEASES READERS ARE TALKING ABOUT!

REMEMBER YESTERDAY
BY PINTIP DUNN

Sixteen-year-old Jessa Stone is the most valuable citizen in Eden City. Her psychic abilities could lead to significant scientific discoveries, if only she'd let TechRA study her. But ten years ago, the scientists kidnapped and experimented on her, leading to severe ramifications for her sister, Callie. She'd much rather break in to their labs and sabotage their research—starting with Tanner Callahan, budding scientist and the boy she loathes most at school.

The past isn't what she assumed, though—and neither is Tanner. He's not the arrogant jerk she thought he was. And his research opens the door to the possibility that Jessa can rectify a fatal mistake made ten years earlier. She'll do anything to change the past and save her sister—even if it means teaming up with the enemy she swore to defeat.

OLIVIA DECODED
BY VIVI BARNES

This isn't my Jack, who once looked at me like I was his world. The guy who's occupied the better part of my mind for eight months.

This is Z, criminal hacker with a twisted agenda and an arsenal full of anger.

I've spent the past year trying to get my life on track. New school. New friends. New attitude. But old flames die hard, and one look at Jack—the hacker who enlisted me into his life and his hacking ring, stole my heart, and then left me—and every memory, every moment, every feeling comes rushing back. But Jack's not the only one who's resurfaced in my life. And if I can't break through Z's defenses and reach the old Jack, someone will get hurt…or worse.

WAKE THE HOLLOW
BY GABY TRIANA

Forget the ghosts, Mica. It's real, live people you should fear.

Tragedy has brought Micaela Burgos back to her hometown of Sleepy Hollow. It's been six years since she chose to live with her father in Miami instead of her eccentric mother. And now her mother is dead.

This town will suck you in and not let go.

Sleepy Hollow may be famous for its fabled headless horseman, but the town is real. So are its prejudices and hatred, targeting Mica's family as outsiders. But ghostly voices carry on the wind, whispering that her mother's death was based on hate...not an accident at all. With the help of two very different guys—who pull at her heart in very different ways—Micaela must awaken the hidden secret of Sleepy Hollow...before she meets her mother's fate.

Find the answers.
Unless, of course, the answers find you first.

CHASING TRUTH
BY JULIE CROSS

At Holden Prep, the rich and powerful rule the school—and they'll do just about anything to keep their dirty little secrets hidden. When former con artist Eleanor Ames's homecoming date commits suicide, she's positive there's something more going on. The more questions she asks, though, the more she crosses paths with Miles Beckett. He's sexy, mysterious, arrogant...and he's asking all the same questions. Not only is she sure Miles isn't telling her the truth...but she knows there's a good chance *he* could be the killer.